Luke Jensen,
Bounty Hunter:
Bad Men Die

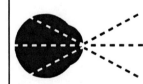

This Large Print Book carries the
Seal of Approval of N.A.V.H.

LUKE JENSEN, BOUNTY HUNTER: BAD MEN DIE

WILLIAM W. JOHNSTONE
WITH J. A. JOHNSTONE

WHEELER PUBLISHING
A part of Gale, Cengage Learning

GALE
CENGAGE Learning·

Farmington Hills, Mich • San Francisco • New York • Waterville, Maine
Meriden, Conn • Mason, Ohio • Chicago

GALE
CENGAGE Learning·

LIBRARY OF CONGRESS CATALOGING-IN-PUBLICATION DATA

Johnstone, William W.
  Luke Jensen, bounty hunter: Bad men die / by William W. Johnstone ; with J. A. Johnstone. — Large print edition.
    pages (large print) ; cm — (Luke Jensen, bounty hunter) (Wheeler Publishing large print western)
    ISBN 978-1-4104-8226-6 (softcover : large print) — ISBN 1-4104-8226-X (softcover : large print)
    1. Bounty hunters—Fiction. 2. Large type books. I. Johnstone, J. A. II. Title. III. Title: Luke Jensen, bounty hunter.
PS3560.O415B33 2015
813'.54—dc23   2015019380

Published in 2015 by arrangement with Pinnacle Books, an imprint of Kensington Publishing Corp.

Printed in the United States of America
2 3 4 5 6   19 18 17 16 15

LUKE JENSEN, BOUNTY HUNTER: BAD MEN DIE

CHAPTER 1

Luke Jensen curled the fingers of his right hand around the butt of the Remington revolver holstered on his left hip in a cross-draw rig. He pressed his back against the faded wallpaper in the hotel corridor, eased closer to the door at his left, and listened intently.

Snores came from inside the room. The sound of them put a faint smile on his rugged, deeply tanned face. He was a tall, rangy man dressed in black from head to foot, although the trail dust that had settled on him during the past week had given his hat, shirt, trousers, and boots a grayish tinge.

He had spent that week tracking down Frank McCluskey, the outlaw who snored peacefully on the other side of the door, blissfully unaware that his freedom and his life as a lawless desperado were about to be over. Luke had finally caught up to him in the little settlement called Rimrock, in

Wyoming Territory.

Poised to pull the Remington, lift his foot, and drive his heel against the door next to the knob, Luke could see his plan playing out in his head, plain as day. When the door crashed open, he would rush in and wallop the startled McCluskey before the outlaw knew what was going on.

Before he could put the plan into operation, he heard footsteps down at the other end of the hall where the stairs from the first floor reached a landing. Someone was climbing those stairs — and singing softly. He couldn't make out the words, but he could tell the voice belonged to a woman.

He bit back a curse and took his hand off his gun. Even though he intended to take McCluskey by surprise and capture him without any shooting, he couldn't guarantee it would go smoothly. He couldn't risk lead flying around with an innocent bystander in the corridor, especially a woman.

Early in his career as a bounty hunter, he might not have worried much about anybody else being hurt, as long as he captured the fugitive he was after and collected the reward. Age had softened him a little, he supposed, as had being reunited with his brother Smoke after many years apart.

Now and then, Luke worried about that. A man in his line of work, tracking the most dangerous outlaws west of the Mississippi, couldn't afford to get soft.

It was a good way to wind up dead in a hurry.

He turned toward the landing as the woman reached it. He figured he could amble down the corridor as if he were a guest leaving one of the other rooms, give her a pleasant nod as they passed, and let her go into her own room. Then he could return to McCluskey's door and resume his plan.

The woman stopped singing to herself as she started along the hallway and saw Luke coming toward her. She was a short woman with brassy blond hair and a voluptuous figure in a dark blue dress made to show it off. She looked at Luke with frank, open appraisal and smiled as if she liked what she saw.

Luke knew good and well that he wasn't what anybody would consider handsome. His face was craggy and the thin dark mustache didn't do anything to relieve the natural grimness of his mouth. But for some reason most women seemed to find him attractive, and he knew that, too. He returned the smile and reached up to touch a finger

9

to the brim of his flat-crowned black hat.

"Good morning," the woman said.

"Ma'am," Luke greeted her politely. He didn't pause but moved to the side to go around her.

"I don't recall seeing you around. Are you staying here in the hotel?"

"That's right," he lied. He kept moving, not wanting to stand in the hallway and have a conversation with her. She needed to just go on into her room, close the door, and let him get on with his business.

"My name's Delia Bradley."

"Luke Smith," he said, giving her the false name he used sometimes. "If you'll excuse me . . ."

"Oh, of course." She waved a hand with long fingernails painted red to match her lips. Rings adorned several of her fingers, as well. She definitely had a flashy look about her, and Luke wondered if she might be a soiled dove visiting someone in the hotel.

He had just stepped past her when that thought went through his mind, followed immediately by the possibility that she might be headed to McCluskey's room. He couldn't help but glance back over his shoulder and saw her taking an over/under derringer out of the little bag she held. Her flirtatious smile had disappeared, but she

10

was still baring her teeth at him in a hate-filled grimace.

Luke lashed out with his left hand as she jerked the derringer up. Grabbing her wrist, he thrust it toward the ceiling as she pulled the trigger, firing the upper barrel. The gun made a little popping sound as it went off, no louder than a man clapping his hands.

At the same time, he struck with his right fist, clipping her on the chin with a short, swift blow. His hand wasn't clenched tight, so he didn't do any real damage, but the punch was enough to stun her. He wrenched the derringer out of her hand as she sagged toward him.

He caught her under the arms to keep her from thudding to the floor and realized she was shamming. She lifted her knee toward his groin in a vicious strike.

He twisted to the side and took the blow on his thigh, where it was still painful but not incapacitating. "Damn it. Settle down!"

Not much chance of that, he realized as she opened her mouth and screamed, "Frank! Frank, get out of here!" She started fighting like a wildcat, clawing at Luke's face with her free hand and trying to gouge his eyes out with those long fingernails.

Anger welled up inside him. He hit her again, still pulling his punch, but not as much. The blow drove her head to the side and caused her eyes to roll up in their sockets. She couldn't fake that reaction. Her knees buckled, and Luke let her fall.

McCluskey might have slept through that derringer going off, but Luke knew the outlaw must have heard the blonde's warning scream. He bounded past her, drawing both Remingtons, and paused just long enough to lift his foot and kick the door open.

He dived to the floor, twisting so that he landed on his belly with both guns up. Shots roared inside the room, coming so close together they sounded like one thunderous blast. Bullets whipped through the air a couple feet above Luke's head and punched through the wall on the other side of the corridor.

He hoped nobody was in that room.

McCluskey crouched beside the bed, gun in hand, wearing only the bottom half of a pair of long red underwear. He was medium height, a little stocky but powerfully built in the arms and shoulders. He had close-cropped dark hair on a squarish head and a slab-like jaw usually thrust out belligerently. That was certainly the case as the hammer of his gun fell on an empty chamber.

He had emptied the revolver without doing a damn bit of good. That was all right with Luke. He didn't have any qualms about shooting an unarmed man who had just tried to kill him — especially when the reward on McCluskey was good dead or alive.

Luke triggered both Remingtons, but Mc-Cluskey was fast as he flung himself onto the bed. He had to be to have stayed alive as long as he had. Luke's bullets narrowly missed. Rolling off the mattress's other side, McCluskey came up and plunged toward the room's lone window.

Luke surged to his feet and was drawing a bead on the fleeing owlhoot when something landed on his back. The impact made him stumble forward a couple steps.

"I've got him, Frank!" the blonde screeched in Luke's ear. "Get away while you can!"

She went after his eyes again, reaching around with both hands as she wrapped her legs around his torso and clung to him like a tick. Her fingernails raked stingingly across his cheek, dangerously close to his right eye. He flung himself back and forth violently as he tried to throw her off, but she hung on to him for dear life.

McCluskey could have made it through the window then if he had tried, but he thought it was too good an opportunity to rid himself of one of the bounty hunters on his trail. He dropped the gun he had emptied and snatched up a bowie knife lying on the little table next to the bed. As he shouted a curse, he lunged toward Luke and thrust the heavy blade at his chest.

McCluskey's impulsive attack had brought him within reach. Luke knocked the bowie aside with the Remington he held in his left hand and struck out with the right-hand revolver, slamming it into McCluskey's head. A blow like that could crack a man's skull and kill him, but just then Luke didn't care about that. He didn't want McCluskey trying to swipe that bowie at him in a nasty backhand.

McCluskey went down hard. Luke figured he would be out for several minutes — but he had thought that about Delia, too, and she had recovered her wits quicker than he'd expected. He needed to deal with her while he had the chance.

She had knocked his hat off when she jumped on him. He hunched his shoulders and lowered his head to make it harder for her to claw at his face, then holstered his right-hand gun and reached back to grab her. He felt fabric and closed his fingers on it. As he bent forward at the waist, he hauled hard on her dress and heaved her up and over his head, creating a ripping sound as cloth and stitches gave.

Delia cried out as she flew through the air. With a flash of creamy skin, she landed on the bed and bounced.

Luke was a little surprised to see that she had come right out of the torn dress and lay there clad only in a thin chemise that didn't leave much of her lush figure to the imagination. He still held the dress.

She came up off the bed spitting with fury. He threw the dress over her head, blinding her temporarily, then wrapped his right arm around her and pinned her arms to her sides as he lifted her off her feet. All she could do was scream muffled curses and kick her feet. Her heels banged against his shins, but he did his best to ignore that as he tried to figure out what to do with her.

He was saved from having to ponder that for very long by the arrival of a gray-haired, middle-aged man who appeared in the room's open doorway holding a shotgun. He had a lawman's badge pinned to his vest, and as he leveled the Greener at Luke he barked a command. "Throw that gun on the bed, mister, right now!"

"Take it easy, Marshal," Luke said as he tossed the Remington in his left hand onto the bed. No man in his right mind put up much of an argument when he found himself staring down the twin barrels of a shotgun. "This isn't what it looks like."

"I don't know what you think it looks like, mister. I was told that all hell was breakin' loose up here, and that's sure as blazes how it appears to me!"

CHAPTER 2

Normally, Luke checked in with the local star-packer whenever he arrived in a new town. It was just a reasonable precaution. Some lawmen got proddy when they found out that a bounty hunter was operating in their jurisdiction. Others were relieved that a dangerous outlaw was about to be taken into custody and would offer to help.

Luke hadn't done that because the first man he'd asked about McCluskey, the elderly hostler at the livery stable where he'd left his dun, had pointed him to the hotel and said that a man matching the outlaw's description was staying there. Luke had decided to look into that before paying a visit to the local law.

With the inducement of a five-dollar gold piece, the desk clerk had confirmed that a man who looked like McCluskey was upstairs in Room Seven. The name he'd signed to the register was Pete Yarnell, an alias McCluskey had used in the past.

"He's still upstairs, too," the clerk had said. "Reckon he's sleeping late this morning. From what I heard, he had quite a bit to drink last night at the Powder River Saloon. The night clerk told me he came in drunk as a skunk."

A hungover outlaw was usually a little slower in his reactions and therefore easier to corral. With that opportunity staring him in the face, Luke hadn't been about to waste it by taking the time to hunt up the marshal. He'd gone upstairs, ready to bust into Room Seven and capture Frank McCluskey.

As the shotgun-wielding marshal had put it, all hell had broken loose.

Struggling to hang on to the squirming Delia, Luke said, "Marshal, my name is Luke Jensen. That fella there on the floor is Frank McCluskey. I reckon you've got at least one wanted poster on him in your office, and probably more than that. He's wanted in Wyoming, Idaho, Montana, and Dakota Territories for holding up banks and stagecoaches, rustling cattle, and gunning down at least five men."

"Sounds like a real sidewinder," the lawman said as a frown creased his forehead. "If you know all that, I suppose you must be either a bounty hunter or a deputy U.S. marshal — and I've got a hunch Uncle Sam wouldn't hire anybody as scruffy-looking as you."

Under other circumstances, Luke might have taken offense at that comment. It was true that he was a little dusty and trail-worn at the moment, but several times a year he enjoyed visiting San Francisco, dressing well, and patronizing the city's finest restaurants and clubs. Although he was largely self-educated, he was also a very well-read man and could discuss Plutarch, Hawthorne, and von Clausewitz with equal ease.

But there was no way the marshal could know any of that. Luke shrugged. "That's right. I'm a bounty hunter, and I'd be much obliged to you, Marshal, if you'd let me lock up McCluskey in your jail."

That prompted a fresh round of squealing, cussing, and fighting from Delia, and despite the lawman's grim demeanor, a smile tugged at his mouth for a second under his bushy gray mustache. "What've you got there, Jensen?"

"A wildcat," Luke said dryly. "She says her name is Delia Bradley. Do you know her?"

"Yeah. She's a soiled dove, works over at

the Powder River Saloon. She seems a mite put out with you."

"I believe she's smitten with McCluskey here. She tried to take a shot at me with a derringer and did her best to warn him to get away."

The marshal nodded. "All right. Why don't you put her down? I don't figure she'll try anything else."

Luke wasn't so sure about that, but he pulled the dress off Delia's head and set her feet back on the floor.

She clenched her fists and pounded them against his chest. "Marshal, arrest this man! He attacked me. You can see for yourself that he ripped the dress right off me!"

"That's not exactly the way it —" Luke grabbed her around the waist from behind as she lunged toward the bed and made a grab for the gun he had tossed there at the marshal's command. He swung her away from the bed.

She started kicking and flailing again.

On the floor, McCluskey groaned and moved around a little as he began to regain consciousness.

"Blast it. Quit that!" Luke told Delia. "I'm going to pitch you out that window if you don't stop fighting."

"Here now!" the marshal exclaimed.

"Nobody's pitching anybody out any windows. But I *will* lock you up if you keep raising a ruckus, Delia."

The threat seemed to get through to her. She stopped struggling and said coldly to Luke, "Quit pawing me, mister. I get paid any time a man wants to do that."

Luke set her down where he would be between her and the bed where the Remington lay. He said to the lawman, "Is it all right if I get my gun again, Marshal?"

"Yeah, go ahead," the middle-aged man told him. "I reckon I've got the straight of things now. You say that fella's name is Frank McCluskey?"

"That's right," Luke said as he picked up the iron and pouched it.

"I've heard of him, all right." The marshal moved farther into the room and stepped aside to clear the doorway. "Delia, put your dress on and get out of here."

"But it's torn!" she objected.

"It'll hold together enough to cover you so you'll be decent." The marshal paused, then added, "As decent as you ever are, I should say."

Delia sniffed disdainfully, picked up the dress, and pulled it over her head. It was ripped down the back but covered the front of her well enough.

Luke had an objection of his own. "Wait a minute. She tried to help McCluskey escape. That's against the law."

"Yeah, but he didn't escape, and I can tell you right now, our justice of the peace will just throw out any charge you try to press against her."

"That's right," she said, smirking. "Charlie's not going to put me in jail."

Luke bit back a curse. The fact that Delia referred to the justice of the peace as *Charlie* indicated that he was probably one of her regular customers. He wouldn't likely want her locked up.

As long as she stayed out of his way, Luke supposed he didn't care what happened to her. He nodded his head toward the door. "All right. Get out."

She glared at him, and for a second he thought she might stick her tongue out at him like a little kid. But then she sniffed again, lifted her head, and stalked out of the room in her torn dress as if she possessed all the dignity in the world.

The marshal stepped closer to McCluskey and prodded him with the shotgun.

"Be careful, Marshal," Luke warned. "He's as fast and tricky as a snake."

"I know what I'm doing. He won't be the first outlaw I've locked up, you know." But the lawman backed off a couple steps before he went on. "All right, McCluskey, get up. You're going to jail."

McCluskey groaned again and looked bleary-eyed at Luke. "Damn. You just about busted my head open," he complained.

"That's right," Luke said. "You're lucky your brains are still inside your skull. Don't give us any trouble and maybe they'll stay there."

The marshal covered McCluskey with the Greener and Luke rested his right hand on the butt of a Remington as McCluskey climbed unsteadily to his feet.

"Let's go," the marshal said as he backed toward the door.

"Damn it. Won't you even let me put my pants on?" McCluskey begged. "You can't mean to parade me through town like this!"

The marshal hesitated, shrugged, and looked at Luke, who picked up McCluskey's denim trousers from where they had been thrown over the back of a chair, most likely the previous night while he and Delia Bradley were caught up in the throes of passion.

Luke checked the pockets and didn't find any weapons, only a few coins and a lucky elk's tooth — said luck having run out for McCluskey. He tossed the garment to the outlaw, who pulled it on.

"How about my boots?" McCluskey asked.

The marshal shook his head. "I've already given you the only break I'm going to. Get moving and keep your mouth shut."

With the lawman in front of McCluskey and Luke behind, they took the owlhoot out of the hotel room and down the stairs to the lobby. Quite a few people were gathered there. From the looks of them, some were guests in the hotel and others were citizens of Rimrock. They had all turned out to see what the shooting on the second floor was about. They watched with avid interest as Luke and the marshal took McCluskey out of the hotel.

Luke looked at them as he passed by. Probably would be a good turnout in Cheyenne, too, when the law hanged Frank McCluskey for his crimes.

CHAPTER 3

The marshal's name was Warren Elliott and he had been the law in Rimrock for the past five years, he explained to Luke as he poured coffee from a battered old pot keeping warm on a potbellied stove. "I'd say McCluskey is the worst renegade I've had locked up in all that time." He motioned with his tin cup toward the stack of half a dozen wanted posters he had pulled out from the pile in the bottom drawer of his desk. All of them offered rewards for the capture of the notorious bandit and killer Frank McCluskey.

"He'll get what's coming to him," Luke promised. "All I have to do is get him to Cheyenne."

Elliott scratched at his jaw. "Have you given any thought to how you're gonna do that?"

"I suppose I'll put him in handcuffs, tie him on a horse, and lead him to his appointment with the hangman," Luke said with a shrug.

"How's his gang going to feel about that?"

Luke sank down on the old sofa positioned against the front wall of the marshal's office and cocked his right ankle on his left knee. "McCluskey doesn't have a gang right now," he explained. "He was riding with four or five men, but the others got shot up and captured when they tried to hit the bank in Rock Springs about a week and a half ago. McCluskey was the only one of the bunch who got away. He should have known right then that his luck was starting to turn."

Elliott grunted. "If he got away, I reckon he still had at least a little luck on his side."

"But he got away empty-handed and with nobody to back his play anymore. It was only a matter of time until somebody nabbed him."

"And that somebody was you." Elliott fanned out the wanted posters. "You're gonna collect . . . let's see" — he added on his fingers — "four, five, six thousand dollars, looks like." He whistled. "That's a mighty good reward."

Not so good when you considered how often he had to risk his life to collect that kind of money. But Luke supposed that as a small-town badge-toter, Marshal Elliott sometimes had to risk his life, too — and for a lot smaller payday.

"If I was you," the lawman mused, "I think I'd take McCluskey over to Rattlesnake Wells."

Luke frowned. "I think I've heard of the place. Just a wide place in the trail, from what I recall. Why would I take McCluskey there?"

"You haven't been around these parts for a while, have you?"

"No, not really."

"Rattlesnake Wells is a lot more than a wide place in the trail now," Elliott said. "There was a gold strike up in the Prophecy Mountains not far from there, and Rattlesnake Wells turned into a boomtown. Some mining tycoon name of Browning built a spur line railroad just to haul out the ore."

Luke thought he saw what the marshal was getting at. "Does that spur line connect up with the Union Pacific?"

"Yep. And once you get to the Union Pacific, it's a straight shot over east to Cheyenne. You can be there in about three days from now, countin' the time it'll take you from here to Rattlesnake Wells, instead of the week or more it'd take you to ride all the way, especially as slow as you'd have to move with a dangerous prisoner."

Luke liked the sound of that. The less time he had to spend in McCluskey's company, the better. Not to mention the fact that he would collect the bounty on the outlaw a few days sooner, as well. It never hurt to speed up the money.

"There's a good livery stable and wagon yard in Rattlesnake Wells," Elliott continued. "Run by a fella name of Joe Peterson. You could leave your horse there for a few days while you take McCluskey over to Cheyenne, then come back for him."

"That's a good idea, and I appreciate the advice, Marshal." Luke frowned slightly. "What about that Bradley woman? Is she liable to cause any more trouble?"

"Delia?" Elliott shook his head. "I doubt it. She may be sweet on McCluskey right now, but there's no profit in her being stubborn about it. Did you ever know a soiled dove who was interested in anything except money, when you got right down to it?"

"Not many," Luke admitted. "Maybe one or two."

"Well, there's nothin' special about Delia Bradley. You don't have to worry about her anymore, Jensen. I'd bet a hat on that."

■ ■ ■ ■

Luke was a pretty good judge of jails, and the one in Rimrock looked solid to him. He didn't see any way McCluskey could break out, and Marshal Elliott was too canny to be taken in by any tricks that the outlaw might try to pull. Luke decided it was safe enough to get a good night's sleep at the hotel and start out for Rattlesnake Wells early the next morning.

When he checked in, he asked the clerk, "Nobody was hurt in all that shooting a while ago, were they?"

"No, but I've got some bullet holes in the walls to patch," the man groused. "Rimrock's a pretty peaceful town. We're not used to so much commotion."

"It wasn't my idea for McCluskey to shoot up the place." Luke started to add that the clerk had already collected a sawbuck for his trouble but then decided to be generous. He slid another silver dollar across the counter, in addition to what he had already paid for the room. "That'll buy some plaster."

Yeah, he thought as he carried his Winchester and war bag upstairs to Room Twelve, he was definitely getting soft in his old age.

He dumped the rifle and bag in the room and headed back downstairs.

The hotel didn't have a dining room, but there was a café in the next block run by a Norwegian couple with thick accents. The husband fried up a good steak, and the wife's deep-dish apple pie was as good as any Luke had tasted in a long time. Her coffee was considerably better than Marshal Elliott's, too.

By the time he was finished with the meal, he was comfortably full and a bit drowsy but not quite ready to turn in yet. He stood on the boardwalk outside the café, lit a cheroot, and considered his options.

There seemed to be only one. Rimrock appeared to have but a single saloon, the Powder River . . . where Delia Bradley worked. He gazed diagonally across the broad main street toward the brightly lit building, not sure he wanted to run into her again.

On the other hand, he was damned if he would allow some little soiled dove who didn't weigh more than a hundred pounds soaking wet keep him from going anywhere he wanted to go.

Clenching the cheroot between his teeth, he started across the street. He heard the tinny notes of a player piano coming from inside before he reached the entrance. The merry sound grew louder as he pushed the batwings aside and stepped into the saloon.

The place was about half full, with a number of men standing at the bar and others sitting at tables drinking and playing cards. Luke spotted three women, all with painted faces and wearing gaudy dresses, delivering drinks from the bar to the tables, but none of them was Delia Bradley.

Maybe she was taking the night off because she was too upset about her outlaw beau being captured to work, Luke thought.

Most of the men and all three of the women turned to look at him when he came in. It wouldn't have taken long for word to get around town that a bounty hunter was in Rimrock. He was probably the only stranger in these parts, other than McCluskey himself, so he had to be the manhunter. Some of the saloon's patrons had seen him earlier that afternoon, too, when he and Elliott marched a barefoot, stripped to the waist, sullenly scowling Frank McCluskey to the local *juzgado.*

Luke didn't particularly want the attention. He figured he'd drink a beer, then head back to the hotel and try to get a good night's sleep. He gave the people in the saloon a curt nod, then headed for the bar.

The man on the other side of the hardwood was lean and gray, wearing an apron tied around his waist, a white shirt with sleeve garters, and a brocaded vest. He greeted Luke with a sardonic, unreadable expression and asked, "What'll it be?"

"Beer if it's cold."

"It's what passes for cold around here," the bartender said. "Is that good enough for you?"

Luke chuckled. "I reckon it'll have to be."

Although the beer the drink juggler pulled from a tap was only cool, it tasted good. Luke took a long swallow and nodded in satisfaction.

The bartender finally smiled. "You're him. The bounty hunter."

"That's right."

"You're the reason I've got a girl upstairs crying her eyes out instead of, well, doing what she's supposed to be doing."

Luke shook his head. "I'd tell you I'm sorry, but that's not really my responsibility. Anyway, McCluskey just rode in here yesterday. How could she fall head over heels in love with him that fast?"

The bartender grunted. "You don't know Delia. That girl . . . well, she never does anything halfway. She's all the time pitching a conniption fit over one thing or another.

I'd fire her and run her little round behind out of here if she wasn't so good at what she does."

"Somebody who's that quick to go whole hog about something is usually pretty quick to get over it, too," Luke commented.

"We can only hope," the bartender said, raising his bushy gray eyebrows. "In the meantime, I'd watch my back if I was you, Mr. Jensen."

"I'm sort of in the habit of that." Luke finished the beer and thought about seeing if he could sit in on one of the poker games, then decided he was too tired for cards. He nodded good night to the bartender and walked out of the Powder River, aware that some of the customers were still watching him curiously.

Most of the time, life in a frontier town was so monotonous that any distraction was welcome. Luke knew that and didn't take offense at the staring.

Nobody was in the hotel lobby except the desk clerk, who still didn't look too happy about the prospect of repairing those bullet holes. Luke ignored the man and went upstairs to his room. He smiled a little, though, as he passed the section of wall Mc-Cluskey had done such a good job of ventilating.

His room was on the other side of the hall and a couple doors farther along. As he approached it, he looked at the spot where he had wedged a bit of black thread between the door and jamb, down low, close to the floor. It was still there, telling him that no one had gotten into the room.

Unless they had come in through the window, that is. Since there was no balcony outside — Luke had already thought to check on that — such an invasion would have been difficult. It would have required leaning a ladder against the front wall of the hotel, something that was liable to be noticed in a tranquil place like Rimrock.

He was satisfied that he wasn't walking into an ambush, but had a gun in his right hand anyway as he used his left to unlock the door and swing it open. He'd left the curtain pushed back over the window so some light from the street came in, and he could see well enough to tell that the room was empty except for its simple furniture. He stepped inside, holstered the Remington, closed and locked the door, and pulled the curtain before he lit the lamp on the table beside the bed.

His gun belt and holstered revolvers went on the lone ladderback chair, which he'd pushed over next to the bed so the weapons would be handy while he was sleeping. He dropped his hat on the table next to the lamp. He had taken off his boots and undressed down to his trousers when a quiet knock sounded on the door.

He stiffened for a second and then reached down to slide one of the Remingtons from its holster. Knowing how easy it was to fire a shotgun through the flimsy panels of the door, he stood to the side and well back in the room so it would be more difficult for someone in the hall to pinpoint his location by the sound of his voice as he called, "Who's there?"

"Delia Bradley."

Not many things surprised Luke after the life he'd led, but that answer did. He stayed where he was and asked, "What do you want, Miss Bradley?"

"Just to talk," Delia said through the door. "I promise. I . . . I'd like to apologize for my behavior earlier today, Mr. Jensen."

Luke didn't trust her for a second, but he was curious. She sounded calm and rational enough. Of course, that could be an act. Still, there was only one way to find out.

In his bare feet, he moved to the door in utter silence and turned the key slowly and carefully. It didn't click in the lock to alert Delia that he was right on the other side of the door.

He backed off and told her, "It's open. Come on in."

CHAPTER 4

Luke had the Remington leveled and the hammer thumbed back as the door opened. Delia didn't seem bothered by having a gun pointed at her as she stepped into the room, but she said, "You don't need that. I give you my word, Luke."

He had gone from Mr. Jensen to Luke mighty fast, he thought, especially considering that a few hours earlier she'd tried to shoot him and then claw his eyes out. Maybe she really did want to apologize.

She wore a simple gray dress, although it was cut low enough to leave her shoulders mostly bare and reveal a considerable amount of the valley between her full breasts. A lacy shawl was draped around her shoulders to entice more than it concealed.

It wouldn't do much to keep her warm, Luke thought.

He lowered the Remington but didn't put

it away, holding it at his side. "I didn't really expect to see you again before I left town, Miss Bradley."

"Please, call me Delia." She smiled a little as she moved a step closer. "I'm used to men being on an, ah, informal footing with me, if you know what I mean."

Luke grunted. He was well aware that she was running her eyes over his bare chest, shoulders, and arms, and the flirtatious look he had first seen in the hotel corridor that afternoon was back in her eyes.

She had looked at him like that just before she'd pulled that derringer and tried to shoot him in the back, he reminded himself. It wasn't fooling him.

When he didn't say anything, she went on. "I just wanted to tell you that I know I got carried away earlier today. You were just doing your job, and I shouldn't have tried to hurt you because of it. Really, I . . . I don't know what came over me. Goodness gracious, I hadn't even known that man, that Mr. Yarnell, for twenty-four hours. If I'd known he was a wanted outlaw, I never would have caused so much trouble."

Well, that was a bald-faced lie, thought Luke. She had called him *Frank* when she'd screamed the warning to him, so obviously McCluskey had told her who he was. Guess she thought a seductive smile and a look down the front of her dress would be enough to distract him into forgetting about that.

It might have worked on a lot of men. Even Luke had to admit that the view was mighty damn appealing. But whenever somebody tried to kill him he had a hard time forgetting it. "I accept your apology. Now, if there's nothing else, it's been a long day and I'm tired."

"You probably want to turn in."

"That's right."

"You don't have to do it alone, you know." She slid the shawl off her shoulders and dropped it over the top of the chair. "After everything that happened, I feel like I owe you something, Luke. I'd be glad to spend the night with you, and it won't cost you a thing." She started to slip the dress down off her left shoulder.

"You can stop right there."

She froze, and anger flashed in her eyes. "Are you sure about that? I promise, I can make the time pass mighty pleasantly for you, honey. In fact, I guarantee it."

"And then what? You try to talk me into busting McCluskey out of jail and letting him go free so you can run off with him? Is that the sort of romantic notion you've got

39

in your head, Delia?"

She forced an expression of surprise on her face, but Luke could tell it wasn't genuine.

"What are you talking about? Such a crazy thought never even entered my mind! I just feel bad about what happened earlier and want to make it up to you."

With his free hand, Luke rubbed his chin as he frowned in thought. "I'd wager you know how much bounty McCluskey is worth to me, so you'd figure I wouldn't bust him out no matter what you did in bed," he mused. "That means you probably planned on getting me unarmed and then getting the drop on me so you could use me as a hostage. You could march me over to the jail at gunpoint and threaten to kill me unless Marshal Elliott released the prisoner."

Her eyes were fairly glittering with anger, but she still tried to make her voice honey-sweet. "Why, I'd never do anything like that. You're just such an attractive man —"

Luke's harsh laugh interrupted her. "Now I know you're just putting on an act, Delia. It's not going to work, so you might as well take your cleavage and get on out of here."

The fake smile disappeared as she snarled at him. "You damn fool. You don't know what you're passing up."

"Whatever it is, I reckon there's a good chance I'll live longer without it."

"Oh!" She snatched up the shawl but didn't put it back on as she turned to the door.

"You'll get over McCluskey," Luke told her. "He's just a two-bit outlaw. A week from now you'll have forgotten that you ever met him."

She jerked the door open, stalked out, and slammed it behind her hard enough to make it shiver in its frame.

Luke locked the door, holstered the Remington, and went to bed.

He fell asleep quickly and didn't dream.

Breakfast at the café was just as good as supper had been the night before, and Luke felt well-rested and well-fed as he went to the livery stable to get his horse and McCluskey's mount. Once he had the horses saddled and ready to ride, he led them to the general store, which had just opened for the day.

Marshal Elliott had told him it would take about a day and a half to ride to Rattlesnake Wells, so Luke wanted to make sure he had enough provisions for that journey. His weeklong pursuit of McCluskey had exhausted some of his supplies.

With that errand taken care of, he headed for the marshal's office.

"Is that a fresh pot or left over from yesterday?" Luke asked as he came into the office. He gestured toward the coffeepot on the stove in the corner.

"The grounds are still good," Elliott said defensively. "The town doesn't pay me what you'd call an extravagant wage. Man's got to be thrifty to live on it. I'll pour you a cup, though, if you want it."

"No, thanks." Luke had already had an extra cup at the café, figuring he would need it to stay alert on the ride to Rattlesnake Wells.

"Suit yourself." Elliott picked up a ring of keys from his desk. "I already fetched the prisoner some breakfast awhile ago, so he's ready for you, I reckon."

"I'm obliged to you for your help, Marshal."

Elliott unlocked the cell block door. "I'm just glad we were able to corral that jasper. I don't like the idea of an outlaw like him being in my town and I didn't even know it."

"You didn't have any reason to suspect McCluskey was in these parts," Luke pointed out. "There's no telegraph office here, so you wouldn't have gotten a wire about that bank robbery over in Rock Springs. You wouldn't have known to be watching for him."

"And the stagecoach only comes through once a week. That's the only news we ever get. Since it was westbound last time, word of the holdup never got here. But it all worked out all right, I suppose." Elliott swung the thick wooden door open. "Can't say as I'll be sorry to see McCluskey go. You need to be mighty careful with him on the way to Rattlesnake Wells, Jensen. He's liable to try to escape."

"I'll be ready for any tricks he pulls." Now that he had captured McCluskey alive, Luke would just as soon keep him that way and turn him over to the authorities in Cheyenne. But if the outlaw tried to make a break and Luke had to kill him, well, that wouldn't be any cause for lost sleep.

McCluskey was fully dressed, wearing the clothes that had been brought over from the hotel. He stood at the cell door, grasping the bars and glowering at Luke as the bounty hunter and the marshal entered the cell block.

Luke drew one of his Remingtons and covered McCluskey as Elliott unlocked the cell. The lawman stepped back quickly and drew his own gun. "Come on out now," he told the prisoner.

"And don't forget all the posters on you say dead or alive," Luke added.

McCluskey swung the door back and said sullenly, "I'm not gonna try anything. I'm smart enough to know when the odds are against me."

"Just not smart enough not to take up a life of crime," Elliott said.

McCluskey sneered at the marshal but didn't have any other response.

"Hands behind your back and turn around," Luke said.

"You're gonna cuff me like that?" McCluskey asked indignantly. "Hell, a man can't ride with his hands cuffed behind his back."

"You can. I'll be leading your horse. You don't have to worry about the reins."

"Maybe not, but it'll be blasted uncomfortable."

"Not as uncomfortable as the coffins where all the men you've killed are spending their time now."

McCluskey smirked. "Hell, I'll bet they're not feelin' a thing."

Luke suppressed the impulse to pistol-whip the man again. "Turn around."

McCluskey did, and Luke snapped a pair of handcuffs on him. With that done, he grasped the outlaw's shirt collar and jerked him through the marshal's office and outside where he helped him up into the saddle as Elliott stood by with gun still drawn. Once McCluskey was mounted, Luke ran a length of rope under the horse's belly and tied the outlaw's ankles together.

"If this jughead runs away or falls down, there won't be a damn thing I can do about it," McCluskey complained bitterly. "I'll be stuck up here."

"It's your horse and your worry," Luke said. "You'd know better than I would how likely that is."

"You're hopin' I don't make it to Cheyenne alive, aren't you?"

"I'm not worried about it one way or the other," Luke replied honestly. "If I really want you dead, I can just shoot you in the head as soon as we've left town. Nobody would ever know the difference, or care overmuch if they did. You'd do well to remember that."

The frown McCluskey gave him was enough payment for that jibe, Luke thought as he chuckled to himself.

Even though the hour was fairly early — the sun had just come up — quite a few people were on the street, and Luke realized they had turned out to watch him leave Rimrock with his prisoner. Having the notorious desperado Frank McCluskey captured in their town was probably the most exciting thing that had happened in the settlement in years. It was possible nothing would ever take place in Rimrock to top it. Some of the townspeople were probably even sorry to see them go.

Luke wouldn't regret putting the place behind him. He glanced across the street at the Powder River Saloon, which was dark and quiet at the early hour. Delia Bradley was probably asleep. He was confident that what he had told her was right. She would soon forget all about Frank McCluskey.

Luke swung up into the dun's saddle. Elliott handed him the reins of McCluskey's horse.

"Thanks again, Marshal," Luke told the lawman.

"My pleasure. Just be careful, Jensen. You never know what you might run into."

Luke nodded and heeled his horse into motion. Leading McCluskey's mount, he rode out of Rimrock, on his way to collecting six thousand dollars.

As they passed the saloon, he thought he saw a curtain in one of the windows twitch, but he wasn't sure about that and didn't figure it mattered anyway.

■ ■ ■ ■

Delia let the curtain fall closed. She couldn't bear to watch McCluskey humiliated like that, being paraded in front of those stupid townspeople as a helpless prisoner while Jensen took him out of town. She hadn't known McCluskey long, but she knew what a proud man he was and how that display had to be eating at his guts.

It was just one more thing Luke Jensen would pay for, sooner or later, she swore to herself. Her eyes were red-rimmed and gritty. She'd been awake all night, crying and plotting her revenge.

That damn bounty hunter would rue the day he first set eyes on her, she thought as she stripped off the thin wrapper she wore and started cramming her few belongings into a threadbare carpetbag.

CHAPTER 5

Southwest Wyoming was a wide basin broken up occasionally by ridges and buttes and gullies. The rugged, snowcapped mountains in the distance were the Prophecies. Rattlesnake Wells was located at the base of that range, on the closest side of the peaks.

In the thin, clear air, the mountains looked almost close enough to reach out and touch, but Luke and McCluskey were still a day and a half's ride away, assuming they didn't run into any delays.

They rode steadily toward the mountains and stopped only occasionally to let the horses rest. McCluskey complained almost constantly, but after a while Luke was able to just ignore him, almost as if he couldn't hear it.

During the years he had spent as a bounty hunter, a lot of his prisoners had done the same thing, and the only other options were to gag them or knock them out, both of which were too much trouble as far as he was concerned. It was easier to not pay attention to the profanity-laced tirades.

When the sun was high overhead, Luke called a halt in the shade of some scrubby aspens that grew along the edge of a gully. The wash was dry, but he supposed water ran in it during rainstorms, which accounted for the trees. Their roots could reach down far enough to find some moisture.

"I've got some sandwiches I brought from the café back in Rimrock, and I'll boil up a pot of coffee," he told McCluskey when he had dismounted and let the dun start grazing on the sparse grass beneath the trees. "You think you can stop flapping your gums long enough to eat?"

"How the hell am I gonna eat with my hands behind my back? I've got to tend to some other business, too, if you know what I mean." McCluskey smirked at Luke. "You gonna help me with that, bounty hunter?"

Luke resisted the impulse to backhand him. He untied McCluskey's ankles and stepped back quickly, drawing one of his guns. "Get down," he ordered.

McCluskey kicked his feet free of the stirrups, swung his right leg over the horse's back, and slid to the ground. He landed awkwardly and almost fell before righting himself.

"Turn around." Luke didn't holster the Remington until McCluskey was facing away from him, then he took a pair of leg irons from one of his saddlebags and snapped them around McCluskey's ankles. The chain had just enough play to let the outlaw shuffle along a few inches at a time.

When his ankles were secure, Luke unlocked the handcuffs, again stepping back swiftly so McCluskey wouldn't have a chance to spin around and make a grab for him.

"There are some bushes right over there," Luke told him. "Go take care of your business, then we'll have something to eat."

Moving slowly and tentatively, like a little old man, McCluskey headed toward the bushes.

"Stay where I can see your head and shoulders," Luke added as he started gathering fallen branches to build a fire on a rocky spot near the edge of the gully.

He glanced toward McCluskey now and then as he got the fire going and set the coffeepot at the edge of the flames to boil. After a few minutes the outlaw emerged from the brush and shuffled over to stand next to the fire, across from Luke.

"How about leaving the cuffs off until after we've eaten?" he asked. "It'd sure make things a lot easier."

"For you or for me?" Luke asked.

"Hell, for both of us. You don't want to have to feed me and give me drinks from a coffee cup, do you?"

As a matter of fact, Luke didn't. As he straightened, he reached for his gun, thinking he could make McCluskey back off, then set the man's food and drink on the other side of the fire and cover him while he ate.

He didn't get the chance. Before he could draw the Remington, McCluskey launched himself across the flames in a diving tackle that caught Luke around the waist.

Caught by surprise, Luke was slow to react just enough to give McCluskey a chance. The impact of their collision drove Luke backward, and suddenly there was nothing underneath his boots except empty air. McCluskey had knocked him off the edge of the gulley.

A second later, Luke's feet hit the sloping side of the wash, but it was too steep for him to catch his balance. He kept toppling toward the bottom with McCluskey hanging onto him. As they rolled over and over, the outlaw grabbed desperately for one of Luke's guns.

Luke's head smashed against a rock on the side of the gully with stunning force. Barely aware that his prisoner had succeeded in snatching one of the Remingtons from its holster, the realization shot through Luke's brain just in time for him to wrap his left hand around the barrel and shove it aside as McCluskey pulled the trigger.

The gun's muzzle was so close to Luke's ear that the shot slammed against it like a physical blow. The bullet screamed past his head and plowed harmlessly into the side of the gully. As they rolled, McCluskey's face loomed above him, so Luke jabbed a fist into it, striking the outlaw squarely in the nose.

He knew from experience that being hit like that stung like blazes and was enough to incapacitate a man for a few seconds. Luke tried to seize that advantage by locking his right hand around McCluskey's throat. He squeezed hard enough to make McCluskey's eyes bulge out.

They hit the bottom of the wash with enough force to jolt them apart. Luke grabbed for the other revolver, but he found only an empty holster. The gun had come out during their mad tumble down the slope.

He rolled and kicked just as McCluskey tried to bring the Remington to bear on him. The toe of his boot struck McCluskey's wrist and knocked the gun out of his hand. It flew a good ten feet before it thudded onto the bottom of the sandy, rock-littered wash.

Luke scrambled after the weapon, but before he could reach it McCluskey was on him again. He dropped his feet over Luke's head, snaring him with the chain between the leg irons. Luke grabbed the chain just as McCluskey jerked his knees back, and his grip was all that prevented the iron links from crushing his windpipe.

McCluskey dragged him over onto his back and tightened the stranglehold. At the same time, the outlaw picked up one of the rocks scattered around the bottom of the gully and swung it up, then brought it down toward Luke's head.

The rock was the size of two fists put together, and it would have crushed Luke's skull like an eggshell if it had landed. Luke saw the blow coming just in time to jerk his head aside. The rock slammed into the ground a couple inches from his right ear.

Luke let go of the chain and immediately

started to gag as the pressure increased on his throat. He reached up and behind him with both hands and caught hold of McCluskey's knee. From that angle he couldn't exert as much strength as he would have liked, but he forced the joint in the wrong direction as best he could. It was enough to make McCluskey cry out in pain, and the grip on Luke's neck eased.

He twisted and shoved, and his head popped free of the hold McCluskey had had on him. He levered himself up on his left arm and buried his right fist in McCluskey's midsection. McCluskey rolled onto his side, gasping for breath.

Luke knew the feeling. His lungs were starved for air, but he couldn't afford to take the time to catch his breath. He went after McCluskey, scrambling up and throwing punch after punch. He pounded the outlaw's head from side to side. Blood splattered from McCluskey's nose and mouth. He put up his hands, but he wasn't fighting. He was pawing feebly in an attempt to block Luke's punches and making little mewling sounds.

Luke drove one last punch to McCluskey's jaw. The outlaw's eyes rolled up as he went limp. He was out cold.

With his chest heaving, Luke pushed

himself to his feet and stumbled back a couple steps so he could look around. He spotted both Remingtons and hurried to pick them up before McCluskey regained consciousness. When he had both guns in his hands and had backed off about a dozen feet to cover the prisoner, he finally had the chance to catch his breath and gather his strength.

His throat ached from the chain. He growled as he thought about stomping McCluskey's face in. He wasn't the sort to kill a man in cold blood or even beat up an unconscious opponent, so he ignored the impulse and waited for the outlaw to come to, using the few minutes to regain breath and strength.

The outlaw began to groan and twitch. Luke had seen the man regain consciousness before, so the sight was a familiar one.

McCluskey blinked and gradually pushed himself up to a sitting position with his back against the side of the gully. "Damn you," he said thickly through bloody, swollen lips. "That's the second time you've knocked me out. It's not gonna happen again."

"Damn right it's not," Luke rasped. "The next time you give me any trouble, I'm going to kill you, McCluskey. Consider that fair warning."

"Big talk."

"Not if I can back it up." Luke motioned with the left-hand Remington. "Get up. You're going to crawl back to the top."

"I can't climb with these leg irons on!"

"Figure out a way," Luke told him coldly.

McCluskey rolled over so that he was facing the slope. He had to pull himself up with his hands and push his body along with knees and toes. The wash was only about fifteen feet deep, but by the time McCluskey crawled out of it and collapsed on the ground, his hands were bloody and the knees of his trousers were shredded and had blood on them, as well.

From twenty feet away, Luke had kept his guns trained on the outlaw every inch of the way, staying even with him on the slope.

Now that they were both out of the gully, Luke said, "Roll onto your face, McCluskey, and put your hands behind your back."

McCluskey cursed, "You told me I could have my hands loose while I ate."

Luke laughed in astonishment at the man's gall. "Well, that's moot now. The coffee's boiled away and I sure as hell don't feel like hand-feeding you. You can do without until we make camp tonight."

"That's not right!" McCluskey protested. "You can't starve me like that."

"You're lucky I don't cut your throat," Luke snapped. "Now roll over."

Still complaining, McCluskey did as he was told. Carefully, Luke put the handcuffs on him. Then he took the leg irons off and lifted the prisoner to his feet.

A short time later, they were on their way. McCluskey was tied onto his horse again, a steady stream of profanity spewing from his mouth.

CHAPTER 6

By the middle of the afternoon, McCluskey fell into a sullen silence. Eventually he dozed off as he rocked along in the saddle.

Luke noticed. The peace and quiet was more than welcome.

McCluskey remained subdued when Luke made camp next to a small creek that evening. With one hand free and the other cuffed to his saddle weighing him down and preventing him from making any sudden moves, he was able to feed himself and drink the coffee Luke brewed. He even said, "I'm obliged to you for the meal — and for not killin' me."

Luke didn't trust this new, meek, co-operative McCluskey for a second. He knew the man was still a ruthless killer. His life wouldn't be worth a plugged nickel if McCluskey ever got the upper hand. Luke was determined that wasn't going to happen.

After they had eaten, Luke propped Mc-

Cluskey, once again in handcuffs and leg irons, against a tree trunk and wound rope around him, binding him securely to the tree. With that done, Luke was able to stretch out in his bedroll and sleep soundly — or better than McCluskey did, anyway.

They were on their way again early the next morning, and by the middle of the day they were approaching Rattlesnake Wells. McCluskey hadn't caused any problems since the day before at the dry wash. His shoulders slumped as he rode along, he looked like he had given up hope.

Maybe it was just a pose, Luke told himself. He kept a wary eye on the outlaw. But McCluskey seemed mired in despair as they rode into the settlement.

Marshal Elliott had called Rattlesnake Wells a boomtown, and that was an apt description. Main Street was crowded with wagons, buckboards, buggies, and riders on horseback. The boardwalks thronged with people. The town had been there before the gold strike in the mountains that loomed above it. Several large springs — the wells that had given the place its name, along with an accompanying nest of diamondback rattlers — provided water for immigrants passing through the area on their way to Oregon and Washington. Because of that history, a number of permanent buildings stood along the street, but the boom had brought in quite a few tent saloons and stores and other business establishments.

Luke had seen it happen before — sleepy little hamlets becoming thriving cities almost overnight. Rattlesnake Wells would go back to being small and sleepy as it once had been almost as quickly if the gold vein ever petered out.

The most important result of the boom, as far as Luke was concerned, was that the railroad had come to Rattlesnake Wells. He had seen the tracks running into the settlement from the south as they'd approached, along with the poles carrying telegraph wires. The tracks ended at a large, red-brick depot building and roundhouse at the far end of the street.

It would have been too much to hope that a train was in town, soon to pull out and head south to the junction with the Union Pacific. Luke would have gotten on that train with McCluskey and spent as little time in Rattlesnake Wells as possible.

But there was no locomotive at the station puffing smoke from its diamond-shaped stack as it built up steam, so Luke knew he would have to spend at least one night there, which meant his first priority was to get McCluskey safely behind bars again.

A lanky old-timer with a bald head under a tipped-back hat perched on the driver's seat of a wagon parked in front of a store set up in a big tent. A sign tacked to a post pounded into the ground read ALBRIGHT'S MERCANTILE.

Luke reined in and nodded to the old-timer. "Excuse me, mister, can you tell me where to find the marshal's office?"

The old man looked at McCluskey with wide, interested eyes. "Got yourself a prisoner there, I see. You a lawman, son?"

"You could say that," Luke answered with deliberate vagueness. Plenty of people didn't like bounty hunters and considered them one step above the reptiles that had congregated around the springs in times past.

"What'd he do?" the old man wanted to know.

Luke kept a tight rein on the impatience he felt. "Enough to get himself in plenty of trouble. If you could point me to the marshal's office . . . ?"

"Oh, sure." The old-timer leveled a gnarled hand. "Just go on down this street. It's yonder a couple blocks on the left-hand side."

Luke nodded again. "Obliged to you."

"Gonna lock him up?"

"That's the idea."

"He don't look all that dangerous."

It was true. At the moment, McCluskey looked more pathetic than he did like a menace.

Luke knew just how deceptive that was and heeled the dun into motion. He weaved through the traffic in the street, leading McCluskey's mount. The outlaw drew a lot of interested stares, but Luke didn't stop to offer explanations. He didn't draw rein until he was in front of the stoutly built log building that housed the RATTLESNAKE WELLS MARSHAL'S OFFICE AND JAIL, according to the sign.

A little boy about ten years old, with bright red hair, stood in front of the marshal's office and stared up at Luke and McCluskey.

Luke said, "Son, do you know if the marshal's inside?"

The youngster had a little trouble finding his tongue before saying, "Yes, sir, he is." He added with barely controlled excitement, "That's Frank McCluskey!"

"That's right," Luke said, a little surprised that the boy knew who McCluskey was. "Would you mind fetching the marshal for me?"

"Sure!" The kid hurried to the door, threw it open, and called, "Pa! Pa, come quick! A fella out here's got Frank McCluskey in irons!"

Well, that probably explained it, Luke thought.

Seeing as the boy's father was the marshal, the boy spent a considerable amount of time in his pa's office and could have studied all the reward dodgers that came in. The drawings of McCluskey that decorated some of those posters were reasonably accurate, with enough of a resemblance for the kid to recognize the genuine article when he saw it.

A tall young man with the same red hair as the boy emerged from the office. He was hatless and had an open, honest, friendly face with a faint dusting of freckles. He wore a Colt on his hip and looked like he knew how to use it. A lawman's badge was pinned to his vest.

A whistle of admiration came from his lips as he looked at Luke and the prisoner. "That's Frank McCluskey, all right. Good eye, Buck." To Luke, he said, "Who are you, mister, and what are you doing with this desperado? Although I reckon I can make a pretty good guess."

"Name's Luke Jensen. McCluskey's my

prisoner, and I'm taking him to Cheyenne to turn him over to the authorities there."

"And collect all the rewards on him, I'll wager," the marshal said. When Luke didn't respond to that, the lawman went on. "I'll bet you want to take him on the train."

"That's the idea," Luke said. "When's the next one due?"

"Ten o'clock tomorrow morning."

That was a relief, Luke thought. He and McCluskey would have to spend only one night here. He had nothing against Rattlesnake Wells, but the sooner he took in McCluskey and had the reward money in his pocket, the better.

"I was hoping —"

"That you could lock him up here overnight? I reckon that can be arranged. My name's Bob Hatfield, by the way. Some folks call me Sundown, on account of my hair." Marshal Hatfield put his hand on the boy's shoulder. "This little heathen is my son Bucky."

Luke nodded to the youngster. "Pleased to meet you, Bucky. And I'm obliged to you for your help a minute ago."

Buck grinned. "Shoot, all I did was open a door and yell for Pa."

Luke swung down from the saddle. "If it's all right with you, Marshal, I'd like to go ahead and get McCluskey safely behind bars."

Hatfield frowned. "He looks a little banged up, and your throat's a mite bruised, Mr. Jensen. The two of you have some trouble on the way here?"

"Yeah, yesterday," Luke admitted. "On the way here from Rimrock. That's where I caught up with him."

Hatfield nodded. "I know Marshal Elliott over there. Good man." He drew his revolver, and the smooth ease with which the Colt slid out of its holster told Luke he'd been right in his estimation of the young marshal. "I'll keep him covered while you get him down. Buck, you run on back to the house."

"Aw, Pa, I want to stay here and watch," the boy objected.

"No, you go on and do what I tell you. I want you to let Consuela know she'll need to cook up enough food for a couple guests tonight." The marshal added to Luke, "That's my housekeeper. She feeds the prisoners here in the jail, and the town pays her a little."

Luke nodded, but he didn't really care about Hatfield's domestic or financial arrangements. He just wanted to get McCluskey behind bars again.

Ten minutes later, he'd accomplished that. The outlaw continued to cooperate. He sank onto the bunk inside the cell, clasped his hands together between his knees, and stared expressionlessly at the floor.

As Hatfield turned the key in the cell door and stepped back, he commented, "I'm not complaining, mind you, but from everything I've heard about him, I expected Frank McCluskey to be more of a ring-tailed wildcat."

"He seems to have tamed down some," Luke said as he looked at the prisoner. "But you and your deputies, if you have any, shouldn't trust him. He knows he's got a hang rope waiting for him. A man like that is usually desperate enough to try anything."

"We'll be careful," Hatfield promised. "You're welcome to bunk here tonight if you want to, just to keep an eye on him. There's a cot in the storeroom you can use."

"I'll think about it," Luke promised. "I might just take you up on that. Right now, though, I could use a drink and something to eat."

Hatfield grinned. "Bullock's Saloon, on the other side of the street in the next block, puts out a decent free lunch, if you want to kill both of those birds with the same stone."

"I'll do that."

"Stop back by any time," Hatfield said.

"And you're having supper at my house tonight."

The invitation took Luke by surprise. Most lawmen treated bounty hunters like something they'd scrape off the bottom of their boots.

"I wouldn't want to put you out —"

"You won't be putting anybody out," Hatfield insisted. "I know what you're probably thinking. I don't have anything against bounty hunters, though. Every outlaw you put behind bars — or in the ground — is one less hardcase to wander into my town and cause trouble. Keeping the peace here in Rattlesnake Wells is my one and only concern, Mr. Jensen. Well, that and my boy."

"All right, then." Luke's instinctive liking for this young man grew. "I'll be back by later, after I've tended to my horse and gotten something to eat. Can you point me to Peterson's Livery Stable? Marshal Elliott over in Rimrock recommended it."

Hatfield gave him directions, they shook hands, and Luke took his leave of the young marshal. He led both horses down the street until he came to the cavernous livery barn.

After turning over the mounts to the proprietor, a gangling, dark-haired, garrulous man, and making arrangements for them to be kept there until he returned from Cheyenne, Luke headed for Bullock's Saloon.

Having been in business for a while, it was one of the permanent buildings in town, a fairly impressive two-story frame structure. He crossed the street, dodging wagon teams and saddle mounts along the way, and had just stepped up onto the boardwalk in front of the batwing entrance when a hand fell hard on his shoulder and jerked him around.

"Luke Jensen!"

CHAPTER 7

Instinct made Luke's hand flash to the butt of a gun. He pulled and had the Remington halfway out of leather before he realized the man who'd accosted him wasn't making any threatening moves.

The man stood there on the boardwalk staring at Luke as if he couldn't believe his own eyes. "Luke?" he asked in an astonished voice. "My God, Luke Jensen. Is that really you?"

The man was as tall as Luke but leaner, wearing brown whipcord trousers, a gray shirt, and a darker brown hat. His slightly lantern-jawed face was clean-shaven but as rugged and weathered as Luke's. Obviously, he spent most of his time out in the open, as well. His hair was sandy and starting to gray.

As soon as Luke saw the man, a chord of recognition went through him. He was certain he knew the hombre from

69

somewhere, but he couldn't come up with a name or recall where they had met.

The man had called him by his real name, which meant Luke probably didn't know him from the years spent as a bounty hunter. Most of that time, until the past couple years, he had used the name Luke Smith. He knew he hadn't met the man that recently, or he would have remembered him.

"I'm sorry —"

"I thought you were killed at Richmond." The man grabbed both his shoulders. "But you're alive!"

That was all it took. The mention of Richmond made the memories come flooding back into Luke's mind. *The long, bloody siege that had left most of the once beautiful city in ruins. The growing sense of numbing despair and defeat. The last-ditch plan to smuggle a fortune in Confederate gold to safety so that it could continue to finance the struggle against the Yankees. Greed, betrayal, sudden death, the smashing pain of a bullet in the back . . .*

Luke shook his head to clear out the memories. But Derek Burroughs hadn't been there for that part of it. That was the man's name. Luke knew it now as well as his own. Burroughs had fought side by side with him in the hellish battles of the Wilder-

70

ness and Cold Harbor, when General Lee was trying desperately to keep that butcher Grant from closing in on Richmond. Luke and Burroughs had been friends — not close friends, but the comradeship known only to men who have been through combat together. The last time Luke had seen him was when Burroughs was wounded at Cold Harbor.

"I heard you made it and were sent back home," Luke said.

"They told me you'd been killed, just before the war ended."

"I'm still breathing."

"I can see that." Burroughs paused. "You know who I am now, right?"

"Of course I do, Derek."

Burroughs laughed and pulled Luke into a hug, pounding him on the back. Luke returned the embrace, glad to see his old comrade. The war had been a grim, dark time, and he had never gone out of his way to look up any men he had known then. The only ones he wouldn't have minded seeing again — the men who had betrayed him and left him for dead — had been brought to justice by another member of the Jensen family, gunned down by Smoke years ago when he believed he was avenging the murders of his pa and his older brother, long before he'd discovered that Luke was still alive.

It was good to see Derek Burroughs, no doubt about that. As the man stepped back, Luke said, "What brings you to Rattlesnake Wells?"

"I was about to ask you the same thing!" Burroughs exclaimed. He pointed at the batwings with a thumb. "Why don't we go inside and catch up over a drink?"

"That's exactly what I was thinking."

Bullock's Saloon was a nice enough place, very similar to hundreds of other saloons Luke had been in over the years. Sundown Bob Hatfield was right about the free lunch being good. Luke assembled a sandwich from several pieces of ham and a couple thick slices of fresh bread, then put it on a plate with three hard-boiled eggs and carried the food over to a table, along with a mug of beer.

Burroughs said he had already eaten, but he had a beer, too. He sat with his long legs stretched out and his hat thumbed back. "You've got to tell me how you wound up alive, Luke. Everybody I ever talked to from the old outfit believed you were dead."

Luke shook his head. "It's too long a story to go into, but you've probably heard how it was in Richmond at the end. Pure insanity.

It's a wonder anybody ever got anything right about what happened in those days."

Burroughs nodded solemnly. "I didn't just hear about it. I was there. I was in a hospital in Richmond during the bombardment. The cot would shake day and night from the shells falling nearby. It got to where I wished one of them would go ahead and land on me, just to get it over with. But it never did. The sisters said it was a miracle the hospital was never hit worse than it was. They said God was watching out for us. I don't have any better explanation."

Luke swallowed the big bite of the sandwich he'd been chewing while Burroughs talked. "I'm glad you made it out alive. A lot of good men didn't."

"Truer words were never spoken." Burroughs lifted his beer mug. "To absent friends."

"Absent friends," Luke said as he lifted his own mug.

Both men drank.

As Luke set his beer down, he went on. "What have you been doing since then?"

"Oh, I went home after the war, when I had recovered enough." Burroughs shook his head. "There was nothing for me there. A bunch of Yankee carpetbaggers had come in and taken my family's land. All my friends, the boys I ran with growing up, were dead. I was the only one of my bunch who made it back from the war. There was a girl . . . but she'd had enough time while I was away to decide she didn't really want me after all. She married a Yankee judge instead." His shoulders rose and fell. "I didn't see any reason to stay. So I lit out for Texas, you know."

Luke knew. It was a story that had been repeated thousands of times over as defeated Confederate soldiers returned home.

"Ever since then I've been drifting," Burroughs continued. "Never could seem to settle down any one place. I drove cattle from Texas up to the railheads in Kansas for a while and thought about becoming a rancher, but I just couldn't see it. When folks struck gold in the Black Hills, I went up there and thought I'd make my fortune." He laughed and shook his head. "Gold and I just seem to have a natural aversion to each other." He leaned forward. "All right. I rambled on and let you eat, because I know a hungry man when I see one. But now you can tell me what you've been doing for the past fifteen years."

"There's not a lot to tell." Luke didn't like to talk about the past.

"You're not getting off that easy," Burroughs said. "Did you go home after the war? Where was it? Missouri, right? The Ozarks?"

Burroughs had a good memory, being able to recall those details from late-night conversations around a campfire. That was where the Jensen family farm had been, all right. Luke's little brother Kirby — known to one and all as Smoke, these days — had kept it going, along with their mother and their sister Janey while Luke and their pa Emmett had gone off to fight.

That part of the Jensen family had endured its own tragedies during the conflict that had split the nation apart, things that Smoke didn't like to talk about, even to this day. But after he and Luke had been reunited, he had shared the truth.

Luke shook his head. "No, I never went home. After everything that had happened, it just didn't seem like the right thing to do. I did like you — went on the drift." He swallowed some of the beer. "Wound up getting into bounty hunting work."

"A bounty hunter," Burroughs repeated.

Luke looked for signs of disapproval but didn't see any.

"Well, I can't say that I'm surprised. You were always the toughest fella I ever knew, Luke." Burroughs grinned. "That's why I always tried to keep track of where you were when we were fighting the Yankees. I figured most of their shots would be aimed at you, so if I could keep a little distance between us, I'd be safer."

Luke chuckled. He knew that Burroughs was exaggerating. The man hadn't been foolhardy or reckless, but he had never lacked for courage and had given a good account of himself in every battle.

"What brings you to Rattlesnake Wells?" Burroughs went on. "You hunting an outlaw?"

"Nope. Already caught him. He's locked up over at the jail, and I'll be getting on the train with him in the morning and taking him to Cheyenne."

"Well, how about that? Good reward on him?"

Luke nodded. "Good enough."

"I'm glad to hear it." Burroughs grew serious. "I imagine it's a hard life, but I wish you the best with it, Luke, I really do."

"How about you?" Luke asked. "Why are you here?"

"Well . . ." Burroughs let out a rueful laugh. "I said that gold and I have a natural aversion to each other, but that doesn't mean I've stopped trying to find it. I was thinking about staking a claim up in the

Prophecies and giving prospecting another shot."

"Good luck to you, if you do."

"Oh, I'll have good luck. I consider the two of us meeting like this to be an omen. It's not every day you run into an old friend, you know."

"I reckon not," Luke agreed. He wasn't sure he believed in omens, though.

But he believed in luck, no doubt about that, and he hoped his would continue to run as smoothly as it had since that ruckus at the dry wash the day before.

Joe Peterson was working on a wagon in his wagon yard — had a wheel off so he could grease the axle — when the buggy rolled up in front of the livery stable next door. His hands were pretty dirty, so he grabbed a rag from the wagon seat and wiped them as he walked toward the buggy.

A woman was at the reins, he noted with interest. She wore a prim blue dress with little flowers on it and a blue sunbonnet with blond curls peeking out from under it. A thick book with black leather binding — a Bible, more than likely — lay on the seat beside her.

She greeted him with a big smile. "Good afternoon, sir. I was wondering if I could leave my buggy and my team here with you?"

A couple fine brown horses were hitched to the buggy, which was a nice, well-cared-for vehicle. The woman was nice, too — young and pretty with a wholesome innocence about her.

She didn't have a wedding ring on her finger, he noted. "You sure can, miss. I'll take good care of the critters for you."

She picked up the Bible and held it in both hands as she said, "Would it be all right if I looked inside, just to assure myself that conditions are suitable? I mean no offense, of course. It's just that I love all of God's creatures so much, even the beasts of burden, and I want to be sure they'll be treated properly."

Peterson was a little annoyed, but he didn't show it. He smiled and nodded. "Why, sure, that would be fine. Let me give you a hand . . ." He helped her climb down from the buggy and led her inside the barn. It was cooler there, out of the sun.

She kept her Bible clutched in front of her chest, as if to ward off any evil that might come at her.

"This is the finest livery stable between Laramie and Rock Springs, if I do say so myself," he told her.

"I do believe you're right, Mister . . . ?"

"Peterson, ma'am. Joe Peterson."

She paused in front of the two most recently occupied stalls, the ones that held the horses brought in by Jensen. "These animals look like they're quite happy," she commented.

"Like I said, I take good care of the animals stabled here." Peterson gave in to the curiosity he felt and asked, "Ma'am, are you some sort of, I don't know, missionary? I couldn't help but notice that you're carryin' a Bible."

"That's right, Mr. Peterson," she said, giving him another of those dazzling smiles. "A missionary is exactly what I am. I've come to spread the good news to Rattlesnake Wells. You can call me Sister Delia."

CHAPTER 8

Derek Burroughs left after reminiscing for a while, saying that he had to make arrangements for supplies for his prospecting trip. Luke agreed to meet his old friend back at Bullock's that evening, after he'd had supper at Marshal Hatfield's house.

With nothing to do that afternoon, Luke sat in on a poker game at the saloon. The stakes were low, the play friendly, the company convivial. He kept his wagers small and didn't bluff wildly, so when he cashed out late that afternoon he was forty dollars ahead. Not a bad day's work, he thought, especially since the time had passed pleasantly.

He lit a cheroot and strolled back over to the marshal's office. Other than the usual commotion from the large number of people in the boomtown, it had been a quiet afternoon in Rattlesnake Wells, so he was confident that the prisoner hadn't caused any trouble. But it never hurt to check on things. And he'd realized that he didn't know where Bob Hatfield lived. Whoever was in the office, either the marshal or a deputy could tell him.

Opening the door, Luke saw that Hatfield wasn't there. Behind the desk was a heavyset young man with dark, curly hair, an eager expression, and a deputy's badge pinned to his shirt. He appeared even younger than Sundown Bob. From what Luke had seen so far, Rattlesnake Wells didn't have an abundance of experienced lawmen, but the town didn't seem any the worse for it.

"Something I can do for you, mister?" the deputy asked.

"I'm Luke Jensen. I brought in that prisoner McCluskey earlier today."

The deputy got to his feet quickly. "I'm Fred Ordway. Bob told me about you, Mr. Jensen. He said I was to give you a hand if you needed anything."

"Pleased to meet you, Fred. All I need is for you to tell me where the marshal's house is. He asked me to have supper with him and his boy tonight."

"Oh, sure. Go two blocks up Main to Dodge Street and turn left on Dodge. It'll be in the second block, on the right. It's a pretty white house with a flower bed full of roses out front. You can't miss it."

Luke nodded. "I'm obliged, Deputy. One more thing. I'd like to take a look at the prisoner."

"He's doin' fine. He'll be gettin' supper from Señorita Consuela, too. Better than he deserves, I'm thinkin'." Deputy Ordway took the ring of keys from the nail on the wall where it hung. "But you can check on him if you want. It's no trouble at all."

He unlocked the cell block door, and he and Luke went in. McCluskey was stretched out on his bunk, hands behind his head, staring at the ceiling. He turned his head a little to glance at Luke, then resumed his staring.

"He's been like that ever since I got here," Ordway said. "Not a lick of trouble. Bob told me to be careful with him, though. Said he might be tricky."

"That's right," Luke agreed. "Anything he tells you, you can figure there's a good chance he's lying."

"Yes, sir. I'll sure keep that in mind."

Things seemed to be well under control, but worry still nagged at the back of Luke's mind. He couldn't accept the change in Mc-Cluskey's attitude. The outlaw wouldn't give up that easily.

But as long as he wasn't trying to escape,

there really wasn't anything else Luke or the local lawmen could do. He and Ordway went back into the office, and Ordway locked the cell block door.

"I suppose I'll head on over to the marshal's house now," Luke said.

"Don't you worry about a thing," Ordway assured him. "I'll keep a close eye on the prisoner."

Luke shook hands with the deputy and thanked him, then walked up Main to Dodge Street.

Ordway was right. The well-kept white house with the neat flower bed full of red roses out front was no trouble to find. Luke went up the walk, past the flowers to the porch, and knocked on the front door.

The woman who responded to the knock wasn't exactly what he'd expected. She was maybe twenty-five years old and extremely attractive, with smooth olive skin and long raven hair parted in the middle. She wore an apron over a dress that clung to her rich figure. "Can I help you, señor?"

Maybe she was the housekeeper's daughter, Luke speculated. He took off his hat and held it in his left hand. "My name is Luke Jensen —"

"Of course!" she broke in as she gave him a smile that made her even prettier. "Señor

Hatfield told me you were coming to supper. Please, come in, Señor Jensen."

"I hope I'm not too early," Luke commented as he stepped inside. To his left was a comfortably furnished parlor. Everything seemed to be spotless and exactly in its place.

"No, not too early at all. I am Consuela Diaz." She offered him her hand, and as he took it he realized that she must be the housekeeper and cook after all, despite her youth and beauty.

"Señor Hatfield and Bucky are out back," she told him. "You are welcome to join them while I finish preparing the meal."

That was confirmation of her identity, he thought. But he was curious about something else. "And Mrs. Hatfield?"

The smile on Consuela's face was replaced by a solemn expression. "I'm sorry to say, Señora Hatfield passed away two years ago, not long after the family came here."

"I didn't know that," Luke said. "Thank you for telling me, Señorita Diaz. That way I won't say anything to the marshal that might be awkward."

"Of course. You would have no way of knowing." She pointed along a hallway that led toward the back of the house. "You can go out that way, Señor Jensen."

Luke nodded his thanks, put his hat on again, and found the back door. He thought about what he had just learned from Consuela Diaz. It seemed the young marshal was a widower and had a mighty pretty housekeeper and cook to help him raise his son.

Whatever else she might help him with was none of his business, Luke told himself, but he was human enough that he couldn't help wondering about it.

When he stepped out into the yard, he spotted Marshal Hatfield and the boy standing under a cottonwood tree, facing away from him toward a fence about twenty feet from them. Empty cans were balanced on three of the fence posts. It was obvious to Luke what Hatfield and Bucky were doing.

For one thing, Bucky was wearing a gun belt and holstered revolver, too. The gun was a Smith & Wesson .32 with no trigger guard, lighter, with a shorter barrel than the Colt Peacemaker Hatfield carried, and more suited to the youngster.

Neither of them seemed to have noticed Luke.

As he approached, Hatfield said to his son, "All right, Buck, let's see your draw. Remember, you want it to be fast, but it needs to be smooth, too. That's even more important. Don't jerk the gun. It's liable to throw off your aim if you do."

Bucky nodded, concentrating on the cans atop the fence posts. His right hand was poised for a hook and draw. He grabbed the .32 and pulled it from the holster.

The draw was pretty swift for a kid, Luke thought, and clearly Bucky had been listening to his pa's advice because the gun came out slick and smooth. He lifted it, thumb curling over the hammer and drawing it back, and when the gun came level Bucky squeezed the trigger.

The hammer clicked as it fell on an empty chamber. Bucky cocked and dry-fired the revolver twice more, rapidly shifting his aim each time.

Hatfield clapped him on the shoulder. "Not bad, son. Not bad at all. I think you might've gotten all three of those cans."

"I agree," Luke said.

Hatfield looked back at him casually. His lack of being startled made Luke realize the marshal had been aware of his presence all along.

Bucky looked around quickly, though, and exclaimed, "Mr. Jensen! The bounty hunter!"

"Some men don't like being called that, Bucky," his father advised.

"It's all right," Luke said with a little wave of his hand. "That doesn't bother me. It's exactly what I am."

"Have you been by the jail?" Hatfield asked.

"Just a little while ago. Your deputy seemed to have things under control."

Hatfield nodded. "Fred's a good man. He hasn't been packing a badge for very long, but he's eager to learn and he's taken to the job well."

Bucky spoke up. "My pa's teachin' me how to be fast on the draw, Mr. Jensen."

"I saw that," Luke told him. "It looks like you're learning, too. I don't think many youngsters your age could get a gun out that slick."

"You should see Pa draw and shoot. He's the fastest there is!"

Hatfield said, "Don't exaggerate, Bucky. There are plenty of men faster than me."

"Show him, Pa," the youngster urged. "Show Mr. Jensen your draw."

"No, I'm sure Mr. Jensen has better things to do than stand around and watch me shoot."

"As a matter of fact," Luke said, "I don't. I'm just waiting for supper to be ready, and your housekeeper talked like it would still be a few minutes."

Hatfield's eyes narrowed. "You wouldn't be wanting to get some idea of how you'd stack up against me, would you, Mr. Jensen?"

"Not at all," Luke answered honestly. "I'm always interested in how a man handles a gun, though. I guess it goes with being in my line of work."

"You see, Pa!" Bucky said. "Go ahead and draw."

"Well . . ." Hatfield shrugged. "I suppose it won't hurt anything. Folks around here are used to hearing shots coming from back here when Bucky's practicing." He turned toward the fence, stood there for just a second, and then in a draw too fast for the eye to follow, the Colt fairly leaped into his hand and spat flame as he triggered three swift shots from the hip. Each of the cans flew into the air, neatly drilled by a bullet, and then thudded to the ground.

Bucky let out a shrill whistle of admiration.

Luke was impressed, too. He didn't possess the blinding speed with a gun that his brother Smoke did, or even their adopted brother Matt Jensen, but he was faster on the draw than most hombres.

However, Bob Hatfield would have shaded him if they'd been facing off. The marshal was that fast.

He would have given Smoke a run for his money, Luke thought, although he firmly believed that Smoke was faster.

Seeming a little embarrassed as he turned away from the fence, Hatfield lowered the gun's barrel, from which a few tendrils of smoke still curled. He took three fresh cartridges from the loops on his shell belt and started replacing the ones he had fired. "It's always best to reload as soon as you can, Buck. You never know when you might need a full wheel."

Luke heard the hint of a drawl in the marshal's voice that he hadn't noticed before, and it jogged something in his brain.

From the back door, Consuela called, "If you men are through shooting up the place, supper is ready!"

CHAPTER 9

The food was excellent. If Luke had been expecting something like he would have gotten down in Texas or south of the border, he would have been disappointed, because Consuela served fried chicken, corn on the cob, greens, and some of the tastiest, fluffiest biscuits he'd had in a long time. He decided that her excellence as a cook matched her fastidiousness as a housekeeper . . . and her beauty.

Luke decided if Sundown Bob Hatfield hadn't given some thought to marrying the woman, he was a damn fool. Two years of grieving for his late wife was long enough. But again, the marshal's personal life was none of his business, Luke reminded himself.

After they had eaten, Consuela announced, "I'll take supper over to the jail for the prisoner now, Señor Hatfield."

Instantly, the marshal got to his feet. "I'll

come with you."

She waved him back into his chair. "There is no need. It's only a few blocks, and despite its growth, Rattlesnake Wells is still a peaceful town."

Luke had noticed the same thing, and he understood better why that was so. Word must have gotten around about what a gunslick the young marshal was, and nobody wanted to cross Sundown Bob.

That wouldn't last forever, Luke thought as his mouth tightened briefly into a grim line. Sooner or later some hombre who fancied himself a fast gun would show up to test Hatfield's speed, looking to make a reputation for himself. Even if Hatfield survived that encounter, there would be another and another and another. . . .

Luke's brother Smoke was one of the few truly fast guns to survive very long, and even he sometimes found himself challenged now and then by some foolish kid hungry for fame and glory.

"I'd be glad to walk with you, Señorita Diaz," Luke offered. "I'm going back over to the jail anyway. I decided to take you up on that offer, Marshal. I'll sleep on the cot in the storeroom."

"All right," Hatfield said. "I told Fred you might do that. I'll be by later. I always make some late rounds after Bucky goes to sleep."

The youngster said, "I think you ought to take me with you on your rounds, Pa. I'm not sleepy."

Hatfield chuckled. "You say that now, son, but I know good and well you'll be asleep two minutes after your head hits the pillow."

A few minutes later, Luke and Consuela left the house. She had a wicker basket containing the food intended for McCluskey. Luke offered to carry it for her, but she said, "No, that's all right, Señor Jensen. It's not heavy."

As they turned onto Main Street, Luke saw that Rattlesnake Wells was loud and boisterous, but there wasn't any real trouble going on. "Marshal Hatfield seems to have the lid on this town pretty tight."

"Sí, the people respect him and try not to cause too much trouble," Consuela agreed. "Of course, how could they not respect him? He is a fine man. I have known him for many years."

"Then you must have known his wife."

"Priscilla? Yes, she and Señor Hatfield were older than me, but we all grew up together down in . . ." Her voice trailed off and she didn't finish what she was saying.

But it had been enough to jog another

memory in Luke's brain. "Down in Texas, right? In the border country? I remember hearing something a few years ago about a young fella down there who was mighty fast with a gun. Had red hair, too, as I recall. But he wasn't named Hatfield or called Sundown Bob, for that matter. Seems like they called him the Devil's River Kid."

He heard the sharp intake of breath from Consuela as he spoke that name. She stopped short and turned to face him on the boardwalk in front of a hardware store that was closed for the night. "Señor Jensen, I . . . I don't know what you're talking about."

"The Devil's River Kid was an outlaw, wanted for murder," Luke went on. "He shot up a bunch of hired guns working for a wealthy local rancher. I don't remember all the details, but it seemed like he was in a bad spot and didn't have much choice but to do what he did."

She stood stiff as a steel rod and said quietly, "Please, Señor Jensen . . . no one here knows who Bob really is or what happened down in Texas. He just wants to live here in peace and raise his son."

"Might not be easy to do, as fast on the draw as he is. Sooner or later, somebody's going to hear about him and remember the same things I just did and figure it out. They'll show up and try to take him back to Texas. Either that or beat him to the draw and get famous that way."

"Perhaps. Perhaps not. If there is any justice in the world —"

"Well, that's sure something nobody can count on," Luke said.

"But if there is," Consuela insisted, "Bob will have a good life here. I will do everything in my power to make it so." She moved a step closer to him. "Anything you wish of me, Señor Jensen, to leave him alone, it is yours."

"Hold on a minute," Luke said with a frown. "What makes you think *I'm* after him?"

"You are a bounty hunter, and . . . and . . ."

"And there's still a reward out for the Devil's River Kid. But not for Marshal Bob Hatfield of Rattlesnake Wells, Wyoming. As far as I'm concerned, that's who I just had supper with. A very pleasant supper, I might add."

"Then you . . . you didn't come here to arrest him and . . . take him back to Texas, as you said?"

"Señorita, all I want from that young man is the use of his jail for the night. That's the

94

honest truth. I didn't figure out who he really is until just a few minutes ago, and I'm not going to cause trouble for anybody who's been so friendly and hospitable."

"He is a good man, a very good man, *es verdad.*" Even in the shadows under the awning over the boardwalk, he could see her sag a little in relief. "Thank you, Señor Jensen. Thank you so much."

"No need to thank me. I'm just going on about my business." He took her arm. "So let's just head for the jail —"

Shots blasted somewhere down the street, and even as the echoes rolled through the night, Luke had a pretty good idea where the shots were coming from and what they meant.

Frank McCluskey was making a break!

CHAPTER 10

Deputy Fred Ordway sat in the office with his feet propped up on the desk, wondering if he might be able to sneak a piece of chicken out of the basket before he took the food in to the prisoner. The marshal had mentioned Consuela's fried chicken earlier and it was about as close to heaven as a man could find, at least in that part of Wyoming.

From time to time Fred thought about asking Consuela to one of the box supper socials the town held several times a year. From the looks of it, Bob was never going to get around to asking her, despite the fact that his wife had been gone for a couple years.

Of course, every time Fred started thinking like that, he got over it and told himself to forget it. No girl as beautiful as Consuela Diaz would ever go to a social with somebody like him. Besides, she was in love with Bob. Anybody with a pair of eyes could see that.

Except, evidently, Bob his own self.

Fred was musing on such universal mysteries of life when the door of the marshal's office opened. Not wanting to be caught with his feet up on the desk, Fred swung his legs down quickly and straightened in the old swivel chair. He tried to look official and efficient, but he wasn't sure that was possible under the best of circumstances.

He thought the visitor might be Consuela bringing the prisoner's supper, but that wasn't the case. The person who came in was female, though, and like Consuela, young and pretty. Blond and fair, however, not dark and sultry. She wore a blue dress and bonnet and carried what looked like a Bible in front of her like a shield.

Fred got hurriedly to his feet. "Can I help you, ma'am?"

"Are you the marshal?"

Her voice was sweet as apple pie, Fred thought. "Uh, no, ma'am. I'm the deputy, though. Deputy Fred Ordway, at your service."

"Why, I'm just so pleased to meet you, Deputy Ordway. My name is Sister Delia."

"Sister?" Fred repeated with a slight frown.

"Oh, I know I'm not a nun. But I *am* a missionary, come to minister to the good people of Rattlesnake Wells — and the not-so-good people, too, of course. They need to hear the word of the Lord more than anyone else, don't you think?"

"Well, I, uh, suppose so." Fred wasn't sure what this woman was doing there, and she didn't seem to be in a hurry to explain. "Have you had a problem? Need to report a crime?"

"What?" She seemed genuinely puzzled, then her expression cleared and she laughed. "Oh, no, nothing like that! I'm here because I heard that you have a prisoner locked up in the jail."

"Yes, ma'am. I mean sister, we do. A vicious outlaw named Frank McCluskey."

Her blue eyes widened. "Oh, dear. He sounds terrible. But Deputy, we mustn't forget that no matter what Mr. McCluskey has done, he is one of God's creatures. And as such, he needs the comfort of the Holy Word." She lifted the Bible she held. "I would like to go share that comfort with him."

Fred stared at her for a second, then emphatically shook his head. "No, ma'am. I'm sorry, but the marshal would skin me alive if I ever let a lady like you into the cell with an outlaw! I know you're just tryin' to help, but I can't do it."

"Goodness gracious. I don't want to actually go into the cell with him." A little shudder went through Delia. "If I could just go into the cell block, so that I can speak to the man through the bars, that would be sufficient for me to follow my calling and do my sacred duty."

"Well, I don't know . . ."

"You'd be right there with me, of course. To protect me."

Fred liked the sound of that. Something about the woman made him want to protect her. Still, he was a little leery about taking her into the cell block to preach to McCluskey. For one thing, he didn't think it would do a blasted bit of good. He had never seen or heard of a truly repentant outlaw, unless maybe it was one who was walking up the thirteen steps to a gallows to keep an appointment with the hangman.

"Tell you what," he suggested. "Marshal Hatfield will be stopping by here later when he makes his evening rounds. If you'd like to wait, you could ask him about it. If he says it's all right for you to talk to the prisoner, then it's fine with me."

"Well, how long will that be?"

Fred scratched his head. "Hard to say for

sure. An hour or so, I reckon."

"I'd really hate to wait that long, Deputy. None of us know for certain how long we have left in this world. No one knows the day and the hour of the last trumpet. Why, if the Lord were to return in the next hour, poor Mr. McCluskey would be lost in a state of sin, when salvation awaits him right here." She patted one hand against the Bible's black leather binding and gave Fred a soulful look.

He felt himself weakening. He was pretty sure that Bob would be fine with what Sister Delia wanted. It wouldn't hurt anything to let her talk to McCluskey for a few minutes. Anyway, Consuela would be there soon with the prisoner's supper, and he could use that as an excuse to shoo the pretty little missionary gal out.

"All right," Fred said reluctantly. He was acting against his own better judgment and hoped it wouldn't come back to cause him trouble. "But I warn you, you may be able to stay for only a few minutes."

"That's all right," Delia said, warming the room with her smile. "A few minutes is all I need."

Fred took the ring of keys down, unlocked the cell block door, and swung it open. As Delia started forward eagerly, he held up a hand to stop her. "Better let me go first. Just to make sure McCluskey's not doin' anything that might, uh, be improper for a young lady to see."

"Why, you're so kind and thoughtful to look out for me like that, Deputy Ordway."

"You might as well call me Fred."

"I'd be delighted to . . . Fred."

Feeling better about his decision, the deputy put his hand on the butt of his gun and stepped into the cell block. A lantern hung at the end of the short corridor between the cells, and its glow revealed McCluskey still stretched out on the bunk. He wasn't doing anything except lying there.

"Get up, McCluskey, you've got a vis—"

The unexpected feeling of a ring of cold metal pressed to the back of his neck made him stop short in what he was saying. He started to turn, but the object prodded him harder and a voice he barely recognized as belonging to Sister Delia said, "That's a gun muzzle. Stand still, you damn fool, or I'll kill you."

While Fred stood there frozen and shocked beyond belief, McCluskey swung his legs off the bunk and stood up quickly. He practically lunged at the cell door and wrapped his hands around the bars. "Delia!" he exclaimed. "Is that you?"

"Of course it is, Frank. You didn't really think I'd let you rot in jail, did you?"

McCluskey threw back his head and laughed. "Gal, you're just full of surprises. Get me out of here!"

"In a minute. I want to make sure this fat boy doesn't get even more stupid and try anything."

Fred felt her lifting his revolver from its holster. He felt sick to his stomach, not only because he knew how upset and disappointed Bob would be that he'd let a prisoner escape, but also because he was disgusted with himself for letting a pretty face and a honeyed voice fool him so easily. He knew that if he allowed Delia to take his gun, he'd have no chance at all of stopping this.

He felt the gun at the back of his neck waver and realized it was probably the only opportunity he'd have. He jerked away, twisting around, and flung out his arm toward the phony missionary. He made a grab for his gun and tried to knock her aside at the same time.

The little pistol in her hand cracked. Fred felt a line of fire rake across the side of his neck and knew the bullet had grazed him. He got hold of his Colt and tried to wrench it out of her grip, but he fumbled and the gun slipped away from both of them. It thudded to the floor at their feet.

"Frank!" Delia cried as she kicked the revolver and it slid toward McCluskey. Panic bloomed inside Fred as he saw the outlaw bend over, reach through the bars, and scoop up the Colt.

McCluskey came up shooting, flame spouting from the barrel of the gun.

CHAPTER 11

The door of the hardware store was set back in a little alcove. Luke grabbed Consuela's arm and pushed her into it. "Stay there," he told her sharply as he reached for one of the Remingtons. "You ought to be out of the line of fire."

"But what is happening?" she asked, her voice full of alarm.

"A jailbreak, if I had to guess." He couldn't waste any more time talking to her. He had to hope she would stay where she was.

Quite a few other people were on the street. All of them would be in danger if bullets started to fly around. As he broke into a run along the boardwalk toward the jail, he waved his left arm at them and shouted, "Get off the street! Off the street now!"

Men yelled curses and questions, but thankfully most of them also began to scatter. Riders galloped away from the gunfire, and men on wagons turned their teams toward the nearest alleys and cross streets.

On the far side of the street, the door to the jail stood partially open with lamplight spilling through it. Suddenly someone flung it wider. Two figures appeared, dark against the light behind them as they rushed out of the building. The man lunged into the street and leaped at a man trying to ride past.

The rider let out a yell as he was grabbed and flung out of the saddle. He landed hard with his face in the street.

As Luke ran closer, he got a better look at the two people who had rushed out of the marshal's office. Frank McCluskey was the one who had just unhorsed the rider. As the woman grabbed the mount's dangling reins, Luke realized he could think of only one female who'd try to bust the outlaw out of jail.

"Delia!" Luke grated. Was that woman going to plague him forever?

McCluskey grabbed the saddle horn, stuck his foot in a stirrup, and hauled himself up into the saddle. He took the reins from Delia and extended his other hand toward her. She grabbed it and swung up behind him, pulling her dress up brazenly to her thighs so she could throw a leg over the horse's back. The hurried movement caused her sunbonnet to tumble backward off her blond curls and dangle behind her by the strings tied around her neck.

That was Delia, all right, Luke thought as he raised the Remington in his hand and bellowed, "McCluskey!"

The outlaw jerked the horse around and rammed his boot heels into its flanks. The animal leaped ahead and raced straight at Luke. McCluskey leaned forward over the horse's neck to make himself a smaller target as he fired at the bounty hunter.

The slugs kicked up dirt in the road not far from Luke's feet, but McCluskey's gun blasted only twice before the hammer fell on an empty chamber. Luke hated like hell to shoot a horse, but he drew a bead on the charging animal and squeezed off a shot. The horse screamed and collapsed, its front legs going out from under it so that McCluskey and Delia sailed off its back and over its head.

McCluskey hit hard but rolled and came up on his feet. Luke fired again and narrowly missed. A second later, McCluskey crashed into him and they both went down. The outlaw grabbed Luke's wrist and twisted, forcing the gun to fall and skitter away in the dust.

Luke swung his left fist into McCluskey's jaw, driving the outlaw to the side, but he managed to stay on top of Luke and hammered a punch to the side of his head. McCluskey got a hand on Luke's throat and bore down hard.

Damn sick and tired of McCluskey trying to choke him, Luke bucked up violently from the ground and threw McCluskey off. They rolled away from each other, and as each man came up on one knee, Luke saw to his dismay that McCluskey had wound up next to the fallen Remington. The outlaw snatched the gun from the ground and swung it up.

Luke braced for the shock of the bullet.

Before McCluskey could pull the trigger, a shadow flashed behind him and something thudded. The outlaw sagged forward, the Remington slipping from his fingers and dropping to the ground again. As McCluskey toppled onto his face, out cold, Luke was surprised to see Derek Burroughs standing there, gun in hand. Clearly, his old friend and comrade-in-arms had just buffaloed McCluskey, saving Luke's life.

The danger wasn't over, though. Delia had pushed herself up onto hands and knees. She shook her head as she tried to recover from the fall off the horse. Seeing the small pistol lying beside her, she grabbed it.

Footsteps pounded in the street close by. Luke looked over to see Marshal Bob Hatfield rushing toward them. Hatfield didn't know who Delia was and had no reason to think she was a threat. To him she would just be a woman knocked down in the street who needed help.

"Marshal, watch —"

Delia fired at Hatfield. The lawman stumbled and fell.

Luke's shouted warning had come too late.

He scrambled up and dived at Delia as she tried to turn the gun toward him. He knocked it aside and rammed into her. She cried out as he knocked her sprawling again. He grabbed both of her wrists, shook the gun loose from her hand, and then used his left hand to pin her wrists above her head. She bucked and kicked as he straddled her, but she couldn't throw him off.

"Derek, cover McCluskey," Luke said. To the townsmen who were still on the street, he snapped, "Somebody see how bad the marshal's hurt! Some of you men need to go check on the deputy, too."

Delia was still struggling as Luke tore the bonnet off her head and used its strings to bind her wrists together. She spit and snapped at him like a wildcat.

She was pure-dee crazy, he thought, consumed with hate and obsessed with a no-good outlaw.

When he was satisfied that she couldn't get away, he stood up and drew his left-hand Remington, which had stayed in its holster. He looked at Burroughs still covering McCluskey. The owlhoot showed no signs of regaining consciousness yet.

"You all right, Derek?"

"Yeah, I've got this one, Luke. He's not going anywhere."

Luke hurried over to the men who had gathered around Hatfield. When the crowd parted a little and he saw that Hatfield was sitting up.

"Looks like he was just creased on the hip," one of the townies reported. "He'll be all right."

"I'll be the judge of that," Hatfield said as he lifted a hand. "Somebody help me up."

"I'm not sure you should be walkin', Marshal —"

"Damn it, I have to see if Fred's all right."

Luke understood the worry over the deputy. If Ordway was still hale and hearty, it was unlikely McCluskey would have gotten out of the jail.

Luke clasped wrists with Hatfield and

lifted the young man to his feet. Hatfield's jeans were dark with blood at his left hip, but the injury didn't stop him from heading for the office, although he limped badly along the way.

Consuela hurried to meet him, still carrying the basket containing McCluskey's supper. She said anxiously, "Bob!" In her fear for him, she obviously wasn't worried about keeping things formal between them.

"I'm all right, Consuela," he told her as he reached the boardwalk in front of the marshal's office. "At least I reckon I will be." He disappeared inside with her right behind him.

Luke reached down and grasped Delia's arm. She kicked at him as he hauled her to her feet. He turned her around so she was facing away from him, took hold of both of her arms, and marched her toward the marshal's office.

"I don't know how the hell you got here from Rimrock," he told her, "but you're going behind bars just like McCluskey."

She flung out curses that would have done a mule-skinner proud.

Luke ignored them. "And if you killed that deputy, I wouldn't be surprised if you wound up hanging for it."

"That fat fool's not dead," Delia said.

Luke hoped she was right.

As he shoved her into the marshal's office, he saw Hatfield and several other men through the open cell block door. They had Fred Ordway propped up against the bars of an empty cell. The deputy's left shoulder was covered with blood, but at least he was alive and conscious. Consuela knelt beside him, mopping at the blood around his wound.

Hatfield turned toward Luke, swayed, and almost fell. He caught himself with a hand against the doorjamb and asked, "Who's this?" as he nodded toward Delia.

"She's the one who shot you and tried to bust McCluskey out of here," Luke explained. "She may be dressed prim and proper now, but she's just a saloon girl from over in Rimrock who fancies herself in love with him."

"I *am* in love with him!" Delia screeched. "And I'll kill all of you to save him!"

"It would be a good idea to lock her up, Marshal," Luke said.

Hatfield nodded. "I was thinking the same thing. Put her in that cell across from the one where McCluskey was."

Luke forced Delia into the cell and clanged the door closed behind her. He asked the marshal, "How's your hip?"

"Hurts like blazes, but the bullet just creased me. Didn't break any bones as far as I can tell. I'll live. I'll just be a mite gimpy for a while. Where's McCluskey?"

"A friend of mine knocked him out and is keeping an eye on him."

"We need to get him back behind bars."

"I'll take care of that." Luke went to the door and motioned to several of the men crowding onto the boardwalk to peer into the marshal's office. "Some of you fellas pick up McCluskey and carry him in here."

They toted the senseless outlaw into the building and dropped him none too gently on the bunk in the cell he had occupied previously, causing some signs of coming around to appear. It was the third time he'd been knocked out in the past few days.

It was a wonder his skull wasn't getting a little mushy by now, Luke thought.

Seeing that Burroughs had followed the men carrying McCluskey into the jail, Luke nodded to him. "I'm sure obliged to you, Derek. You not only saved my life, you made sure McCluskey didn't get loose to keep on robbing and killing."

"Well, I couldn't just stand by and do nothing when I saw him about to shoot you, now could I?" Burroughs said with a grin. He clapped a hand on Luke's shoulder.

"What are old friends for if not to save each other's lives every now and then?"

"Well, it's a debt I won't forget," Luke said.

A little bird-like man in a dark suit hurried into the office. Seeing the medical bag in the man's hand, Luke pointed to the cell block door. "Your patients are in there, Doctor."

The sawbones nodded and bustled past them.

A moment later, Hatfield came out of the cell block, being helped by Consuela. "I told Doc to tend to Fred first. He's hurt a lot worse than I am."

"You need medical attention, too," Consuela said to the marshal.

"I'll get it, as soon as I know that Fred's going to be all right. Just help me sit down. I'd just as soon get off this leg."

Luke and Consuela helped lower him into the chair behind the desk. Once Hatfield was sitting, he frowned and reached out to pull a book lying on the desk toward him. "What's this?"

"It looks like a Bible," Consuela said.

"That's what it was." Luke took hold of the leather-bound volume and opened it to reveal that someone had carved out a space in the pages. When the book was closed, no one would be able to see what had been done to it. "I knew Delia must have smuggled a gun in here somehow and then gotten the drop on Deputy Ordway. I guess when he's up to it he can tell us exactly what happened. But for now it's enough to know that she-devil tried to help McCluskey escape — and failed."

"It's a good thing we've got her locked up, then," Hatfield said.

Luke nodded solemnly. "Truer words were never spoken, Marshal. That's exactly where she belongs."

CHAPTER 12

Marshal Hatfield's only other deputy was Chuck Helton, a middle-aged part-timer whose main job was as a hostler at Peterson's Livery Stable. Having heard the shooting, he showed up a short time later, was introduced to Luke, and took over the office.

Several men carried Fred Ordway over to the doctor's house on a stretcher, since he was hurt badly enough to need quite a bit of care for a while. The sawbones believed that Ordway would recover, which was a relief.

He cleaned and bandaged the wound on Hatfield's hip and sent the lawman home with Consuela. By that time, Hatfield had started to worry about Bucky having been left there alone.

"I expect that boy of yours is fine, Marshal," Luke told him. "From what I saw, he's pretty level-headed and can take care of himself."

"Well, I hope so, but he's only ten years old," Hatfield said with a frown. He limped out of the office, leaning on Consuela.

She would get him home all right, Luke was certain of that.

Helton seemed relieved that Luke was going to spend the night at the jail. He said as much once everybody had cleared out. "I'm glad you're here, Mr. Jensen. The only law work I've ever done is helpin' Bob haul in a few drunk cowboys or prospectors every now and then. I never had to be responsible for prisoners like those two."

"They're behind bars now where they can't hurt anybody," Luke said. "Just be careful and keep your distance from them, and you'll be all right."

It had been a long day. Weariness gripped him. He went into the storeroom, stretched out on the cot he found there, and closed his eyes. Sleep didn't come right away, however.

He could still hear Delia cursing and carrying on in the cell block. He had a feeling he might wind up hearing that unpleasant sound in his dreams.

Or in his nightmares, more likely.

Luke had agreed to meet Derek Burroughs

for breakfast the next day, before the train pulled out. The meal was going to be on him. It was the very least he could do to repay his old comrade for saving his life and preventing McCluskey's escape.

Delia had finally run out of steam, stopped pitching a fit, and gone to sleep sometime during the night. McCluskey was asleep, too, when Luke checked on them the next morning.

The outlaw had never gotten his supper the night before, but Luke couldn't muster up any sympathy for him, not after the way he had gunned down Fred Ordway in addition to all his other crimes.

"Morning," Deputy Helton greeted when Luke entered the marshal's office. "What do you think Bob will do with that lady prisoner? Are you gonna take her to Cheyenne with you, Mr. Jensen?"

Luke leaned a hip on the corner of the desk and frowned in thought. After a moment, he said, "As far as I know, the only place where charges would be against her are right here in Rattlesnake Wells or maybe over in Rimrock. From what Deputy Ordway was able to tell us last night, she came here posing as a missionary. She had to get here somehow, so she must have stolen a horse and a buggy or a wagon in Rimrock.

Maybe when the marshal feels a little more spry, he can ask around and find out. But there's no point in me taking her to Cheyenne." With a grim smile, Luke shook his head. "As long as she stays locked up until I'm on that train later this morning, I don't really care *what* he does with her. She's the one who shot him, so I imagine he'll charge her with assault and attempted murder for that. She'll probably go to prison."

With that settled, as much as it could be, Luke left the marshal's office and headed over to the café where he and Burroughs were supposed to meet. He found his old friend already there, drinking coffee. Luke signaled the waitress for a cup of his own, then sat down at the table.

Burroughs grinned. "I've already got flapjacks, bacon, and eggs on the way for both of us, Luke. That sound all right to you?"

"It sounds just fine to me. We sure would have enjoyed a meal like that during some of those campaigns in the war, wouldn't we have?"

"Shoot, I'd have settled for real coffee instead of that muddy water they had us drinking!"

Luke grimaced. "I don't think either of us

118

would ever want to go back to those days."

"No, sir," Burroughs agreed. "I've had enough of war to last me the rest of my life." He took a sip of his coffee. "I'm a peace-loving man now."

"I try to be," Luke said with a sigh, "but somehow it never seems to work out that way."

There was a lot of truth to that. Clearly, in his line of work a man couldn't expect much peace and quiet. Death and danger were his frequent companions, in fact.

But there were times when he wasn't chasing outlaws, and even then trouble seemed to have a way of finding him.

Maybe it was the Jensen name, he mused. Judging by what he had heard from Smoke and Matt, the same thing happened to them. No matter where they went or what they did, sooner or later somebody wound up shooting at them.

The food was good, and Luke enjoyed the meal. He kept an eye on the time, though. He didn't want to miss that train and have to wait for the next one. He had nothing against Rattlesnake Wells — in fact he liked most of the people he had met — but he was ready to put the place behind him.

After checking his turnip watch one last time, he slipped it back into his pocket and said, "I've got to be going, Derek." He laid a couple silver dollars on their table, which would more than pay for their meals. "It was really good to see you again, and a stroke of excellent luck, too." Luke smiled. "In all likelihood, I'd be dead now if you hadn't been around last night."

"Right place, right time." Burroughs held out his hand as both men stood up. "Maybe we'll run into each other again one of these days."

"I hope so." Luke clasped Burroughs' hand for a moment and then left the café to head for the marshal's office.

Consuela had been there while he was gone, he discovered. She'd brought breakfast for both prisoners.

"It was more than they deserve," Helton told Luke. "Especially the gal. She called poor Señorita Diaz all sorts of ugly names. But she's a *real* lady, the señorita is. She never turned a hair. It beats me why Bob hasn't married her yet."

"Wondered the same thing myself," Luke admitted, "and I haven't even been around here very long."

Helton chuckled. "He'll come to his senses one of these days, maybe." The deputy stood up and reached for the keys. "I reckon you're ready to take McCluskey down to the depot."

"That's right."

As if to punctuate Luke's words, the shrill sound of a steam whistle came through the open front door of the office. The train was about to roll into Rattlesnake Wells.

After leaving the café, Derek Burroughs walked at a deliberate pace along Main Street until he reached the livery stable.

Joe Peterson greeted him by saying, "Got your horse ready to go just like you asked, Mr. Burroughs."

"Thanks, Joe," Burroughs said with a friendly smile. His saddlebags and rifle were already on the mount. He had brought them over earlier, before meeting Luke for breakfast.

"You think you'll ever be coming back to Rattlesnake Wells?" The liveryman didn't seem offended that Burroughs checked the cinches. Any man who spent much time in the saddle wanted to be sure everything was as it should be before he mounted up.

"I don't really know," Burroughs replied to Peterson's question. "Maybe one of these days I'll mosey back in this direction."

"Well, if you ever do, you know where to bring your horse. It's been a pleasure doin' business with you."

"Same here, Joe." Burroughs handed an extra silver dollar to the liveryman. Everywhere he went, he tried to be as pleasant and easygoing as possible. Everybody was glad to know him and sad to see him go.

That was the way Burroughs wanted it.

He swung up into the saddle, lifted a hand in farewell, and turned the horse to ride out of the settlement and head into the mountains to the north. As he started up the slopes, he heard the whistle of the locomotive. The train was pulling in, and in less than an hour it would roll out of Rattlesnake Wells, heading back to the junction with the Union Pacific.

Burroughs smiled as he thought about what that train was going to be carrying, in addition to a bounty hunter and a prisoner.

CHAPTER 13

The train's passengers disembarked fairly quickly, then with much clanging of metal and hissing of steam, the locomotive backed the caboose onto a siding where it was uncoupled. It pulled forward again and was uncoupled from the coal tender, the two passenger cars, and the two freight cars that made up the train.

With that done the locomotive rolled into the roundhouse to be turned so it could head back the way it had come. Luke felt his impatience growing as minutes passed and the locomotive didn't reappear.

He stood on the platform next to McCluskey, who was wearing cuffs and leg irons again. Luke kept his left hand on the outlaw's right arm. The other passengers getting ready to board the train kept their distance.

"You'll never get me to Cheyenne alive," McCluskey said as he scowled.

"That's a foolish thing to say, McCluskey," Luke replied. "I'd think you would understand by now, I don't care if I get you there alive. I'd just as soon get you there dead."

"You won't get me there at all, damn you."

"Yesterday you were so cooperative," Luke said dryly. "What happened?"

"I knew something would happen to get me loose."

"You knew that crazy Delia would show up?"

"No. I just knew it would be something. And I still do. I won't die at the hands of the law, and that includes bounty hunters. I had a vision."

"Good Lord," Luke muttered. "Spare us from two-bit bandits with visions."

"I mean it," McCluskey insisted. "I know my destiny. I'm not gonna hang, and you're not gonna kill me, Jensen. You just wait and see."

"That's exactly what I intend to do. Actually, I don't attend many hangings. But I'm going to make a point of watching you dance on air, McCluskey, hopefully not too far in the distant future."

And that future was coming closer, Luke thought. The locomotive had finally rolled out of the roundhouse and was pulling past the platform again on another siding so it could get in front of the cars. Once that coupling was made, the train would pull past the caboose on the other siding and then back up so it could be hooked on.

It was a laborious and hazardous process for the railroad workers who handled the coupling and uncoupling, but it was the only way to turn a train around at the end of a spur line like Rattlesnake Wells.

The blue-uniformed conductor moved onto the steps of one of the passenger cars and bellowed, "All abooarrdd!"

The people waiting on the platform, including Luke and McCluskey, moved toward the cars.

Luke Jensen and his prisoner were gone, and Chuck Helton was pouring himself a cup of coffee from the pot on the stove when the part-time deputy heard noises coming from the cell block.

He frowned and turned in that direction as he tried to figure out what was going on. It sounded almost like a cat had gotten in the cell block somehow and was squalling. That was impossible, though.

Or was it? Helton supposed a cat could have squeezed in through one of the barred windows in the cells. The blasted critters could get in places you never thought they could. He liked having them around the livery stable where he worked because they kept the mice and rats down, but other than that, he'd never warmed up to them.

If a cat had gotten in there, it could just get back out on its own, he decided.

The whimpering and crying sounds continued, and after a minute, he started to get worried. He still had a prisoner in there, after all, and with Marshal Hatfield and Fred Ordway laid up, she was his responsibility.

He carried the coffee over to the desk and set it down. "All right, all right. Hold your horses."

He got the keys from the nail where they were hanging and went over to the cell block door. The sounds were louder as they came through the barred window in the door. "Hey, are you all right in there?"

The prisoner didn't answer, but Helton could tell that the pitiful noises were coming from her cell. Muttering a curse under his breath, he unlocked the door and swung it open. "Lady . . . whatever your name is . . . are you all right?"

He still got no response, so he stuck the keys in his pocket, drew his gun, and stepped into the cell block. Jensen had warned him to be careful, and so had the marshal, but the prisoner was a woman, after all, and just a little bit of one, at that.

Helton stepped closer to the cell door. The light was dim, but he could see well enough to tell that the blonde was huddled on the bunk, doubled over and clutching her stomach. She lifted her head, and he was shocked to see how pale and haggard her face looked, beaded with sweat.

"That greaser woman . . . poisoned me!" she gasped.

"N-now hold on," Helton stammered. "I'm sure Señorita Consuela wouldn't do that. Anyway, McCluskey ate the same thing you did . . ."

"That's right. He's not here anymore. You don't know if he's sick or not."

Helton started to back off. "I'll go get the doc—"

"Maybe you could . . . get me some water first?"

He'd been told to keep his distance from her, but she was so sick there was no way she could be a threat. He had sense enough to step back into the marshal's office and lay his gun on the desk, though, just to make sure she didn't try to grab it away from him.

He poured some water from a pitcher into one of the cups they used for coffee and carried it into the cell block. "You're gonna have to get up and come get it. I'm not unlockin' that door."

"All right. Th-thank you . . ." She struggled up from the bunk and stumbled toward the cell door. When she reached it, she leaned against the bars and clung to them with one hand while she reached through with the other arm. That hand trembled violently, so Helton had to step closer and press the cup into her fingers with both of his hands.

He felt a slight impact against his belly, almost like somebody had tossed a rock and hit him, and looked down to see the handle of a knife protruding from his body. His eyes widened as crimson began to spread on his shirt around the blade. He gasped. "How —" He didn't know where she'd had the knife hidden. He hadn't even seen her other hand move.

His knees folded up and he dropped the cup. Clattering loudly, it fell onto the stone floor. The prisoner grabbed his shirtfront with her other hand and jerked him closer. She was surprisingly strong for a woman, especially one so sick.

But she wasn't sick at all, Helton realized as he looked into her face from a space of a few inches and felt the cold steel going in and out of his body as she stabbed him again and again. His weight dragged him down, and she knelt with him as she continued to thrust the knife into him through the bars.

He couldn't believe it was happening.

He died that way, with his mouth still hanging open in amazement.

"Please, I need a ticket."

The clerk at the ticket window in the station looked up and saw a young woman. She wore a blue dress and looked a little disheveled and pale, but she was still attractive, other than the look of desperation on her face.

"Ma'am, the train's about to leave —"

"I know. That's why I have to hurry."

"Well, you might make it . . . How far do you want to go? All the way to Cheyenne?"

She nodded. "That's fine. How much?"

"Let's see . . ." He could tell she was getting more impatient, but such things couldn't be rushed. The railroad didn't pay him for making careless mistakes. "It'll be two dollars and fifty cents."

She thrust a bill through the wicket.

"There's five dollars. I don't need any change back, just the ticket."

"Well, now, ma'am, I'm not sure it's wise

throwin' money around like that —"

"Please. It's a matter of life and death."

Some folks, it was just a waste of time arguing with them. The clerk wrote up the ticket, tore it out of the book, and handed it to her.

She'd been telling the truth about not wanting the money she had coming back to her. She turned and ran from the lobby, across the platform, and swung up onto the last passenger car after it had already started rolling. Couldn't be easy for her to do that, a little thing like her.

The clerk shook his head. It took all kinds in this world, he supposed.

He looked down at the five-dollar banknote she had given him and saw the dark stain along its edge. A frown creased his forehead. It looked almost like . . . He shook his head. That didn't make any sense.

The stain looked almost like blood.

Derek Burroughs rode onto a rocky promontory where he could look down at Rattlesnake Wells. The train was just leaving after getting the caboose hooked up again, clouds of white smoke billowing from the Baldwin locomotive's diamond-shaped stack as it pulled out.

Horseshoes rang loudly on the rocks

behind Burroughs. He glanced around as more than a dozen hard-bitten, well-armed men rode out of the trees. He was expecting to see them, so he wasn't surprised by their appearance.

As the group of riders reined in, the man in the lead asked, "Is that it? The train with the gold?"

"That's it," Burroughs confirmed. "It stayed extra time in the roundhouse so the shipment could be hidden in the cab of the locomotive, just like my source at the mine told me it would be. Once they're well out of town, they'll stop and transfer it to the caboose."

"A hundred and twenty-five thousand dollars in gold," the other man said with an avaricious grin. "We're all gonna be rich men once we take it off that train."

"Yes, we are," Burroughs agreed, nodding. He wasn't thinking about the gold as much as he was about Luke Jensen. He sincerely hoped that his old friend wouldn't try to interfere when he and his men stopped the train.

He'd really hate to have to kill Luke, he mused, especially after saving his life just the night before.

CHAPTER 14

The first thing Luke had done when he boarded the train with McCluskey was to seek out the conductor. That hombre's eyes had widened at the sight of the outlaw shuffling along in handcuffs and leg irons. Others who had seen the prisoner seemed upset, looking askance at Luke and McCluskey and giving them a lot of room.

"You can't bring that man on my train like that," the conductor said.

"I don't have any choice in the matter," Luke declared. "I'm sure not taking these irons off him. This is Frank McCluskey. He's wanted all over this part of the country, and I'm taking him to Cheyenne to turn him over to the authorities there."

The conductor's forehead wrinkled in a frown. "I don't see a badge on you, mister, so I suppose that means you intend to collect the reward on this fellow when you turn him in."

"That's right," Luke said evenly. He heard the contempt in the conductor's voice plainly enough but knew from experience it was best for him to keep a tight rein on his temper in such situations.

"Well, you can't have him in the regular cars. It'll frighten the other passengers too much. You'll have to put him in the caboose, and I won't stand for any argument about it."

Since that was exactly what Luke wanted, he didn't intend to argue. He wasn't going to admit that to the conductor, though. The man might change his mind just to spite him.

Luke nodded curtly. "All right. If that's the way it has to be, I guess that's what we'll do."

The conductor sniffed as if to say *Damn right you will.* Luke looked down to hide the grin that flashed across his face for a second.

"Let's take him on back there now," the conductor said.

By that time, the caboose was hooked up again to the train, which rolled slowly along the rails, building up speed as it left Rattlesnake Wells. The three men walked through the passenger cars, which were behind the baggage cars, and into the car bringing up the rear that served as the conductor's office and a place for the brakemen to take it easy when they weren't working.

The brakies weren't in there at the moment.

The conductor told Luke, "You might as well put your prisoner on that chair over there in the corner. He can't get loose, can he?"

"Not likely." Luke steered McCluskey over to the ladderback chair and sat him down in it. He took out another pair of handcuffs and looped one end around one of the rungs in the back of the chair and the chain between McCluskey's cuffs. By snapping it shut, he ensured that McCluskey couldn't get up and go anywhere without taking the chair with him. As awkward as it already was having his ankles fastened together like they were, getting around while fastened to the chair would be almost impossible.

"There's coffee on the stove," the conductor said with grudging hospitality.

"Much obliged." Luke poured himself a cup but didn't offer to do the same for McCluskey. He was through showing the outlaw any consideration. "How long does it take to get to Cheyenne?"

"We'll arrive about seven o'clock this

evening, if there aren't any delays."

"What's the country like between here and the junction?"

"Mostly flat, which means we make good time." The conductor's attitude was warming up a little. Talking about the train that was his responsibility probably helped with that. "There's one range of pretty rugged mountains to get through."

Luke nodded. Normally he would have worried about the train slowing down to take the grades in the mountains. That would make it easier for someone who wasn't supposed to be there to get aboard.

But McCluskey didn't have a gang that would set out to rescue him, Luke reminded himself. The only person who seemed determined to set the outlaw free was Delia, and she was locked up safely back in Rattlesnake Wells.

Luke frowned slightly as he sipped the coffee. She had been behind bars when he left the marshal's office and jail earlier that morning, but he had no way of knowing if she was still there, he realized. She was shifty as a sidewinder. The likelihood of her causing any more trouble was small, but he couldn't rule it out one hundred percent.

He would be glad when Frank McCluskey was off his hands and the reward money was in his pocket.

The door of the caboose opened, and a man in a gray suit and darker gray derby hat stepped in. He had a successful, well-fed look about him, with a beefy face, thick dark mustache, and bushy side-whiskers. A short black cigar was clamped between his teeth. He stopped short as he saw Luke and McCluskey, and an angry flush began turning his face an even darker red.

"Damn it, Hitch!" he exploded. "What are these two doing in here?"

Delia sat beside the window and tried to collect her thoughts as she watched the flat terrain covered with scrub brush rolling past outside. She was still a little out of breath from rushing to the train station and from the strain of worrying that the stupid deputy's body would be discovered before she could get aboard and leave Rattlesnake Wells behind.

Killing the lawman had been a calculated risk. When she'd taken the knife from the sheath strapped to the inside of her left thigh and put it in the man's belly, she hadn't known whether he had the key to the cell on him or not. It was the only chance she had to free herself and help Frank, so she'd taken it.

She had never murdered anybody before. She'd killed two men in the past, customers of hers who'd gotten too rough with her and then lost their temper when she fought back. Those killings had been self-defense, and she'd never lost a bit of sleep over them.

She didn't think the deputy's death would bother her for very long. After all, Frank's life was at stake and she loved him. Whatever she had to do to save him was justified as far as she was concerned. She would have killed the damn bounty hunter, too, and the marshal, and the marshal's Mexican slut, and anybody else who got in her way and threatened her man.

If anyone had asked her why she'd fallen so hard for Frank McCluskey, Delia couldn't have said. All she knew was that from the moment he had put his arms around her and kissed her, she was his forever and would do anything for him.

Someone slid onto the empty half of the seat beside her, next to the aisle, and interrupted her musing about McCluskey. She turned, saw a man in a cheap suit. He had weaselly eyes over a long, whiskey-veined nose. A drummer of some sort, Delia thought, trying not to shudder as he boldly ran his eyes over her. She was used to being looked at like that by men, as if they could see right through her clothes to the ripe body beneath.

"Hello. Traveling by yourself, miss?"

"No," Delia said primly. "My husband is with me."

That statement had some truth to it. Someday she and Frank would be married. She was sure of it. And while he wasn't exactly with her at the moment, he was somewhere on the train, and that was close enough for her.

Being told that she was married seemed to take some of the starch out of the drummer, but he didn't deflate too much. "Oh? Where is he, then?"

Maybe he was used to women lying to avoid his unwanted attentions.

"He's gone to talk to the conductor," Delia said without missing a beat. "He's an important man. Everyone on the railroad knows him."

"Is that so? I ride this line pretty often. Maybe I know him, too."

"Oh, I doubt that." Delia's haughty tone made it clear that the traveling salesman would be beneath her mythical husband's notice.

"Well, I'm sure you won't mind if I keep you company until he gets back." And with that he slid a little closer so his hip was touching hers.

Delia felt her self-control slipping away. She slid her hand into the pocket where she had put the knife so it would be handier and turned slightly toward the drummer. He wore a look of slightly surprised anticipation on his fox-like face.

He was about to be even more surprised, she thought, leaning toward him and putting a little weight on the knife. The tip of its razor-keen blade penetrated the man's coat and shirt and pricked into his side. "I think it would be best if you went and found somewhere else to sit, instead of annoying me."

His eyes widened and his rather prominent Adam's apple bobbed up and down as he swallowed hard.

He stammered, "I-is that —"

"Yes, it is," Delia said. "And I'm perfectly capable of carving out your liver with it if you don't do exactly what I told you."

He had gone pale, which made the veins in his nose stand out even more. "For God's sake, lady, be careful with that! You're sticking me."

"I'm about to do worse than that," Delia told him.

He scooted away from her on the bench.

She made the knife disappear back into her pocket.

"Take it easy," he muttered. "I'm going, I'm going. You don't have to be so damn touchy. All I wanted was a little pleasant conversation to pass the time."

"All I want is for you to go away. And don't even think about going to the conductor and complaining about the crazy woman with the knife. If you do, I warn you I'll find you. Some night when you least expect it, I'll be there." She smiled at him. "And then I'll cut out your eyes and your tongue, but not before I've done some cutting elsewhere. I won't leave you with any of the things that are so important to you, mister."

He practically leaped up from the seat and hurried away.

Satisfied, Delia settled back in the seat and looked out the window again, thinking.

She had been through both passenger cars after she came aboard. Since Frank and the bounty hunter hadn't been in either one, they were in one of the freight cars or in the caboose. She considered the caboose the more likely possibility and had settled into a seat in the second passenger car closest to it.

What she would do after getting into the caboose would have to wait until she was actually in the caboose, and then she could figure it out. The goal was pretty simple, though.

Set Frank McCluskey free . . . and kill Luke Jensen.

Luke looked at the man in the derby and said in a deceptively mild tone, "Most men wouldn't take kindly to being talked about like that, mister — and I'm one of them."

The newcomer ignored him and continued glaring at the conductor. "You know there's not supposed to be anyone in this caboose except railroad employees and my guards. Who are these men?"

The conductor had a look of dismay on his face. "I'm sorry, Mr. Bertram. I completely forgot about the shipment."

"Forgot?" Bertram repeated. "My God, man, how could you forget about that much —" He stopped short, glanced at Luke and then at McCluskey as if thinking that he'd been about to say too much. "Who are you?" he demanded.

"My name's Luke Jensen. This is my prisoner, Frank McCluskey."

Bertram's piggish eyes widened. He had heard of McCluskey, even if the conductor hadn't. "Frank McCluskey the outlaw?" His voice had a little squeak of alarm in it.

"Here?"

"Better calm down, mister," Luke advised. "If your face gets any redder, you're liable to pop a blood vessel."

Before Bertram could respond to that, the door of the caboose opened again and a hard-faced man carrying a rifle came in. "We're ready to stop and make the switch, boss."

Bertram gestured curtly at him to stop him from saying anything else.

It didn't matter. Luke was no fool and had already figured out what was going on. "Exactly how much gold are you shipping out in secret on this train, Bertram?"

The man stared at him for a second, then said, "What? Gold? I don't know what you're —"

"Don't waste your breath denying it," Luke said. "You're working for the mine owners who have pooled their gold to ship it to Cheyenne. It must have been refined down to ingots. I thought I saw a smelter back in the hills above Rattlesnake Wells. Raw ore would weigh too much, but you could pack a fortune in gold bars into a couple fairly small strongboxes. Let me guess. They're up in the cab of the locomotive right now. That would explain why it was in the roundhouse longer than usual.

The engineer is going to stop the train and your hired guards will carry the boxes back here to the caboose and lock them up. That's how the plan goes, isn't it?"

Bertram looked more and more astonished, not to mention angry, as Luke spoke. He roared, "Who the hell *are* you? Chadwick, cover this man! If he reaches for a gun, kill him!"

The conductor quickly answered, "He's a bounty hunter, Mr. Bertram. Like he told you, that other man is a prisoner he's taking to Cheyenne."

"I don't believe it! He's got to be an outlaw himself! These two are working together! They're after the gold —"

"Not hardly," Luke interrupted in a flat, cold tone. "I told you the truth, Bertram. I didn't know anything about your precious gold until you came in here, lost your temper, and started flapping your gums. Figuring it out from there wasn't difficult." He paused. "Maybe the mine owners should have hired someone a bit more . . . discreet, shall we say? . . . to get their gold to Cheyenne." He smiled and drank some more of the coffee.

Chadwick, evidently one of the hired guards, took a step forward. "He knows too much, Mr. Bertram. Want me to take his guns and tie him up?"

Before Bertram could answer, Luke added to the tension by saying softly, "I don't think you want to try that, friend." He didn't like having guns pointed at him.

That could have led to trouble, but Bertram was canny enough to realize that he was creating problems where they didn't have to exist. He held out a hand toward Chadwick and motioned him back, making a visible effort to be the voice of reason, rather than the blustery hardnose he had been mere moments earlier. "Let's all settle down. Jensen, do you swear you didn't know about that gold and aren't on this train to make a try for it?"

"I stand by what I said," Luke snapped. "I don't intend to take a damn oath, if that's what you mean. But it's the truth." He nodded toward McCluskey, who sat on the ladderback chair with a wolfish grin on his face. "I can't say the same for McCluskey, but in his current situation there's not much he can do to cause trouble for you."

Bertram frowned. "I don't like having a notorious outlaw on the train, whether he's locked up or not. But I don't suppose there's anything I can do about it now, short of throwing you both off and making you walk back to Rattlesnake Wells."

"The boys and I can do that if it's what you want, Mr. Bertram." Chadwick sounded like he would welcome the opportunity.

Bertram heaved a sigh and shook his head. "No, we're going to try to make the best of the situation. Go ahead and let the engineer know he can stop any time he wants, and we'll transfer the strongboxes back here."

"He'll be glad to get 'em out of the way," Chadwick muttered.

"As for the two of you" — Bertram addressed Luke, including McCluskey in the statement — "I want you out of here. You'll have to ride in one of the passenger cars."

The conductor looked like he was about to object to that idea. It had been his idea to take them back there, after all. He wanted to cooperate with Bertram since the man worked for the mine owners and their business was important to the railroad, but he also felt like he had a responsibility to the other passengers.

Luke could practically see those thoughts going through his head.

"I really don't think that's a good idea," the conductor finally said. "Seeing McCluskey shackled like that might frighten and upset the passengers."

Bertram chewed his cigar. "You think I care about the other passengers?"

145

"Well, I do," the conductor said with a small show of defiance. "Look, Mr. Bertram, you have half a dozen very competent guards. Jensen won't have any chance to get his hands on that gold. And even if he did, what could he do with it? One man couldn't carry off those strongboxes. It takes two men just to budge one of them."

"Are you saying we should allow them to stay in here?" Bertram asked, seeming astounded again.

"I just don't see that it can hurt anything. Let's just get on to Cheyenne as quickly as possible and get this job finished."

Clearly, Bertram didn't like it, but after a moment, he nodded. "All right." He jerked a hand at Chadwick. "Get moving. The sooner we get this done, the better."

Chadwick nodded and hurried out of the caboose. A few minutes later, the train began to slow.

McCluskey looked up at Luke and asked, "How much are those rewards on me?"

"They add up to six thousand," Luke replied. "A very tidy sum."

"And how much are two strongboxes full of gold bars worth?" McCluskey asked, still wearing that savage grin on his face.

"Considerably more," Luke acknowledged. He smiled and shook his head. "You remind me, McCluskey, of just how inconvenient it is at times to be an honest man."

CHAPTER 15

After the train had stopped, Luke watched the conductor, whose name he still didn't know, leave the caboose. He figured the man was going to reassure the passengers that nothing was wrong and that the halt was only temporary. Since he was in charge, more than likely, he had already figured out some plausible story to explain it.

Bertram left, too, and Luke had no doubt he was going to supervise the transfer of the strongboxes full of gold to the caboose.

Left alone in the caboose with McCluskey, Luke considered what was about to happen. He could understand the logic of the plan. Secrecy was the goal, and loading the strongboxes into the locomotive's cab while it was in the roundhouse had accomplished that. The gold had probably been delivered to the roundhouse in the dead of night.

It seemed like it would have been simpler

to leave the strongboxes in the cab, rather than going through the business of stopping the train and carrying them back to the caboose, but after a few minutes of thought, he had that figured out, as well. The locomotive wasn't going all the way to Cheyenne. It would stop at the junction with the Union Pacific.

Once there, the caboose would be shunted onto a siding, then switched to an eastbound train to finish the journey with the gold safely inside.

Such elaborate precautions usually meant the mines had had trouble in the past getting their gold shipments out. He wondered if that was the case or if the mine owners were being extra careful because of the size of the shipment.

"You'd better think long and hard about this, Jensen. We're talking about enough money that you could give up bounty hunting for good. You could buy your own ranch if you wanted to. Hell, you could buy *two* ranches!"

Luke knew that if he wanted, his brother would be happy to let him live out the rest of his days on the big Sugarloaf Ranch down in Colorado. As much as he liked Smoke, that idea didn't appeal to him.

"What makes you think I even *want* a ranch?"

The outlaw grinned at him again. "You mean to tell me you really enjoy gettin' shot at and dealing with lowlifes like me all the time?"

"The part about dealing with men like you does get tiresome," Luke admitted. "But I've been doing it so long I'm afraid I'm too old to change."

"This life will be the death of you."

"Sooner or later, everybody can say the same thing, no matter what they do," Luke said.

A short time later, Chadwick and another heavily armed guard came in, followed by several burly, unarmed men in work shirts and overalls carrying a pair of wooden strongboxes strapped by iron bands. From the way the men handled them, it appeared the boxes were heavy.

Bertram and four more guards brought up the rear. "Put them in the corner," he ordered, pointing.

From his seat, Luke watched the men toting the boxes — probably railroad employees, he thought — place them on the floor in the front left corner of the caboose, next to the conductor's desk.

As they straightened up and brushed their

hands off, Bertram went on. "Remember, you men are sworn to secrecy. You can't ever tell anyone about this, in case the mine owners want to use this method again."

That warning was a waste of time, Luke thought. Sooner or later, someone would let it slip what they had done. Probably as soon as he found himself in a saloon with a few drinks inside him. He would want to brag about how he had handled such a valuable load of gold ingots.

And there wasn't anything a stuffed shirt like Bertram could do to stop it.

The men had nodded their agreement and left the caboose.

Bertram continued. "Chadwick, you and three of your men will stay in here with the gold. I want two men in the next passenger car to keep anyone who doesn't belong from coming back here. Try not to let it be too obvious that you're guarding something, though. We don't want to make the passengers curious."

Chadwick nodded and picked two of the men to go up into the passenger car. He and the remaining three men made themselves comfortable, two of them sitting down on a sofa, another reversing a ladder-back chair like the one on which McCluskey sat, and Chadwick himself pouring coffee for all four of them. None seemed curious about the presence of Luke and McCluskey, so Luke assumed their presence had been explained.

Not long after that, the conductor came in and asked, "Are we ready to roll?"

"As far as I'm concerned, we are," Bertram told him.

The conductor glanced uneasily at the strongboxes, pulled a handkerchief from his pocket, mopped sweat from his face with it, and muttered, "We can't get to Cheyenne soon enough to suit me."

Delia was sitting with her head slumped forward a little, brooding as she tried to think of a way to get to Frank McCluskey. As she felt the train's speed slackening, she sat up straighter and looked out the window.

They were still passing through the same sort of terrain that had surrounded them ever since the train rolled out of Rattlesnake Wells. As far as she could see, there was no reason why the train should be stopping.

As it lurched to a halt, a buzz of mystified conversation went through the car as people asked each other what was going on. No one sat next to Delia, so she didn't get that question, but she wondered about it.

A few minutes later, the conductor entered

the car at the rear and started up the aisle, saying in a loud voice, "Nothing to worry about folks, just keep your seats. We'll only be stopped here for a short time while the engineer and the fireman do a little work up in the cab."

"The train hasn't broken down, has it?" a middle-aged woman asked. "I have to get to Cheyenne. My daughter is having a baby any day now!"

"No, ma'am, nothing like that," the conductor assured her. "It's just a minor matter and won't take long to fix, and then we'll be on our way again. Why, I wouldn't be surprised if the engineer will be able to pour on enough steam that we'll still make it to the junction right on schedule."

That explanation seemed to satisfy the passengers, and the conductor moved on to the other car.

Delia wasn't satisfied, though. Surprised, but not satisfied. Maybe she was just naturally suspicious, but she had a hunch something else was going on, although she had no idea what it could be.

Looking through the window, she saw a group of men move past the car, heading toward the rear of the train. Four of them were moving a cart of some sort, two pushing and two pulling. Although she couldn't see what was on the cart — it was covered by a blanket — she could tell it was heavy. She frowned. Men walking along with them all carried rifles.

No one else in the car seemed to pay any attention to the odd procession, but when the conductor came back through, she held up a hand to stop him. "What were those men doing outside the train a little while ago?"

"Men? What men?" the conductor asked.

Delia saw right through that. No man could lie to her and get away with it. She knew good and well he knew what she was talking about. "Close to a dozen men," she said with a frown. "They were moving something on a cart."

"Oh, that."

Delia didn't believe his nonchalance for a second.

"That was just some, uh, railroad equipment. Something to do with that mechanical problem." He sounded like he was getting a little impatient. "I really don't know all the details, miss. I'm the conductor, not the engineer."

Delia put a simpering smile on her face. "Well, I don't really understand all that sort of thing, either, Mr. Conductor. But I appreciate you trying to explain it to me. I'm sorry if I bothered you."

The act mollified him. He shook his head. "It's no bother, ma'am. I'm here to assist the passengers in any way I can, after all. It's part of my job."

He moved on, and the smile disappeared from Delia's face. She was more convinced than ever that something strange was going on, and it had to do with the caboose. She felt sure Frank was back there, so she was doubly determined to get into the caboose herself.

Not only did she have to rescue Frank, but whatever those men had taken back there might be something well worth the two of them getting their hands on.

The train started moving again a short time later, and just as the conductor had predicted, the engineer poured on the steam. They barreled along the tracks at breathtaking speed.

Delia felt her pulse pounding as she looked out the window at the landscape whipping past. She had been on a train only a few times in her life and never one going so fast.

She told herself sternly not to be distracted by such things. She had work to do, *serious* work. Anyway, the mad dash across the plains didn't last long. The train slowed as the tracks began to climb into the foothills at the base of a small mountain range.

Mountains were good, Delia thought. Mountains provided a lot more places to hide than open plains did.

She stopped the conductor as he came through the car again.

With a slight show of annoyance, he asked, "What is it this time, ma'am?"

"I've never made this trip before. What's it like on the other side of these mountains?"

"We'll be back down on the flats until we get to the junction."

"It shouldn't take long, then."

"No, ma'am. Another hour, maybe."

"Thank you." Once again, her smile made the conductor's irritation vanish.

She was running out of time, she thought as she sat back against the hard bench seat. Surely, someone had already found the slain deputy's body back in Rattlesnake Wells and knew she was missing. The marshal would send a wire to the station at the Union Pacific junction asking that the train be searched and that she be taken into custody. She had to free McCluskey and escape before that happened.

She had to act while the train was still in the mountains.

She felt the train leave the foothills and begin climbing toward a pass. She could see it up ahead, at the top of a long, curving grade.

Once they were through the pass they'd be heading down the other side and the train would probably pick up speed. There was no time to lose.

As the train's engine labored to make the climb, she stood up and turned toward the rear of the car. It wasn't swaying as much now that the train had slowed, but it still moved enough so that Delia had to rest her hand on the back of a seat now and then to steady herself as she approached the door to the rear platform.

She felt a little shock of surprise as she recognized the men sitting in the last seats, one on either side of the aisle. They had been with the group moving the thing on the cart toward the caboose while the train was stopped earlier. Both men were dressed like businessmen — plain tweed suits and flat-crowned brown hats.

As she approached, one stood up and moved to block her path. "Sorry, ma'am, no one is supposed to go out on the platform while the train is moving."

"Really? It's sometimes called an observation platform, isn't it? I want to take a better look at these mountains we're passing through. They're really beautiful."

The man shook his head. "No, I reckon you'd better stay in here. Even though the train's not moving as fast as it was, you sure wouldn't want to fall off."

"Well, you're not the conductor," she said with a frown. "I don't think you have any right to stop me."

"I work for the railroad, ma'am, and I'm asking you to go back to your seat."

She didn't know if he was telling the truth about working for the railroad, but it didn't really matter. His coat was open a little, and she was close enough to see that he wore a revolver butt-forward in a cross-draw holster on his left side. That was perfect for her.

She moved forward, and he moved to get in her way, and for a second they did that little dance people do when they're trying not to run into each other.

Delia's real objective was to get close enough to do what she did next. With her left hand, she brought up the knife she had hidden against her body and plunged the blade into the man's belly just above his waist.

His mouth opened and his eyes bulged as she ripped the knife to the side and felt the hot gush of blood over her hand. As he started to double over, he reached for his gun.

She beat him to it, sliding her right hand under his coat and closing it around the butt of the revolver. She jerked it out of the holster, pivoted, and pulled back the hammer as she aimed at the other man.

He didn't have time to do anything except gape in surprise before she pulled the trigger and shot him in the face.

The gun's roar was loud inside the car. As its echoes bounced back and forth, women screamed and men shouted curses and questions.

Delia ignored them all and shoved aside the dying man she had stabbed, leaving the knife buried in his belly. She was surprisingly strong for her petite size, even more so when she was fueled by rage and madness.

As she stepped through the vestibule and out onto the platform, she saw that the train had reached the pass. With smoke boiling from its stack, the locomotive rumbled through the gap in the mountains and started down the long, steep grade toward a trestle that spanned a fast-flowing river.

She took that in with a glance as she stepped across the narrow gap to the platform on the front of the caboose and reached for the doorknob with a hand smeared with blood.

CHAPTER 16

Bertram and the conductor huddled at the desk in the caboose, no doubt going over the plans for what would take place when the train reached the junction. Chadwick and the other three guards seemed relaxed, apparently confident the plan was working well enough that there wouldn't be any trouble.

Luke kept his eyes on his prisoner. The caboose didn't have any windows except a couple small ones for ventilation, so he couldn't see what was going on outside, but he could tell when they reached the mountains. The train slowed and the angle changed as they began climbing the grade.

Bertram barked at Chadwick and the other guard. "All right. You men look sharp now. There are more places up here for an ambush, and the train's going slower. It would be easier for outlaws to get on board."

"Nobody's going to bother that gold, Mr.

Bertram," Chadwick declared. "If they try, we'll give 'em a hot lead welcome. Anyway, once the train makes it through the pass, we'll pick up speed again on the downhill slant."

Luke didn't share Chadwick's confidence. He'd been thinking about it and had decided that half a dozen guards weren't nearly enough to protect the gold if a large gang of outlaws came after it. Bertram was relying too much on secrecy and trickery and not enough on sheer manpower. Things like that happened when a man was too clever for his own good, as Bertram appeared to be.

McCluskey said quietly to Luke, "You know what I'd do if I was bossing the job of stealin' that gold?"

"No, and I don't want to know," Luke replied, although to be honest, he was a little curious. He didn't want to encourage McCluskey by admitting that, however.

McCluskey didn't need encouragement. "I'd hit this train when Bertram and his boys are least expectin' it, when they're starting to think they're safe."

"On the other side of the pass?" Luke asked, despite his own good intentions.

McCluskey said solemnly, "That's right. And as slow as we're goin', I'd say we're

162

just about there."

Luke thought the outlaw was right. He had ridden enough trains through mountainous country to recognize the sensation of a locomotive laboring up the last few yards of a steep grade.

His head jerked up as he heard what sounded like the flat blast of a gunshot. It was hard to tell because of the rattling racket the train made, plus the wind in the mountains whipped sounds away quickly.

He wasn't the only one who heard it. Bertram bolted to his feet and exclaimed, "What was that? It sounded like a shot!"

Instantly, the guards were alert.

Chadwick said, "Hard to tell. Could have been. I can send one of the men to check —"

"No!" Bertram cried. "Don't open that door under any circumstances!"

The train leveled out as it reached the top of the pass, which was a short one. After only a moment, the floor of the caboose slanted again as the train started down the slope.

The doorknob rattled loudly as someone tried to turn it on the other side and found it locked. Tensely, Chadwick and the other guards pointed their rifles at the door.

On the small platform at the front of the

caboose, a woman screamed. "Outlaws!" she shrieked. "They're killing everyone! Let me in! Oh, God, please let me in!"

Chadwick looked hard at Bertram. "What do we —"

His face was covered with sweat. He was torn with indecision, as was obvious from his wild-eyed stare. He twitched as the woman screamed again.

"Bertram, what do we —"

"Let her in!" he burst out.

Luke was on his feet, gun in hand. Suspicion roiled inside him. The idea of outlaws boarding the train was easy enough to swallow. No matter how secret Bertram had tried to keep the shipment, word of that much gold almost always slipped out. But how could outlaws be killing everyone on the train when only one shot had been fired?

Luke was about to call to Chadwick to stop, but the leader of the guards had already reached the door and turned the key. He grabbed the knob, twisted it, and flung the door open.

Flame lanced through the gap as a gun roared again. Chadwick rocked back and dropped his rifle as he gasped in shock and pain.

Luke raised his Remington, hoping to get a shot at whoever was on the platform. He had a pretty good idea who that was.

A dull boom sounded over the noise of the train's wheels, but it didn't sound like it came from elsewhere on the train. Whatever it was had an immediate result.

The train lurched violently as the engineer in the cab threw on the brakes for all they were worth. The wheels screeched against the rails like all the banshees out of hell.

The men in the caboose were thrown off their feet. McCluskey, still sitting in the chair, toppled forward and crashed heavily to the floor. As Luke glanced up, he caught a glimpse of the woman who had shot Chadwick flying backward toward the gap between the caboose and the last passenger car. Her petite size, blond hair, and blue dress told him his hunch was right.

Somehow, Delia had gotten out of jail in Rattlesnake Wells and was trying once again to free her lover McCluskey.

She screamed for real as she dropped out of sight.

That she had slipped between the cars, falling to a grisly death under the train's wheels flashed through his mind in the instant before he slammed to the floor hard enough to knock the breath out of him and stun him. Somehow, he managed to hang on to the revolver.

The train continued to shudder and jerk and act like it was going to fly off the rails at any moment. Luke pushed himself up onto hands and knees and looked around. The rest of the men were still down, and McCluskey —

McCluskey rammed into his side and knocked him sprawling. The Remington slipped out of his fingers and slid along the sloping floor.

The chair had broken when McCluskey was thrown forward so violently. His hands were still cuffed behind his back and he still wore the leg irons, but he had writhed free of the chair's wreckage. He rolled, swung his legs up, and drove them out in a double kick that smashed into Luke's ribs and kept him from retrieving the gun.

Luke grunted and tried not to pass out. He pushed himself out of McCluskey's reach and fought his way to his feet, staggering as the train swayed and the brakes continued to scream.

Whatever was waiting at the bottom of the grade, it had to be bad.

Delia clung with all her strength to the front edge of the platform. She had grabbed it with one hand and had one foot hooked over it, and those were the only things holding her up. If she lost her grip, she would fall, bounce off the coupling, and land under the train. That was certain death.

Before the mysterious explosion, before the train had braked and thrown her off the platform, she had caught a glimpse of Mc-Cluskey through the open door. Knowing he was in the caboose, so close to her, gave her strength she didn't know she had. Slowly, she began to pull herself back up onto the platform, even as the whole train continued to shake.

Delia got her other hand on the platform, and as she solidified her grip she was able to pull herself up and roll onto the steel floor. She looked through the open caboose door and saw McCluskey kick Luke Jensen. Frank was still in irons, but he hadn't given up. He was still fighting. That determination was just one of the things she loved about him.

She had dropped the pistol when she was thrown off her feet, but a rifle lay just inside the door. Realizing the man she had shot had dropped it, she scrambled up onto her hands and knees and lunged toward the weapon before anyone inside the caboose noticed her.

Jensen had gotten away from McCluskey and managed to stand up again. Delia lifted the rifle and swung it up. It was heavy, but she didn't care. She pointed it at Jensen and fired.

The whip crack of the shot was loud in the caboose. With the train shaking so much, accuracy was almost impossible, and she was disgusted to see that Jensen was still on his feet. She worked the rifle's lever and fired again, but just as flame spouted from the muzzle, one of the other men lurched upward, trying to stand.

The slug caught him in the throat. Blood spurted from the wound in a red fountain as he went over backward, gurgling grotesquely.

Cursing her bad luck, Delia levered the rifle and fired again. She screamed, "Stay down, Frank!" and sprayed lead around the caboose. She didn't care who she hit, as long as it wasn't McCluskey.

Jensen kicked the caboose's rear door open and vanished through it. Delia cursed again.

And the train finally ground to a halt.

Luke still had his second Remington, but he never got a shot at the crazy woman blazing away at him with the rifle. He wasn't sure where she got the strength to wield the weapon, unless it was the pure insanity that drove her.

One of the slugs chewed splinters from the doorjamb as he ducked through the opening. He wanted to get out of the close confines of the caboose. He had seen what happened to Bertram and knew that the more wild slugs flew around, the better the chance of dying.

Out in the open, he thought he might be able to get on top of the car, race to the front of the caboose, and drop down behind her, taking her by surprise.

Besides, he wanted to find out what the hell was going on. Was that an explosion he had heard, right after Delia shot Chadwick?

He didn't have a chance to put his plan into operation. The train finally shuddered and shivered to a stop. A rifle cracked somewhere close by, and a bullet ricocheted off the iron railing around the tiny platform at the rear of the caboose.

"Hold it right there, mister!" a man shouted. "Drop that gun and get your hands up!"

Luke looked around. The rails passed between two fairly steep slopes dotted with boulders. He spotted several rifle barrels protruding from behind those rocks and knew he was covered. Whoever those hidden gunmen were, they could riddle him with lead before he made a move.

He had no choice but to let his Remington thud onto the platform as he let go of it.

The train had come to a stop about fifty yards short of a trestle across a river that flowed through the mountains. Keeping his hands in plain sight so the riflemen on the slopes wouldn't get trigger-happy, Luke leaned his head to the side and peered along the train toward the bridge. He saw twisted steel rails curling up in the middle of the span and knew what had happened. Outlaws had blown a hole in the bridge so the train had to stop or crash into the river. That was the explosion he had heard.

Men began emerging from behind the rocks and working their way down the slopes toward the train. As they closed in from both sides, Luke counted almost a dozen. They spread out, a couple heading for the cab, others splitting up to cover the two passenger cars and the caboose.

Suddenly, shots cracked from inside the cars. Some of the passengers were armed and willing to put up a fight. The outlaws dropped behind cover and returned the fire. Luke heard glass shatter as owlhoot lead raked through the windows of the passenger cars. Screams and angry shouts counterpointed the gunfire.

A shot roared inside the caboose, then a moment later another report sounded. Luke didn't think whoever fired those shots was trying to defend the caboose against the outlaws.

His hunch proved correct. A moment later, Frank McCluskey appeared in the doorway, holding a revolver. He was free, although a cuff was still locked around each wrist. Short lengths of chain dangled from the cuffs. The leg irons were in the same shape. Luke knew the shots he had heard inside the caboose were Delia blowing the shackles apart and freeing McCluskey.

The outlaw grinned at the sight of Luke standing there unarmed, with his hands up. McCluskey stayed back enough that he wouldn't be spotted by the bandits approaching the train. "You see, Jensen?" McCluskey gloated as Delia peeked around him at Luke, smirking. "I told you something would happen. It was just a matter of time."

"You're not out of the woods yet, McCluskey," Luke said. "The men who stopped this train aren't your friends. As far as they're concerned, you're just one more obstacle standing between them and those strongboxes full of gold."

"That's where you're wrong." McCluskey

leaned out a little and raised his voice. "Hey! Back here! The gold's in the caboose!"

A couple outlaws ran along the tracks, rifles held ready for instant use. They arrived at the caboose's rear platform and leveled the weapons at Luke.

He looked over the barrel of one of the rifles and felt a shock go through him like a hard punch to the belly. The man pointing the Winchester at him, clearly ready to kill him if he made a wrong move, was his old friend Derek Burroughs.

CHAPTER 17

Burroughs didn't seem surprised.

But then again, he wouldn't be, Luke thought. "When you told me you were going to do some prospecting for gold, Derek, I assumed you meant something else."

"Sorry, Luke. I didn't enjoy lying to you. Just don't try anything. Nobody else has to die here." Burroughs circled out a little so he could see into the doorway. "McCluskey! Throw that gun down."

McCluskey edged back and to the side so he could use the doorjamb for cover. "The hell I will! I don't know who you are, mister, but I've got the gold. That means you have to deal with me."

It was true, Luke realized. McCluskey didn't know who Burroughs was. Burroughs had hit him from behind, knocked him out, and hadn't been around the jail after McCluskey had regained consciousness.

"Derek here is an old friend of mine,"

Luke told McCluskey. "He's the one who saved my life last night by buffaloing you just as you were about to shoot me."

"Is that so?" McCluskey sneered. "Well, I don't reckon it matters that much now. I'm not your prisoner anymore, Jensen, and like I said . . . I've got the gold."

"What are you going to do with it?" Burroughs asked. "You can't haul it out of there. It's too heavy for one man to handle. And we've got the train surrounded."

That was true. The shooting from the passenger cars had stopped. Either the men who'd been putting up a fight were all dead, or they had realized how futile their resistance was and had surrendered. Burroughs' gang appeared to be firmly in control of the situation.

McCluskey was just a wild card — but sometimes wild cards could determine the outcome of the game.

"Listen, mister, you owe me," McCluskey said quickly. "There were four guards in here. They're all dead, thanks to me and my lady friend. You can waltz right in and take the gold without losing any men. Don't you think I deserve something for that?"

The outlaw with Burroughs said, "Why don't we just kill this loudmouth, too?"

Burroughs shook his head. "No, he's got a

point. Maybe we should cut him in for a share."

"I ain't sure the rest of the boys would go along with that idea."

"They will if I say so, and if they know what's good for them." Burroughs' voice was cold and hard as steel as he spoke, and the look on his face gave Luke a glimpse into what his old friend had become. He had turned outlaw, like so many former Confederate soldiers who had returned home to devastation and corruption. There was no mercy left inside him.

Or not much, anyway. Burroughs had spared his old friend's life — so far.

Luke had no doubt that could change in a heartbeat.

"I'm coming in there, McCluskey, and we can talk about this." Burroughs went on. "Luke, you go back inside, too. I want you where I can keep an eye on you myself. You're too tricky to trust otherwise."

McCluskey frowned as he considered that, then he said, "All right, mister, but you're the only one who comes in. The rest of your bunch stays out there, and if you try anything funny, you won't leave this caboose alive."

McCluskey backed away and motioned for Luke to follow him into the caboose.

Burroughs came up the steps with his rifle. Caught between the two of them, Luke stepped back into the caboose.

All the bullets Delia had thrown around in here had resulted in a bloodbath. Luke had seen Bertram and Chadwick gunned down. The other three guards were dead, too, sprawled in limp heaps on the floor.

The only one who had survived was the conductor, who sat huddled against the wall nursing a wounded left arm. The sleeve of his uniform coat was dark with blood, and crimson ran down his hand and dripped from his fingers. Delia stood over him with a revolver in her hand, watching him.

Burroughs followed Luke into the caboose, looked around at the bodies, and nodded grimly. "Looks like you live up to your reputation as a killer, McCluskey."

Luke didn't say anything about how Delia was the one responsible for slaughtering the guards, and McCluskey didn't correct Burroughs' assumption, either.

As for Delia, she looked like she didn't care whether McCluskey got credit for the killings. All that mattered to her was that she had been reunited with the outlaw she loved with such unaccountable intensity.

"Where's the gold?" Burroughs glanced around. "Never mind. I see it," he said as his gaze fell on the strongboxes stacked in the corner. He took a step toward them, but McCluskey got in his way.

"I told you, we have to make a deal before you get your hands on those boxes."

Burroughs' eyes narrowed. "You just don't understand, do you? I'm the only thing keeping you alive, McCluskey, and I'm running out of patience. Sure, we can swap lead if you want. Maybe you'll be lucky and live through it. But my men will storm this car and you'll be wiped out, both you and your little blonde."

"Yeah, but us dying won't do *you* a damn bit of good," McCluskey countered, "because you'll be dead, too, and you won't ever get to enjoy any of that gold. Cut me in on it, and everybody gets to live." He glanced at Luke. "Well, everybody but Jensen, anyway. One way or another, that one is a dead man."

Burroughs looked like he didn't care for that idea. "Let's settle the other matters first. I suppose what you've done is worth, say, one bar of gold."

"I was thinking more like ten."

"Good Lord, man!" Burroughs exclaimed. "That's almost a full share, and you're not even one of us. You just happened to be here."

"Right place, right time," McCluskey said with an arrogant grin.

"Two bars," Burroughs said.

"Eight."

"Four."

"How about six?" McCluskey asked. "That's splitting the difference."

"Four is as high as I'll go. My men won't like it if I give you even that much. They won't mutiny over it, though."

"Not even five?" McCluskey wheedled.

Burroughs shook his head. "Four. That's my final offer."

Delia said, "Frank, how much is four bars of gold worth?"

"A lot," McCluskey replied. "All right, Burroughs, you've got yourself a deal." He moved the gun he held toward Luke. "Now, about Jensen —"

Luke knew McCluskey was about to gun him down in cold blood. He tensed his muscles, knowing that he would rather make a desperate leap toward the outlaw and die fighting than just stand there and take it.

Before either Luke or McCluskey could make a move, Burroughs pivoted sharply and struck out with the rifle he held. The butt slammed into the side of Luke's head and knocked him off his feet. Explosions went off inside his skull as he hit the floor.

Burroughs grinned. "You just leave Jensen to me."

It was the last thing Luke was aware of before darkness claimed him.

CHAPTER 18

If somebody had asked Luke, he would have said that the odds of him waking up alive were pretty damn small. But that was exactly what happened.

As awareness seeped back into him, he knew he wasn't dead.

It was the only thing he was sure of. He didn't know how much time had passed or what he would find when he finally succeeded in forcing his eyes open.

He took stock of his circumstances. He was lying on something hard, but it was too rough to be the floor of the caboose. Light beat warmly against his eyelids, shining through them a little even though they were still closed.

He was outside, he decided, almost certainly lying on the ground.

His arms were pulled back in an uncomfortable position. He tried to move them a little, just to see if he could, but they wouldn't budge. Something rough around his wrists tied his hands together — a lariat.

His feet were bound, too. He was trussed up tightly enough that all he could do was lie there.

But he wasn't blindfolded . . . or gagged, for that matter, although he didn't see what good being able to talk would do him. He opened his eyes to slits and looked around as much as he could without moving his head. If anyone was watching him, he didn't want to reveal that he was awake just yet.

He was lying on the ground, all right, off the cinders of the roadbed and about twenty feet from the rails. He could see the caboose.

A few roughly dressed men moved around. Members of Derek Burroughs' gang, Luke supposed.

As he watched, two of them climbed down from the caboose carrying one of the strongboxes. They struggled with it as if they could barely carry its weight.

"Jensen!" a man's voice whispered urgently. "Jensen, are you awake?"

Luke didn't respond right away. The voice was familiar, but he couldn't figure out who it belonged to.

The man started cursing in a low, monotonous voice about how they were all going to be killed, and Luke suddenly recognized it. He was lying next to the conductor from the train, who was probably tied up just like he was.

Before Luke could open his eyes and let the conductor know he had regained consciousness, a boot toe prodded him in the ribs, which were sore from being kicked by McCluskey earlier. A much more familiar voice said in a normal tone, "Come on, wake up, Luke. I know I didn't hit you that hard."

Luke's eyelids fluttered open. He found himself looking up into the lean grinning face of Derek Burroughs. "You had me worried there, partner. I was afraid I might've accidentally hit you hard enough to do some real damage."

The words felt like rusty nails in Luke's throat as he rasped, "We're not . . . partners."

"Well, not in the formal sense of the word. But figuratively speaking. We've been through a lot together, after all." Burroughs sighed. "When I found out you were going to be on this train, I worried that it was going to cause a problem. I hoped it wouldn't, but I know you too well, Luke. Like we talked about before, trouble just follows you around."

Burroughs wasn't carrying a rifle. He reached down, took hold of Luke's arm, and hauled him up into a sitting position. Luke's head spun crazily for a minute as if the earth had started turning in the wrong direction. When it settled down, he could see what was going on.

The conductor was beside him, as he'd suspected, but sitting up. The man's arms were tied behind his back, and his ankles were bound together like Luke's. His black cap was missing, revealing that he was about half bald. His face was pale and haggard, partly from strain, partly from fear, and partly from the blood he'd lost from his wounded arm. At least the bleeding seemed to have stopped. No fresh blood was running down the man's arm, and the stain around the bullet hole appeared to be drying.

Not far away, quite a few people were sitting on the ground. A mixture of men, women, and children, the passengers from the train had been herded out like cattle.

Four well-armed outlaws stood guard over them, and even though the train robbers were outnumbered almost ten to one, it was obvious none of the male passengers were going to fight back. That would put too many wives and children at risk.

Several railroad employees were in the group, too, including a man in a blue cap and striped overalls who was probably the engineer. He looked up at Burroughs. "You've really taken over, haven't you?"

"That was the idea. Blow up the bridge, stop the train, take the gold." Burroughs chuckled. "You have to admit, it's working like a charm, so far."

Luke looked around. "How are you going to get the gold out? Pack mules? I'm not sure a wagon could make it through these mountains."

"No, I have something a bit more ingenious in mind. I'll show you."

Burroughs reached behind him and drew a knife from a sheath fastened to his gun belt behind his holstered revolver. He leaned toward Luke, but the gesture didn't seem menacing. He used the blade to cut the rope wrapped around Luke's ankles. Then he put the knife away and lifted Luke to his feet.

Again, the movement was enough to make Luke dizzy for a moment, and his muscles were cramped from lying on the ground and being confined. He was unsteady, but Burroughs' hand on his arm braced him until he had his legs solidly under him again.

"Come on." Burroughs led Luke along the

tracks, past the group of prisoners — some of whom regarded him suspiciously, even though he was obviously a captive, too — and on toward the river.

"Where are McCluskey and Delia?" he asked.

"They're down by the river. Don't worry, I'm not going to let McCluskey or that crazy woman kill you."

"McCluskey believes that's part of the deal he made with you."

"I don't care what McCluskey believes," Burroughs said. "We came after that gold. I told the men all along there wouldn't be any more killing than necessary — and no matter what McCluskey thinks, it's not necessary for you to die."

That was where he was wrong, Luke thought.

If he came through this mess alive, he was going to hunt Burroughs down and bring him to justice if it was the last thing he did.

They went down a rocky slope toward the river. Burroughs kept his hand on Luke's arm to steady him on the rough ground. The trestle loomed above them to the left. The arching, intricate framework of crossbeams that supported it was intact except in one place, right in the middle of the trestle. The explosion had separated and twisted the rails and blown some of the beams away.

Even though the trestle hadn't collapsed, the train would have crashed if the engineer hadn't been able to stop. The locomotive would have left the rails when it reached the gap and plunged into the river, dragging the rest of the train with it. There was a good chance everyone on board would have been killed. Burroughs and his men would have had to dig the strongboxes out of the debris — and a pile of corpses.

So the outlaw's holier-than-thou talk about no unnecessary killing was just a bunch of hogwash, Luke thought. Burroughs had been perfectly willing to gamble with the lives of everyone on the train to get what he wanted, and the fact that they weren't all dead was no thanks to him.

The river was about a hundred feet wide at the point Luke and Burroughs stopped. Luke couldn't tell how deep it was, but it had a nice steady current flowing downstream. He could see the water rippling in the afternoon sunlight.

McCluskey and Delia stood on a gravel bar along the near shore. McCluskey had two pistols thrust into the waistband of his trousers, and Delia was carrying a rifle. Her blond curls were loose and moving a little in the stiff breeze that blew along the river.

"Thanks for delivering Jensen to us," McCluskey said, baring his teeth in a savage grin. "We'll take care of him from here."

Burroughs shook his head. "I don't think so."

McCluskey's grin quickly disappeared, replaced by an angry frown. "What the hell are you talking about?" he demanded. "We had a deal."

"What's more important to you? Jensen or your share of that gold?" Burroughs nodded toward the two iron-strapped strongboxes, which sat nearby on the gravel bar with four members of the gang watching over them.

"Jensen deserves to die for all the trouble he's caused me!" McCluskey insisted.

Burroughs shook his head again. "You're going to have to make up your mind. You can't have both. And you'll have to decide pretty quick, too, because our way out is just about to get here."

Luke couldn't figure out what Burroughs meant, but a moment later, he heard a faint rumble, accompanied by a splashing sound. The noises came from downstream, where the river went around a sharp bend, and he suddenly realized what he was hearing.

The shrill cry of a steam whistle confirmed

his guess and made McCluskey and Delia turn and look downstream in obvious surprise. Luke had his eyes on the bend, too, but he wasn't surprised when a riverboat surged into view. The vessel was a sternwheeler, the sort of shallow-draft boat that had been used in earlier years to navigate the Missouri River and its tributaries as part of the fur trade. Droplets of water flung off the big revolving paddles at the back of the boat, glittering in the air as it steamed upriver toward the people waiting on the bank.

CHAPTER 19

Despite the dire nature of his circumstances, Luke almost grinned in admiration of Burroughs' cleverness. "You're making your getaway in a riverboat?"

"That's right," Burroughs replied with a chuckle. "Like you said, a wagon's just not practical in these mountains where there are no roads, and packhorses would have slowed us down too much. By the time they realize at the junction that the train's not getting through, then come out to investigate, we'll be miles upstream. I sent men ahead with most of our horses to the little settlement where the river leaves the mountains. They'll be waiting for us there. We'll split up the gold and scatter, and no one will ever find us."

"What about Delia and me?" McCluskey asked. "Are we coming along on this little riverboat ride of yours?"

"That's up to you," Burroughs replied

with a shrug. "It's all right with me if you do." His voice hardened. "But Luke stays here with the other passengers. The railroad will send another train to retrieve them once they know what happened."

"You're a damn fool to let him live," Mc-Cluskey snapped. He glanced at Burroughs' men grouped around the strongboxes. "I reckon you've got everything on your side right now. We'll play along, won't we, Delia?"

She was tired of the whole thing. "I just want to take our share of the gold and start a new life somewhere, Frank. Settle down and maybe have some kids."

"Uh-huh, sure," McCluskey said.

Luke could see what Delia evidently couldn't. McCluskey had no intention of staying with her, and he sure didn't plan on settling down and having children. He was perfectly willing to let her help him escape, but that was as far as their "romance" went.

He would be wise to take care in his dealings with her, Luke thought. He had a hunch that "Hell hath no fury like a woman scorned" was a saying that applied to Delia Bradley in spades.

Burroughs put his hand on Luke's arm again. "Come on. We're going back up with the others. My men will get the gold loaded."

The riverboat angled in toward the gravel bar. Its draft was so shallow it could come almost get right up to the shore.

As Burroughs led him up the slope away from the river, Luke's mind worked furiously. He didn't see any way to overcome the odds against him and the other prisoners, but the idea of letting Burroughs and his gang get away with damaging the bridge and stealing the gold rubbed him the wrong way. Not to mention the fact that McCluskey and Delia were about to get away. That was the toughest pill of all to swallow.

If he could somehow rally the captives, they might be able to overcome the guards. If they got their hands on those guns, the fight would be a good one. Unfortunately, any such attempt would risk innocent lives. The alternative was to let the outlaws get away.

"You'd better hope our trails never cross again, Derek," Luke said as they approached the group of prisoners.

"Oh, I know that," Burroughs replied. "I wish things were different, but I know you'll carry a grudge about this, Luke. I'll definitely try to steer clear of you in the future. Unless . . . maybe a bar of gold might tempt you to throw in with us?"

"Not hardly," Luke said coldly.

Burroughs shrugged. "I was afraid you'd feel that way. You always were an honest man. It was worth making the suggestion, though."

Luke didn't say anything. Burroughs didn't know how Luke had been betrayed, shot, and left for dead by men he'd considered his comrades in arms, if not his friends, back in the closing days of the war. That betrayal had been over gold, too. Something about that shiny metal did bad things to men, perverted their minds and hearts until they were willing to do anything to obtain it, no matter how evil. Luke had been accused of being mercenary plenty of times — he was a bounty hunter, after all — but he would never stoop that low.

Except for the men guarding the prisoners, Burroughs told the rest of his gang to go on down to the river and board the riverboat. He steered Luke over to where the conductor was sitting, helped him sit down, and bound his hands and feet again. "Sorry to have to do this, Luke."

Then he turned to the prisoners. "Listen to me, folks. No more harm is going to come to you. You'll just have to wait here for a while until someone comes up from the junction to see why the train didn't arrive on time. I'm sure the railroad will take you on to wherever you were going. I'm sorry to cause trouble for you, and I'm sorry for the people who were hurt. Some things just can't be avoided."

Most of the prisoners either gave him surly looks or ignored him.

Burroughs said to the guards, "Your horses are still here, so you'll wait until the boat's gone a mile upstream. We'll stop and blow the whistle. When you hear it, mount up and follow the river until you catch up with us. We'll wait for you."

"You mean to just leave these people here, boss?" one of the guards asked.

"That's what I just told them, isn't it?"

The man shrugged. "Just making sure."

Burroughs turned back to his army comrade. "So long, Luke. I'm sorry our little reunion has to end like this."

"Maybe it hasn't actually ended," Luke said.

Burroughs frowned. "What do you mean by that?"

"Maybe McCluskey was right. Maybe the best thing for you to do is kill me. I'm not going to forget this."

Burroughs laughed and shook his head. "You sound like you're trying to talk yourself into a bullet, Luke. But I know you.

You're just being honest. Like I said, that was always one of your failings."

With that, Burroughs turned and strode away, heading for the river and the stern-wheeler that had been loaded with a fortune in gold.

Luke and the others could see the top of the smokestack rising from the riverboat's boiler, even though they couldn't see the boat itself. They watched the smokestack as the sternwheeler steamed on up the river and went out of sight.

Luke knew it wouldn't take long for the boat to travel a mile upstream. The short interval when the four guards were the only outlaws still on hand represented the best chance of turning the tables, but there was no time to waste.

Unfortunately, tied hand and foot, there wasn't much he could do. He was confident he could work loose from his bonds eventually, but the guards . . . and the riverboat . . . would be long gone by then.

The conductor leaned closer to Luke and said quietly, "I've got my hands loose. Turn a little and I'll see if I can get to that rope around your wrists."

Luke was careful to keep his face expressionless. Making it look like he was shifting around to get more comfortable, he turned so that his back was toward the conductor. A moment later, he felt fingers fumbling at his bonds.

Barely moving his lips, he asked, "How did you get loose?"

"There's a sharp rock here where they dumped me," the conductor replied, equally tight-lipped. "I've been working at it ever since they hauled us out here. It wasn't easy with my arm wounded the way it is, but I knew I had to try. The guards didn't seem to regard me as much of a threat, so they didn't really pay attention to me."

"Their mistake," Luke said.

Time seemed to rush by as the conductor struggled with the knots in the rope, while still pretending that his own hands were tied so the guards wouldn't notice anything wrong. He had only one good hand, and Burroughs had done a good job of tying Luke.

Luke felt the delay gnawing at him. With every minute that went by, the riverboat was traveling farther upstream to the spot where the guards were supposed to rendezvous with it.

To make matters worse, one of the guards took it into his head to stroll over toward Luke and the conductor. The conductor had to stop what he was doing, just as Luke

195

sensed a little more play in the knots.

The hard-faced, beard-stubbled outlaw glared down at Luke. "I think the boss is makin' a mistake lettin' you live, Jensen. I've heard of you. Damn bounty hunter. How's it feel, makin' a livin' off blood money?"

"I've never lost any sleep over it," Luke replied coldly.

The outlaw snarled and looked like he was about to draw back his foot and launch a kick, but he spat and turned away.

Luke supposed he had decided that anything else was too much trouble and let out the breath he'd been holding, happy with the guard's decision. His ribs already hurt.

The conductor went back to work on the knots, grating his teeth together as if in pain.

The ropes came loose and fell away from Luke's wrists. He flexed his fingers to get some circulation going in them again.

Less than a minute later, the high-pitched sound of the riverboat's whistle drifted downstream along the little valley through which the river flowed.

That was the signal. The guards backed toward their horses, keeping their rifles leveled at the prisoners. But they were in a hurry to leave and get to the gold, so they turned their backs as they reached their mounts.

Luke leaned forward, reached for the ropes around his ankles, and tore desperately at them.

Burroughs hadn't been quite as careful with those bonds. The knots came loose without much trouble. Luke threw the rope aside and surged to his feet. His muscles were stiff, but he forced them into action and sprinted across the rocky ground toward the guards as they swung up into their saddles.

It was impossible to rush the outlaws without making some noise. One man still on the ground looked over his shoulder and yelled in alarm. He twisted around and clawed at the gun holstered on his hip.

Luke heard feet slapping the ground right behind him and glanced back to see that half a dozen male passengers and the burly engineer had joined his charge. Seeing his example had been enough to jolt them into action.

As the outlaw's gun cleared leather, Luke left his feet in a diving tackle. The gun roared as he crashed into the man and drove him back into the horses. The animals shied violently from the collision, and the two outlaws halfway into their saddles were thrown clear. They yelled as they sailed through the air.

The shot had gone wild, missing Luke by several feet. He and the guard he had tackled were sprawled on the rocky ground, practically underneath the stamping hooves of the spooked horses. As the guard brought the gun to bear again, a steel-shod hoof came down hard on his hand, crushing bones. The outlaw screamed. Luke ended his pain momentarily by slamming a punch to his jaw that bounced his head off the ground. The outlaw went limp.

Luke heard other shots as he scrambled to his feet. A wild melee had broken out between the prisoners and the other three guards. One of the passengers was down, clutching a wounded leg, but the others were giving the outlaws all the fight they could handle. The train's engineer wrenched a revolver away from one of the outlaws and swung it in a looping blow that caved in the man's head. The remaining two bandits went down in a maelstrom of flying punches and kicks.

The fighting was fierce but short-lived. When the prisoners — former prisoners, now — stepped back, one of the outlaws was dead and the other three were out cold.

Luke picked up a couple pistols that had

been dropped during the fracas and felt better as soon as his hands wrapped around the gun butts. They were Colts instead of his Remingtons, but they would do nicely. "Some of you men grab those horses," he ordered. "We can't let them get away."

The wounded man's wife rushed up to fuss over her husband as Luke checked the man's injury and saw that it wasn't too serious. "He'll be all right, ma'am."

He looked around at the others. "I need three volunteers to come with me. Three who can handle a gun."

The conductor stepped out of the group. He had untied his feet and was making his way around a little unsteadily. "I'll come."

Luke shook his head. "You've done enough, friend. You've lost quite a bit of blood and need to take it easy as much as you can."

The engineer stepped forward. "If you're going after those train robbers, mister, count me in. They killed my fireman. I got a score to settle with 'em."

Two more men spoke up, neither of them married.

That was a good thing, Luke thought. They'd be going up against heavy odds and there was a good chance none of them would come back alive.

But . . . no matter how dangerous it was, Luke was going after Burroughs and the rest of the gang, not to mention McCluskey and Delia. He told his volunteers, "Grab the hats and vests these owlhoots are wearing. Here's what we're going to do. . . ."

CHAPTER 20

Luke and the men going with him had no time to waste. They had to have the element of surprise on their side if they were going to stand any chance against the outlaws. They needed to appear at the rendezvous point before Burroughs started to wonder why his men hadn't shown up.

Not only that, but the outlaws on the boat would have heard the gunfire and had to be curious what the ruckus had been about. Luckily, only a few shots had gone off, so Burroughs wouldn't likely think that the guards he'd left behind had decided to massacre the prisoners.

Wearing the outlaws' hats and vests and armed with weapons they had taken, Luke and his companions mounted up and headed northwest along the river. He figured the stream must have a name, but he'd never heard it. They might as well call it Blood River, he thought grimly. That was likely to be running in it before the day was over.

The engineer, who'd introduced himself as Kermit Winslow, asked as they rode, "Do you really think we can get close enough to jump those hombres without them recognizing us?"

"I hope so," Luke said. "Otherwise, they'll just sit there on that boat and pick us off at their leisure."

The other two volunteers were Craig Bolden, a mining engineer, and Ray Stinson, an unemployed cowboy currently riding the grub line. Both had handled themselves well during the fight with the guards, and Luke hoped that would continue. The odds would be at least two to one against them, so they would need some luck on their side, too.

The going wasn't easy as they rode upriver. In some places the steep slope went down almost to the water, leaving only a narrow trail they could follow. At times, the path was blocked by rocks, and they had to ride into the river a short distance. Fortunately, the stream was fairly shallow despite having a strong, steady current, so the horses didn't have to swim.

Finally, Luke spotted smoke rising into the sky around a bend in the river. He motioned for the others to stop. "I want to go ahead on foot and have a look. We need to know what we're getting into."

He dismounted and left Winslow, Bolden, and Stinson. He used the brush growing close to the water for cover as he slipped forward to reconnoiter.

Reaching the bend, he parted some branches and peered through the gap he'd made. The riverboat was pulled up next to a grassy bank about two hundred yards upstream, and a gangplank had been placed between the deck and the shore so the guards could ride their horses over it when they arrived.

Only those guards weren't coming, Luke thought. One man was dead, and the other three were prisoners, tied up back at the train.

That gave Luke an idea. He faded back along the bank to the spot where he'd left the volunteers.

He explained what he'd seen and what his plan was. "You three are going to ride up to the boat leading the other horse. Keep your heads down so they can't see your faces very well, and there's a good chance you ought to get pretty close before they realize you're not the men they're expecting. They're bound to have heard those shots earlier, so they probably figure some of the prisoners put up a fight. When they see an empty saddle, they'll think the fourth guard was killed in the fighting."

"What are you going to be doing, Jensen?" Winslow asked.

"I'm going to take them even more by surprise. I plan to get on the boat without them knowing I'm anywhere around."

"How do you plan to do that?" Stinson wanted to know.

"The river." Luke nodded toward the stream. "I'm going to stay underwater as much as I can and swim up to the other side of the boat."

Winslow rubbed his jaw and frowned. "That'll be quite a chore, swimming that far against the current."

"If I can make it, we'll have them in a crossfire."

"Yeah, there's that. I guess it's worth a try."

Stinson and Bolden nodded in agreement.

Luke checked the Colts he had taken from the outlaws. Getting wet wouldn't keep them from firing, although being immersed in water wasn't good for guns in the long run. If his plan worked, he wouldn't need those revolvers for very long. He might even be able to recover his Remingtons from whichever of the outlaws had taken them.

He stripped down to his long underwear and tied the pair of Colts into a bundle using his shirt, then tied the sleeves around his waist. "Give me five minutes before you ride around the bend. Take your time as you approach the boat. And remember, keep your heads down." He paused and then gave them a grim smile. "Good luck."

"Good luck to you, too, Jensen," Winslow said.

Luke slipped into the water and stroked out to where the river was deeper. Even though the weather was warm, the mountain streams were fed by a combination of springs and snowmelt, and that made them cold year-round. It instantly drained all the warmth from Luke's body and seemed to steal the very breath from his lungs.

He ignored that and kept moving, knowing he wouldn't be in the water long enough to be in danger of freezing to death. Moving would help warm him up a little. He reached the deeper water and swam against the current, heading upriver.

He hadn't gone very far before weariness began draining the strength from his muscles. Fighting the current was exhausting. As soon as he was around the bend, he had to be careful how hard he stroked and

205

kicked. He couldn't afford to make much disturbance in the water or he risked someone on the riverboat noticing his approach. It would have been easier if he could have circled wide around the boat, gone into the water upstream, and allowed the current to carry him back down, but there hadn't been time for that.

He wondered if he was going to reach the riverboat before Winslow, Stinson, and Bolden did. If he didn't, they would be left on their own once the outlaws discovered they were not three of the guards who'd been left behind. They wouldn't stand a chance unless Luke could board the boat without being seen and take the gang by surprise.

Finally around the bend, he took a breath and ducked his head, going completely under the frigid water. Whenever he needed to take a breath he would have to roll onto his back and allow just his mouth and nose to break the surface. He put that off as long as possible to decrease the chances of being spotted.

With ice seeming to flow in his veins, Luke swam on.

"How long do you plan to wait here?" McCluskey asked as he stood on the deck. He held his left hand out while Delia worked on the lock of that cuff with a sharp piece of metal she had found in the boat's engine room. She had already managed to spring the lock on the right-hand cuff.

Burroughs stood with his hands tucked in the hip pockets of his trousers as he gazed back downstream. His hat was pulled down low over his eyes. "We'll wait as long as we have to for those fellas to join us. We don't run out on our partners."

"What if they're not coming?"

"They'll be here," Burroughs said confidently. "I never knew a man to turn his back on this much gold, did you? Well . . . with the exception of Luke Jensen, and he doesn't really count. Those Jensens aren't normal men. I've heard plenty of stories about his brothers Smoke and Matt."

McCluskey grimaced. He didn't care about Jensen or his damn brothers. He would have liked to have had his vengeance on the bounty hunter, but that was in the past. McCluskey was focused on claiming his share of the gold in those strongboxes sitting on the deck and getting the hell out of there.

He frowned at Burroughs. "We all heard those shots a little while ago. What if the passengers from the train jumped your guards? That's the only explanation that makes any sense."

"Maybe," Burroughs admitted. "But there were only a few shots. That didn't sound like a full-scale battle to me. My men probably had to fire some warning shots to calm things down again."

"I hope you're right. With that much gold at stake, only a damn fool would take chances he didn't have to."

Burroughs narrowed his eyes and gave McCluskey an angry glance, then turned his attention back to the river and the bank along which his four men ought to be riding any time. Obviously, he hadn't cared for McCluskey's veiled insult.

Burroughs wasn't the only one who had heard what McCluskey had to say. Several other members of the gang were standing within earshot, and from the corner of his eye, McCluskey saw them sending speculative glances toward him and Burroughs.

Maybe they were thinking the wrong man was in charge here, McCluskey mused. After all, Burroughs had spared Luke Jensen just because the bounty hunter was an old friend of his. Leaving Jensen alive had been a foolish thing to do. Hell, if it had been him giving the orders, he would have considered killing everybody on the train, including Jensen.

McCluskey wasn't that fond of killing women and children, but the idea of not leaving any witnesses behind was very simple and appealing. It could be that some of those other fellas saw it that way, too.

With a metallic click, the cuff around Mc-Cluskey's left wrist sprang open.

"There!" Delia said, pleased with herself. "I told you I was good at picking locks, Frank."

"It's a handy skill to have," McCluskey said as he rubbed the skin of his wrist where the metal had cut into it. "You think you can do the same with these leg irons?"

"Sure I can. Sit down somewhere so I can get at them."

McCluskey ambled over to the closest strongbox and sat down on it. He stuck his right leg out in front of him. Burroughs gave him a disapproving glance, but he just smirked. What harm was he doing? He wasn't going to hurt the strongbox by sitting on it.

Delia sat down on the deck, pulling up her skirt a little and crossing her legs. She lifted McCluskey's ankle into her lap and went to work on the lock.

That was a pretty undignified position she was in, McCluskey thought, but what did it matter? She was a saloon girl. She had willingly surrendered all her dignity a long time ago.

The more he thought about it, the more McCluskey wondered just how difficult it would be to wrest the leadership of the gang away from Burroughs. He hadn't planned to put together another gang right away, but sometimes opportunities just fell into a man's lap and he would be a fool not to take advantage of them. Anyway, if he took over, he could declare that he was getting a full share of the loot, not just a measly four bars.

Of course, to do that he'd have to kill Burroughs, but that would be okay. In fact, McCluskey was just fine with the idea.

"Here they come." Clearly, Burroughs was relieved, but he tried to sound confident as he looked at McCluskey and added, "I told you they'd be here."

McCluskey gazed back along the river and saw three men riding slowly toward the boat. One of them led a riderless horse. "I thought you left four men behind, Burroughs."

"I did," Burroughs said with a worried tone in his voice. "Something must have happened to one of them."

"I reckon there's not any doubt about

those shots we heard. The passengers from the train put up a fight again, and one of your men was killed."

"That's what it looks like, all right," Burroughs admitted. "I'm sorry about that. But there are always risks in this line of work."

"A smart man runs as few of those risks as he can get away with," McCluskey said, and once again his comment was rewarded with speculative looks from the other members of the gang.

Burroughs was about to say something else — something angry, judging by his expression — but just then Delia succeeded in opening the leg iron on McCluskey's right ankle.

"There!" she said with obvious satisfaction. "One more lock and we'll be done with these shackles, Frank."

"Good job." Grinning, he added, "I knew there was a reason I kept you around, Delia."

She smiled and practically purred under his praise.

In point of fact, he hadn't really kept her around, McCluskey thought. It was more like he couldn't get rid of her. But he had to admit she had helped him a lot. He put his other foot in her lap and let her get to work on that leg iron.

One of the other outlaws muttered, "Those fellas are sure takin' their time gettin' back here. We need to get movin' again."

"Yes, they're dawdling a little," Burroughs agreed. "Maybe one of them is wounded and they're taking it easy because of that. They'll be here in a minute, and we can get started." He turned and cupped his hands around his mouth to call up to the pilothouse, "Better start getting some steam up, Lynch!"

The member of the gang serving as the pilot and captain of the boat waved a hand from the pilothouse with its big open windows on all four sides. Lynch — an unfortunate name for an outlaw, but of course he hadn't started out on a life of crime immediately after being born — was a former river pirate who had been a scourge on the Mississippi and the Missouri. The boat, in fact, had been stolen from a dock in Yankton and brought into Wyoming by following the Missouri, the Yellowstone, and a network of smaller tributaries like the stream they were on.

A low rumble came from the boat's innards as the engine fired up again. The three riders were only fifty yards away.

The leg iron around McCluskey's left ankle sprang open. Delia laughed. "That one was easy. I've really got the knack of this now, Frank, if you ever need me to do it again."

"I won't," McCluskey said. "No man will ever shackle me again. I'll die first."

"Oh, don't say that," she told him as she stood up from the deck and then sat down in his lap. She put her arms around his neck. "We have the rest of our lives to spend together, and I want it to last for a long time."

McCluskey kissed her. He was fond of the crazy woman, no doubt about that, even if he didn't have any interest in spending the rest of his life with her.

A second later, a shout of alarm drove all those thoughts from his head when Burroughs yelled, "Those aren't our men!"

McCluskey bolted to his feet, dumping Delia unceremoniously on the deck. She let out a startled cry.

That sound was swallowed up by the roar of guns as McCluskey, Burroughs, and the other outlaws clawed out revolvers and opened fire on the three men on the bank.

CHAPTER 21

Luke had to come to the surface twice to get a breath during his swim, which seemed to take a lot longer than it actually did. The second time, his face emerged far enough from the water for him to see Winslow, Bolden, and Stinson riding along the bank not far from the riverboat. Luke rolled over and stroked hard, propelling himself against the current. Time was running out.

As in most mountain streams, the water was crystal clear. He could see the boat's hull as he approached it, as well as the paddlewheel at the stern. He swam past the paddle and reached up to grasp the edge of the deck. He knew he might pull himself out of the water and find himself looking down the barrels of half a dozen guns. He was counting on the hope that most of the outlaws, if not all of them, would be on the other side of the boat watching the arrival of the men they thought were their comrades.

As his head broke the surface and he shook it to get water out of his eyes, he heard guns blasting somewhere close by.

That gave his movements added urgency as he heaved himself out of the river and rolled onto the deck. The Colts tied in the bundle thudded against the planking, but that sound was lost in the gun thunder coming from elsewhere on the boat.

He looked around, saw that none of the outlaws were close by, and tore at the knot holding the bundle closed. Seconds later, he had filled both hands with gun butts and dropped the wet shirt on the deck.

Most of the ten-foot-wide deck was taken up by the superstructure that housed the boilers, the engine room, storage space, and a few passenger cabins. As he trotted toward the corner, intending to edge around it and get a look at the fighting, someone shouted above him and a gun blasted. The bullet chewed splinters from the deck near his bare feet.

His head jerked back as he looked up. One of the outlaws was up in the pilothouse and had spotted him. The man leaned out one of the big windows and fired again, coming so close that Luke felt the heat of the bullet as it ripped past his ear. He lifted the left-hand Colt and triggered a hurried but accurate shot.

The outlaw in the pilothouse rocked back, dropping his gun so that it landed on top of the boiler room. He sagged forward again, eyes bulging with pain, and blood trickled from the corner of his mouth just before he collapsed over the window sill and hung there, half in and half out of the pilothouse.

Luke knew the shots from his side of the boat would draw attention, so he wasn't surprised when an outlaw charged around the corner, guns in hand. Spotting Luke, he tried to skid to a stop as he opened fire. His first shot went wild, and he didn't get the chance for another as Luke hammered a slug into his chest and spilled him off the boat into the river.

Luke ran to the corner, put his back against the wall, and risked a quick look. Muzzle flashes came from the trees and clumps of brush scattered along the bank. He counted shots from three men, so he knew his volunteers had managed to get off their horses and make it to cover when the shooting started.

The outlaws had taken cover, too, some of them crouching in doorways and others kneeling behind crates of supplies on the deck. Luke saw a flash of fair hair and spotted Delia Bradley hunkered behind the strongboxes. That was actually a pretty good place to take shelter, he thought. No bullet could possibly penetrate those boxes full of gold bars.

A noise from behind alerted him to trouble coming from that direction. He whirled and found himself facing Derek Burroughs with a leveled gun in his hand.

Luke knew Burroughs could have cut him down, but he didn't fire.

For some reason, he had hesitated.

In the split second they faced each other over gun barrels, the two men's eyes met. Despite everything that had happened, despite the greed that had led Burroughs to turn into a ruthless outlaw with blood on his hands and despite the anger that filled Luke at what Burroughs had done, at that moment, the bond that war had forged between them was still there, and it kept Burroughs from pulling the trigger.

No such bond existed for McCluskey. The outlaw had climbed on top of the passenger cabins and charged across them with a gun in each hand spouting fiery death, yelling at Luke in incoherent, hate-filled rage as he triggered the revolvers.

The slugs fell like hail around Luke. He twisted and threw himself toward the edge of the deck as McCluskey's bullets whipped around him. None of them found him as he dived into the river.

McCluskey didn't stop shooting.

Luke closed his eyes instinctively as he went under the surface. When he opened them again he saw the little trails of bubbles streaking through the water as the bullets searched for him. He kicked hard, knowing that the only safe place for him at the moment was *under* the riverboat.

The shadow cast by the boat enveloped him as he glided underneath it. He hadn't had a chance to grab much of a breath before he went into the river, and his lungs were clamoring for air. He planned to swim to the other side, climb out, and get back into the fight.

The rumble of the boat's engine abruptly got louder, and the paddlewheel lurched into motion. Someone who knew how to run the boat had made it up to the pilothouse. Luke twisted in the water as the wheel began to churn toward him.

He swam hard, knowing that if he got caught in the paddlewheel, it would bust him to pieces. He could get clear faster going back the way he'd come, but some of the outlaws were still shooting into the water. He saw the streaks up ahead left by the bullets.

He couldn't stay where he was. He reached down to the bottom and pushed off hard against it, arrowing through the water and out from under the boat. Rolling over, he jackknifed the upper half of his body out of the water and fired up at the riverboat as it roared past him like a giant primordial beast.

Water blurred his vision, but he could see well enough to shoot. He didn't see Burroughs or McCluskey or Delia. Several outlaws stood on the deck shooting at him. He lanced slugs among them, downing one man and making the others scatter for cover.

The riverboat picked up steam. Luke bit back a curse as it moved on past him and he fell behind. The decks were clear as all the train robbers had hunted holes. All he had to shoot at were the dripping, revolving paddles.

Burroughs and his gang had gotten away — again.

Luke stayed low in the water until the riverboat had vanished around the next bend, just in case anybody was trying to draw a bead on him with a rifle. When the boat was gone, he headed for shore. He stood up when the river became shallow and waded in.

Kermit Winslow and Ray Stinson emerged from the trees, helping Craig Bolden limp along. The mining engineer had taken a bullet through his right calf.

Winslow called, "Jensen, are you all right?"

Luke emerged from the river with water streaming from him. He nodded and said disgustedly, "I'm fine, but they got away with the gold."

"We hurt 'em, though," Stinson said. "I reckon we killed two or three of 'em. That'll make it a mite easier the next time we go up against 'em."

"There's not going to be a next time for you men," Luke said, his voice still harsh with anger, directed mostly at himself. "Bolden's hurt. You need to take him back to the train and wait for help with the others."

"Damn it, we set out to get that gold back and give those outlaws what they got comin'!" Winslow protested.

"Yes, but this was our best chance to do it," Luke said.

"So you're gonna give up?"

Luke reined in his temper. He couldn't blame Winslow for being angry. The man took it personally that someone had held up his train. Luke was sure the conductor felt the same way.

"I never said I was going to give up. I'm going after them. But I'm going to do it alone. Stinson, you and Bolden can ride double back to the train. I'll take the other horse so I'll have an extra mount. I know where that riverboat's headed, and I'm going to see if I can beat it there."

"And if you can . . . ?" Winslow asked.

"I'll have a warm welcome waiting for them." There was nothing warm about Luke's voice.

It was cold and hard as ice.

CHAPTER 22

"Where's a rifle?" McCluskey raged as the riverboat went around the bend. "Somebody give me a rifle! I can still draw a bead on Jensen!"

"Forget it," Burroughs snapped. "Luke's out of sight now, and so are the others."

McCluskey sneered at him as the two men stood on the deck with Delia. "Luke, is it? That's what you call him because the two of you are such good friends."

"We fought together in the war," Burroughs said. "A man doesn't forget something like that, no matter where he finds himself later."

"A man doesn't forget that he needs to be loyal to his partners, either," McCluskey said. "Who's more important to you, Burroughs, the men you ride with now or somebody you knew fifteen years ago?"

"My men know good and well that I'm loyal to them."

"Is that right? You want to explain to them how come you didn't pull the trigger when you had Jensen dead to rights and could have gunned him down?"

One member of the gang was up in the pilothouse, having been sent there by Burroughs after Lynch was killed. Two more were in the engine room, stoking the boiler and keeping the engine running.

But the others, including a couple men who were wounded, were on the deck and heard what McCluskey had to say. They listened with intense interest as the body of an outlaw who'd been killed in the fighting lay uncovered on the stern, a grim, bloody reminder of what had happened back around the bend of the river.

"I didn't have the drop on him —" Burroughs began.

"Yes, you did," Delia piped up. "I saw it, too. You had your gun pointed at him and he had his back to you. All you had to do was pull the trigger."

Burroughs stood with a bleak frown on his face and didn't say anything. He couldn't refute that accusation, and McCluskey and Delia both knew it.

After a moment, Burroughs gave a nod of his head. "What's done is done. Let's just worry about getting on up to Pine City and splitting up the gold —"

"Hold on a minute," McCluskey interrupted. "I know I'm not part of your gang, Burroughs —"

"That's right, you're not," Burroughs said.

"But I've got a stake in this now," McCluskey persisted. "I helped you fight off that ambush Jensen and his friends tried to pull, didn't I? Seems to me that pretty much makes me one of you, doesn't it?"

Several of Burroughs' men muttered in agreement, and a couple others nodded.

Burroughs' frown went from angry to worried as he asked, "What are you getting at, McCluskey?"

"These men know you a lot better than I do, but I'd be worried about a leader who risks not only all that gold but also their lives to spare a man who's trying to hunt them down."

That eloquent comment prompted one of the outlaws to exclaim, "Damn right!"

"I told you it wasn't like that," Burroughs said as he glared at McCluskey. He turned to look at his men. "McCluskey's twisting it all out of proportion. It's true that Jensen had his back to me as I came around the corner, and yes, my gun was in my hand, but I didn't have time to fire before he realized I was there. Before I could do anything, McCluskey started blazing away at him from the top of the cabin and Jensen jumped in the river to get away from the shots. That's all there was to it."

"That's a damn lie." McCluskey knew he was taking a risk by making such a bold charge, but his instincts told him the moment was right.

Delia put a hand on his arm and squeezed in support.

"You had plenty of time to plug him."

Burroughs shook his head and turned away. "I'm tired of arguing with you. You're not one of us, McCluskey —"

"Maybe he ought to be," one of the men said.

Burroughs' head snapped around, and he demanded, "What do you mean by that, Jurgenson?"

The outlaw who had spoken was a hard-bitten man with an old knife scar running down the side of his face. "You gave him a share in the loot from the train. That sort of makes him one of us, doesn't it?"

"That was just a business arrangement, and I didn't have much choice in the matter. It doesn't make McCluskey a member of the gang."

"Nobody's asked me," McCluskey put in, "but from what I've seen so far, I'd be proud to throw in with this bunch."

Another gang member spoke up. "I've heard of this fella McCluskey, boss. He's got a mighty salty reputation. I'd say we ought to think about askin' him to join up with us."

"That's for me to decide —"

"Why?" Jurgenson broke in. "We've let you run the show for a while, Burroughs, but there's nothin' saying it was always gonna be that way. If we don't like somethin', we've got a right to speak up and say so."

"And we don't like you bein' so friendly with a damn bounty hunter," another man added.

McCluskey made an effort not to grin. A couple hours ago, he had never heard of Derek Burroughs and didn't know anything about the man's gang of outlaws.

Now he was not only several bars of gold richer, but he was also close to taking over this bunch, even though they probably didn't realize it yet.

"We've made plenty of money on our jobs," Burroughs argued, "and we've never had much trouble —"

"Until today," Jurgenson interrupted again. "Lynch is dead, Holcroft's dead, and all four of those fellas you left back at the train are probably dead, too. McCluskey's right — we should've just killed all those passengers and train crew and been done with it. Jensen included!"

"That sort of massacre would've had every lawman in the territory on our trail," Burroughs said tightly. "It would have been a foolish thing to do."

"Maybe you just don't have the stomach for it," Jurgenson said with a curled lip.

It was all McCluskey could do not to chortle. Things were falling into place perfectly for him.

Burroughs' face flushed with anger. Trenches appeared in his cheeks as his mouth tightened. "If you think I don't have the stomach for killing, Jurgenson, why don't you push me just a little further and find out for sure?"

Jurgenson was breathing hard as he tried to keep himself reined in. At the same time, he looked wary. Burroughs couldn't have risen to leadership of the gang without being pretty tough, and he was bound to have handled challenges to that leadership before. Naturally, that would make Jurgenson and the other men cautious about pushing him too far.

The difference was that McCluskey hadn't been there to step in and take over. He shook off Delia's hand and stepped closer to Burroughs. "I'm the one who put the burr under your saddle. Why don't you take it up with me?"

Burroughs turned toward him angrily. "What the hell do you think you're doing?"

McCluskey leaned his head toward the rest of the gang. "Letting these men know they've got somebody who wants to be on their side. Somebody who's willing to do the things that need to be done."

The two of them were standing about five feet apart, glaring at each other. McCluskey could tell by Burroughs' stance that the man was ready to slap leather if he had to. McCluskey's hand wasn't far from the butt of one of the revolvers stuck into his waistband.

He suddenly realized he might have a problem. He didn't know how fast Burroughs was. He hadn't seen the man's draw. McCluskey was confident in his own speed — it had kept him alive, after all — but there was always a chance Burroughs was faster. There might be a better way to handle things.

Burroughs said, "I'm starting to think it was a mistake to bring you and your fancy woman with us, McCluskey. Maybe we should have left you back there. Maybe

Jensen wouldn't have come after us if we had."

Delia started to step forward and respond angrily, but McCluskey motioned her back.

"Don't try to blame that on me," he said to Burroughs. "You're the one who let him live. You could have killed him back at the train, or let me kill him, and all your men who died would still be alive."

That was it. He had finally prodded Burroughs over the edge. Burroughs grabbed for his gun.

McCluskey was already moving. He threw himself forward and crashed into Burroughs. His left hand closed around the outlaw's wrist and kept him from completing the draw. The impact of their collision drove Burroughs backward and suddenly both men were at the edge of the deck, toppling out of control into the river.

As they were falling, McCluskey heard some of the gang whooping with excitement. A fight always provoked that reaction in some men. They hit the water and went under, and silence closed in around them.

They continued grappling underwater. McCluskey hung on to Burroughs' wrist to keep him from pulling the gun. He tried to get his other hand on Burroughs' neck, but the outlaw fended him off, lifting a knee into McCluskey's stomach. The blow wasn't a particularly hard one, but it was enough to drive some of the air out of McCluskey's lungs and make him desperate to get back to the surface.

The water churned around them as they battled. McCluskey balled his free hand into a fist and jabbed a punch to Burroughs' face. The blow rocked Burroughs' head back and made red streamers of blood leak from his nose.

Burroughs gave up on drawing his gun and wrenched his wrist free from McCluskey's grip. He splayed that hand over McCluskey's face to dig fingers into his eyes. McCluskey jerked away and landed a punch to Burroughs' throat. Burroughs started to gag, opening his mouth so big bubbles of air escaped. He pulled away and kicked for the surface.

McCluskey went after him.

As soon as he broke into the open air, McCluskey heard the shouting from the boat. The whole gang was gathered on the side of the deck, watching the river. Delia stood in front of the men with an eager yet anxious look on her face. McCluskey knew she wanted to see him defeat Burroughs, but at the same time she was worried about him — and probably a little about herself, too. If

Burroughs killed him, she would be left to the mercy of the gang. She couldn't expect the same sort of treatment a decent woman would have received, even at the hands of the owlhoots.

McCluskey spotted Burroughs a few feet away and lunged at him. He got behind Burroughs, looped an arm around his neck, and forced him below the water. Burroughs kicked and flailed, but McCluskey hung on tightly, bearing down harder and harder on the gang leader's throat, until the man went limp. With a savage exultation surging through him, McCluskey kicked toward the boat and found willing hands ready to reach down and pull him and Burroughs from the water.

McCluskey rolled onto his back, breathing hard from the exertion of the fight underwater. As soon as he could, he pushed himself up onto an elbow and looked over at Burroughs, who lay a few feet away. He figured the gang's former leader was dead, and for a moment it looked that way, but McCluskey saw that Burroughs' chest was rising and falling shallowly.

Delia dropped to her knees beside him and threw her arms around his neck, hugging him tightly even though he was soaking wet. "Oh, Frank! I was so afraid that man would hurt you."

"Not . . . a chance," McCluskey rasped. He pushed Delia aside without being too rough and held up his arm toward Jurgenson. "Give a man a hand?"

Jurgenson grinned as he clasped McCluskey's wrist and hauled him to his feet. He slapped McCluskey on the back. "You're my sort of hombre, mister. That fight didn't last long, but it was a hell of a fracas while it did."

Several other men gathered around to offer their congratulations, as well.

McCluskey grinned as he accepted them. "If you boys will have me, I'd be proud to be one of you."

"One of us, hell!" Jurgenson looked around at the others, got several nods of encouragement, and went on. "We want you to step in and be the boss, like you said."

McCluskey nodded. "I think that'll work out mighty fine for all of —"

"Look out!" one of the men yelled.

McCluskey's head jerked around, and to his surprise, he saw that Burroughs had regained consciousness and managed to climb up off the deck.

Not only was he on his feet, he had clawed his gun out of its holster.

McCluskey had figured he'd be out longer

than that and slapped at his waist, only to realize that his guns must have slipped out while he and Burroughs were fighting in the river.

The sharp crack of a shot sounded, but it didn't come from Burroughs' gun.

Burroughs grunted in pain and hunched over as his own weapon sagged toward the deck. He squeezed the trigger and the gun roared, but the bullet went harmlessly into the planks at his feet. He fell to his knees, then toppled over onto his side.

McCluskey's grin came right back, wider than ever at the sight of Delia standing with a gun in her hand. She had plucked it from the holster of the outlaw standing next to her. A wisp of smoke curled from the revolver's barrel.

McCluskey whooped with laughter and flung up a hand, pointing at Delia. "There's the one who ought to be in charge of your gang, boys! There's your gunslinging outlaw queen. Right there!"

Delia shook her head and handed the gun back to the man she had taken it from. "I just did it to save you, Frank. That's all I care about."

McCluskey laughed and drew her into an embrace. He looked past her at Burroughs' body lying crumpled on the deck. "Get rid of that."

A couple outlaws bent down, grasped Burroughs by the shoulders and ankles, and heaved him into the river with a big splash.

The riverboat chugged on upstream, leaving him behind.

CHAPTER 23

The sun helped dry Luke's long underwear, so by the time Winslow, Stinson, and Bolden started back to the train, the garments were still damp but not unbearable. Luke pulled on his trousers, put on his socks, and stamped his feet down in his boots.

His hat was back at the train, lost somewhere in all the commotion of the holdup. He would have liked to retrieve it but couldn't take the time to go back and search for it. He'd do without for the time being.

He had the two Colts and a Winchester that rode in a scabbard strapped to one of the horses. Those were the most important items he needed, anyway.

Winslow had complained some more about returning to the train instead of accompanying Luke on his pursuit of the outlaws, but in the end he had gone with Stinson and the wounded Bolden. The burly train engineer was tough, but not tough enough for a hazardous pursuit like Luke's was likely to be.

The job needed a professional manhunter — and that's what Luke Jensen was.

He took two horses — a leggy roan and a deep-chested bay. Both animals gave him the impression of having plenty of strength and stamina, which wasn't surprising since they'd been owned by outlaws. A man on the dodge had to have a dependable mount capable of speed for a fast getaway and the ability to go all day whenever there was a posse in pursuit.

Derek Burroughs hadn't named the settlement that he and his men were steaming up the river to and where more of his men would be waiting with the gang's horses. Although he had been through that part of Wyoming, Luke didn't remember a settlement in the area, so it had to be fairly new.

If he wanted to reach that town before the riverboat did, he needed to cross the river, find a way out of the mountains, and head north as fast as he could, keeping the peaks to his left. It would be a good race. The only reason he had a chance was because the river had to follow a twisting and turning course through the mountains and he could take a straight shot north once he was out on the flats again.

With that in mind, he kept an eye out for a good place to ford the stream as he rode the bay and led the roan along the grassy bank.

He had gone a couple miles when he caught sight of something up ahead, but it wasn't a gravel bar that would make crossing the river easier. It was a body sprawled at the edge of the stream, looking like a pile of discarded clothing.

Luke realized it was a man and urged his horse forward at a faster pace. He recognized the clothes.

When he got closer, he was sure of the man's identity. He dismounted quickly and went to the man's side, dropping to one knee. He grasped the man's shoulders and rolled him onto his back.

Derek Burroughs' face was haggard and washed out, with lines of pain carved into it. The river water had diluted the crimson stain on his shirt, but it was still visible and showed how much blood he had lost. The bullet holes in his vest and shirt were mute testimony that he'd been shot.

Luke felt certain Burroughs was dead, but the man's eyes fluttered open. Breath rasped harsh and ragged in his throat. He had trouble focusing until his gaze settled on

Luke, who lifted him and propped him against a knee.

"L-Luke . . . ?" Burroughs asked in a husky whisper, struggling to get the name out.

"That's right, Derek," Luke said. "Just take it easy. Don't try to move around."

"Don't try to . . . tell me . . . I'm going to . . . be all right."

"I wouldn't lie to you that way. You know as well as I do that you're gut shot."

Somehow Burroughs managed to smile, although the expression could have been just a grimace of pain.

"Yeah, I'm . . . done for . . . Should've been dead . . . before now . . . but I hung on . . . managed to get out of the river . . . because I knew . . . you might be . . . coming along to find me. . . ."

"Who shot you, Derek? Was it during that fight back there?" Another possibility occurred to him. "Or was it McCluskey?"

"No, it was . . . that blonde . . . McCluskey's woman. . . ."

"Delia?" That came as a bit of a surprise to Luke, although he knew it shouldn't have, considering everything she had done since he'd known her.

"Y-yeah . . . her. And Luke . . ." Burroughs found the strength to lift a hand and

238

clutch feebly at Luke's arm. "If you go after them . . . you should know . . . McCluskey's taken over . . . the gang. . . ."

Luke's jaw tightened. That news didn't change anything. He was going to have to face McCluskey and the rest of the outlaws anyway if he wanted to stop them from getting away with that gold. But he found it annoying that luck always seemed to break McCluskey's way.

Maybe there was some truth to that hogwash McCluskey had been spouting about having a vision. . . .

Luke pushed that thought out of his mind. He wasn't going to waste time on something so ridiculous. "Don't worry," he told Burroughs. "I'll settle up with both of them for you."

"Be . . . careful. . . . After all this . . . I wouldn't want you to . . . get hurt . . ." His eyes remained open, but a long sigh eased out of him and he seemed to shrink in on himself.

Over the past twenty years, during the war and since then, Luke had seen plenty of men die — too many men — and he knew that Burroughs was gone.

He eased his old friend's head and shoulders back down on the ground, then closed Burroughs' eyes rather than leave him staring sightlessly at the sky. He knew he had more to do. Burroughs had to be laid to rest.

Yet it would take precious time Luke didn't have if he wanted to head off Mc-Cluskey and the other outlaws before they reached the settlement on the other side of the mountains, split up the gold, and scattered. He was sure that was what they had in mind, since it would make it more difficult to track them down. They could get together again later on to plan their next job.

With Frank McCluskey leading them.

Despite all the mental arguments he could make, Luke knew he couldn't ride off and leave Burroughs lying there out in the open for the scavengers. He picked up the outlaw's body and carried it over near the trees, then went to work scooping out a shallow grave, using a knife he found in one of the saddlebags.

It was tiring, time-consuming work, and Luke was all too aware of every minute that went by. But he stayed at it and eventually completed the grim task. He scouted around, found some rocks, and piled them on top of the grave in the hope they would keep animals from digging in it. He would have liked to build a better cairn, but it was the best he could do.

With that done, he sleeved sweat off his face and paused next to the mounded earth long enough to say, "I wish things had worked out differently, Derek. I would have preferred that the time we spent together back in Rattlesnake Wells be my last memories of you, but we don't get to make that choice very often, do we? I hope your soul finds peace, wherever you are."

With that, he went back to the horses, swung up into the bay's saddle, and once again took up his pursuit of McCluskey and his new gang of outlaws.

CHAPTER 24

Luke forded the river a short time later, crossing on one of the numerous gravel bars where the water was less than a foot deep. He searched for a trail that looked like it would take him through the mountains and wished that he knew the area better than he did.

Night fell while he was still trying to find his way. He paused to let the horses rest, trying not to think about the fact that he had nothing to eat. A fire and a pot of hot coffee would have meant even more to him. The day's heat vanished quickly in the thin air, leaving the nights chilly year-round. He didn't want to risk a fire being spotted in the darkness, however.

He wasn't one to dwell on the things he didn't have, so he put food and coffee out of his mind and gave thought to whether to push on or make camp for the night. The horses were tired, he was worn out, and traveling in the dark through unfamiliar country was fraught with danger.

But the smart thing was to move on and just be careful, he realized. The riverboat would *have* to stop for the night. Even with its shallow draft, there were too many obstacles in the river that could tear out its bottom or get it stuck to risk steaming ahead blindly. The man up in the pilothouse had to be able to see where they were going.

If Luke kept moving, he could make up some of the time he had lost while burying Derek Burroughs. Once he realized that, the decision was easy. There were risks involved — but what about his life *didn't* have a lot of risks?

He switched to the roan and mounted up again.

Over the next few hours, with only starlight to guide him, he went up more than one blind trail and had to backtrack and try again. Weariness rode hard on him, clamping its weight to his back and shoulders, but he kept moving. That was the important thing, he told himself.

Once the moon rose, spreading its silvery illumination over the landscape, the going became somewhat easier. The rugged terrain still presented a challenge, but at least he didn't have to worry as much about falling into an unseen ravine and breaking his neck.

He rode until the temperature dropped so far he was shivering and his breath fogged in front of his face. When he finally emerged from the mountains, long after midnight, his satisfaction at achieving that goal was tempered by knowing he was going to have a cold wind blowing in his face as he headed north.

He turned that direction anyway. The horses shied a little, but he forced them on. He lowered his head and hunched his shoulders in a futile attempt to ward off some of the chill.

The temperature wasn't low enough that he was in any danger of freezing, but it was definitely uncomfortable for the next few hours. He pushed on for as long as he could.

When a faint gray tinge appeared in the eastern sky to herald the arrival of the false dawn, he stopped. He unsaddled the horses, rubbed them down, and tied them to some saplings. Walking around, he found enough dry, broken branches among the scrub brush to build a small fire and huddled close to it.

The mountains were between him and the outlaws, so he didn't worry about the flickering orange glow being seen. When the warmth of the flames had seeped into his bones, he rolled up in a blanket he found among the gear on the bay.

Just as exhaustion claimed him, he hoped the dead outlaw hadn't been infested with any vermin.

Sunrise woke Luke a couple hours later. Nothing seemed to be crawling on him, and he was thankful for that.

He pushed the blanket aside and climbed stiffly to his feet, stretching the kinks out of his back. It was hardly the first night he had spent sleeping on the cold, hard ground, but he was getting too old for such things, he thought. Maybe he ought to consider giving up his life as a manhunter.

That was never going to happen, he thought with a faint smile. McCluskey wasn't the only one who could have visions. Luke long since had accepted the fact that manhunting was the only life he would ever know.

The fire had burned down to embers. He stirred them up and added branches until he had a small blaze going again. His belly gnawed at him, but there was nothing to be done about that. He had searched the saddlebags on both horses and hadn't found anything to eat, not even a scrap of jerky.

When he had warmed up again, he saddled the horses and headed north, riding the roan. The riverboat would be chugging along the stream again, he thought as he glanced at the mountains he had left behind.

The golden light from the rising sun washed over the plains, making him feel a little better. The sun climbed steadily, and by mid-morning the temperature was rising, too. Once again, he wished he had his hat. Maybe he could buy one when he got to the settlement, he thought. He had a little money cached in one of his boots.

The first thing he was going to do was find a café and get himself a hot meal. His belly was starting to think that his throat had been cut, as the old saying went.

By the time the sun was overhead at noon, he had started to wonder if Burroughs had been mistaken about a settlement. That seemed unlikely, but Luke thought he should have reached it already.

A short time later, he spotted several columns of smoke rising a mile or so ahead and to the left of him. That smoke was coming from chimneys, he thought as he angled in that direction. Finally, he was close to his destination.

The settlement was nestled at the edge of the pine-covered foothills. It was actually a pretty nice place for a town. It was good ranching country, and in the past few miles he had seen several clumps of cattle grazing here and there. With the river to provide water, it was a natural spot for a settlement to serve as a supply center for the ranches in the area.

As Luke rode in, he spotted a livery stable on his right at the edge of town, reminding him that some of Burroughs' men were already in town. It was possible they might recognize the bay and the roan as belonging to their former comrades in the gang. Best to get the animals off the street and out of sight as soon as possible, he decided.

A middle-aged black man with gray hair came out of the stable to greet him as he rode up. "You look kind of gaunt, mister. Like you been on the trail a long time."

Luke laughed at that comment, but there wasn't much humor in the sound. "Long enough. You have stalls for these two?"

"Matter of fact, I do, but just barely. Some fellas come in yesterday afternoon with a whole dang herd o' horses. Filled up all my stalls and my corral. Only reason I got any space at all is 'cause a couple other fellas rode out this mornin' and took their horses with 'em."

Luke knew the men who had brought in the large group of horses the day before had to be the members of Burroughs' gang. He swung down from the saddle and handed the reins of both horses to the liveryman. "If you could take good care of them, I'd appreciate it. I've asked a lot of them, the past twenty-four hours."

"No more 'n you asked of yourself, from the looks of it. Reckon you'd be in the market for some hot food and coffee, too."

"That would be a lifesaver," Luke admitted with a worn-out nod.

"Go on up the street a couple blocks. You'll see the Pine City Café. My wife's the cook there. A plate of her food and a cup of her coffee will fix you right up, mister."

"I'm obliged." Luke started to turn away, then paused. "Pine City. That's the name of this place?"

"Yep. On account of all the pines on the hills up yonder."

"The settlement hasn't been here very long, has it?"

" 'Bout three years, I'd say. Fella name of Harmon started it. Owns the biggest ranch in these parts, the Leanin' H. Needed the town to take care of supply needs for his ranch and the other spreads hereabouts."

That went along with Luke's thinking from earlier. He nodded his thanks to the liveryman and went in search of the café.

It wasn't difficult to find, and since it was midday, the place was doing a brisk business. Luke eyed the other customers warily as he walked in. He didn't know the outlaws Burroughs had sent on ahead. Any of the men seated at tables or the counter could be members of the gang that had robbed the train.

The good thing was they wouldn't recognize Luke. Of course, it was just as possible the outlaws weren't there at all.

He spotted an empty stool at the counter and angled toward it. Slipping onto it, he glanced at the men to the left and right of him, both of whom appeared to be townies rather than cowboys . . . or outlaws.

One was a bespectacled young man in a brown tweed suit who was probably a clerk in the bank or a store, while the other was a short, stocky man in work clothes. Neither of them seemed to be interested in Luke, although the stocky man gave him a friendly nod without saying anything.

"What can I get you, mister?"

The question came from a woman in an apron who'd come up on the other side of the counter. Luke had already noticed the lunch special chalked on a board hanging on the wall behind the counter — steak, potatoes, turnip greens, cornbread, and peach cobbler, all for fifty cents — and he was about to order that along with a cup of coffee when he glanced up, took a good look at the woman standing before him, and couldn't find words for a second.

The sight of an angel smiling at him would do that to a man.

CHAPTER 25

The woman's blond hair was pulled up in a neat bun to keep it out of her way as she worked in the café. Her eyes were blue and set in a lovely, slightly heart-shaped face that was a little flushed at the moment, probably from going in and out of the hot kitchen on the other side of the swinging door behind the counter. The apron was tied over a blue dress that matched her eyes and flattered her mature, attractive figure. Luke put her age around thirty.

He finally remembered that she had just asked him a question. He found his voice and said, "I'll have the lunch special, please, ma'am."

He had noticed a wedding ring on her left hand. It wasn't surprising that a woman who looked like her was married. She'd probably had plenty of eager suitors from which to choose a husband.

"Coffee?"

"Yes, and keep it coming."

"I had a feeling you were going to say that." Still smiling, she took a cup off a shelf, set it in front of Luke, and filled it from a pot that had been sitting on a potbellied stove behind the counter. Wisps of steam curled up from the black brew. "You take it with anything in it?"

"Not this time." He didn't want anything to dilute the coffee's bracing effect. He picked up the cup, sipped the hot, potent liquid, closed his eyes for a second, and sighed in sheer satisfaction.

When he opened his eyes, he saw that the woman seemed to be trying not to laugh at him. He cocked an eyebrow quizzically at her.

"It's just that I haven't seen very many men who looked like they'd been transported to a state of pure rapture by a sip of coffee," she explained.

"I'm not sure many men have ever wanted a cup of coffee as much as I do right now," Luke told her.

"Well, go ahead and enjoy it. I'll put your order in for you. Shouldn't take but a few minutes to get it ready. My cook is very efficient."

"I met her husband down at the livery stable when I rode into town. He sang her praises, as you might expect."

"Silas? He's a good man. And thank goodness I have Tillie here to help me out, otherwise I'd never be able to keep up." She turned and went through the swinging door to relay his order.

When she came back a moment later she took the coffeepot and went along the counter, freshening the cups of the men seated there. Then she went around the room to the tables and did the same.

Luke sipped his coffee and watched the way she moved. She had an ease and grace that was very pleasing to the eye.

He wasn't the only man in the room watching her. The stocky hombre sitting beside him grunted and said, "Mighty easy to look at, ain't she?"

"I didn't mean to stare," Luke said.

"Oh, hell, it's hard not to when a gal's as good-lookin' as Georgia Walton. To tell the truth, a lot of these fellas would eat lunch here every day even if the food wasn't any good. Luckily, Tillie Grant is as good a cook as you'll find in the whole territory." He stuck out his hand. "I'm Ben McGill."

"Luke Jensen," Luke introduced himself as he shook hands with McGill.

"You must've just gotten here, Luke. I

don't recall seein' you around town before now."

"Just rode in a little while ago," Luke agreed.

"What brings you to Pine City?"

Luke was saved from having to answer that by the arrival of his food, which was heaped on a big platter Georgia Walton brought out of the kitchen and set in front of him.

McGill grinned and waved a hand for him to go ahead. "We can talk later. I wouldn't keep a man from enjoyin' a meal like that."

Luke dug in, forcing himself to eat at a deliberate pace rather than wolfing down the vittles like he wanted to. The food was excellent, as he'd been told it would be, and he wanted to savor every bite of it.

After he had eaten about half the meal, washing it down with coffee, he said to McGill, who was lingering over a cup of his own, "Ever get any steamboats coming up the river?"

"Steamboats?" McGill repeated. "Here? Shoot, I don't think I've seen a steamboat in this part of the territory since I've been here. And that's a good thing, because I own the freight line that runs between here and Sheridan. If there was regular riverboat service, I'd probably be out of business.

There are still some up on the Yellowstone, I think, and farther north on the Missouri, but not in these parts."

Luke nodded. He was glad to hear what McGill had just told him. It meant that the arrival of a riverboat in Pine City would be something out of the ordinary. It would cause a commotion and alert Luke to the fact that McCluskey and the others had arrived.

In the meantime, he could finish his food. He was just wiping up the last of the juices on his plate with the final bite of cornbread when Georgia came over and asked, "How was it?"

"I'm tempted to say it was better than anything I've ever had in San Francisco or Denver," Luke replied.

She laughed. It was a very pleasant sound, sort of like a clear mountain stream dancing over rocks.

"You don't have to go that far," she told him. "We'll just say it was very good."

"And that would be the truth. My name is Jensen, by the way. Luke Jensen."

"I'm Georgia Walton." She offered her hand in a forthright manner.

Luke didn't mention that Ben McGill had already told him her name. He reached over the counter and shook hands with her. "It's an honor and a pleasure."

"Will you be staying in Pine City for long, Mr. Jensen? Or is there a chance you plan to settle down here?"

"I won't be settling down," Luke said. *And I'll be here only as long as it takes to round up McCluskey and the rest of that gang,* he thought.

Worry was starting to gnaw at him, though. He would be outnumbered more than ten to one. How was he going to capture or kill that many men? If he wound up with quite a few prisoners, what would he do with them? He couldn't put them on horses and take them all the way to Cheyenne. It would be too risky. They were bound to try to escape.

McGill had mentioned that he owned a freight line. That meant he had wagons available to him. Luke wondered if he could recruit some drivers and guards from among the men of Pine City and offer them a share of the reward if they helped him transport the outlaws. That would cut down on the amount he'd collect himself, but it might be his best chance.

He was getting ahead of himself, he thought. First came the matter of dealing with the gang, and doing it in such a way that some of the innocent citizens of the settlement weren't hurt. He needed to go see what sort of welcome he could prepare for the riverboat and its passengers.

He slid a silver dollar across the counter to Georgia and stood up.

"The lunch special is only four bits," she objected.

"And easily worth twice that." He wished again that he had his hat, so he could tip it to her. He settled for smiling and lifting a hand in a vague gesture of farewell.

Ben McGill strolled out of the café with him. As they paused on the boardwalk, McGill said, "You know, you never did say what brings you to Pine City."

"Business." Luke wasn't curt about it, but his tone didn't invite further discussion, either.

McGill didn't take the hint. "Well, if you're looking for a good place to invest, Pine City fits the bill. The town's not going to do anything except grow and prosper. I'd be glad to show you around if you'd like."

Luke started to decline the offer, then decided it might not hurt to have a guide. He didn't know how long it was going to take for the riverboat to get there, but it was bound to show up before the afternoon was over. "All right. I'd appreciate that."

As they walked along the street, McGill

pointed out the various businesses with the ebullient air of a true civic booster. The freight company he owned was one of them, and from the looks of the big, sturdy barn and warehouse next to the office, the enterprise was thriving.

Luke was more interested in the general store. As they passed it, he asked McGill, "Do you know if they sell dynamite in there?"

"Sure. Some folks use it for blasting out stumps, and there are some miners up in the hills, putting in shafts. None of them have struck it rich yet, but you never know." McGill paused and frowned a little. "Do you have a need for dynamite, Luke?"

"I might," Luke replied, noting that McGill seemed to consider them on a first-name basis. He didn't offer any explanation for the question.

They passed the marshal's office, according to the sign on the wall of a frame building. The sign also indicated that the local lawman was named Gideon Kent.

"You've got a marshal here," Luke commented. That was good to know. He might have to call on the badge-toter for assistance before the day was over.

"Sure do. A fine one. You were sitting beside him at the café a while ago."

Luke frowned as he looked over at McGill. "I was sitting next to you, and on the other side of me was a scrawny young fella who looked like a store clerk."

"That's Marshal Kent," McGill said. "Don't let his looks fool you. He's a lot tougher than you'd think he is."

Luke didn't think the man had looked tough at all, so that wouldn't take much. He wasn't sure how much help he could count on from Kent.

Maybe it wouldn't come to that. He and McGill had reached the northern end of town, where the river flowed. A bridge constructed of thick wooden beams spanned the stream. The river came through a nearby cut in the hills, and Luke could tell that the current was swift by the way the water boiled around the piers supporting the bridge.

As he looked at the bridge, his brain instinctively began to form a plan. The bridge was too low for the riverboat to get past it. The outlaws would have to put in to shore before they reached it. But they would have to get close to the bridge before stopping, because the banks were too high and steep where the river emerged from the hills.

Luke needed to even the odds, and he didn't see any better way to do it than with a little dynamite. He would have to talk to the local law first, though, since he couldn't just go around setting off explosions.

"Thanks for the tour, Ben," he said as he turned back toward the marshal's office.

"I didn't really show you everything," McGill protested.

"I've seen what I need to see."

Luke strode off, leaving the freighter standing there with a perplexed frown on his face.

Luke hoped Marshal Kent was in his office. Again he had the nagging sense that he was running out of time. He shouldn't have had that meal, he thought, but his hunger had been too great to ignore.

The lawman was at his desk when Luke opened the door of the marshal's office and walked in. Kent had taken off his suit coat, but otherwise he looked like he had in the café. He raised his head from the papers he'd been studying and peered at Luke through rimless spectacles that perched on his sharp nose.

"You're the man who sat next to me in the Widow Walton's place," he said before Luke had a chance to speak. He pushed back his chair. "What do you want?"

Under other circumstances Luke would have taken an interest in the fact that evidently Georgia Walton wasn't married anymore, despite the ring on her finger. As it was, he wondered briefly how long it had been since her husband died and if she was still in mourning.

But he said, "My name is Luke Jensen, Marshal. I've come here to warn you that a whole riverboat full of outlaws is heading for your town."

CHAPTER 26

Marshal Kent looked at Luke as if the bounty hunter had suddenly grown two heads. After a moment he said, "That's insane. There are no riverboats operating in this region."

"There's one now," Luke said. "But there's nobody on it except that gang of outlaws I mentioned. And the only cargo is a hundred and twenty-five thousand dollars' worth of stolen gold bars."

Kent's eyes widened behind the spectacles. "A hundred and . . . That's a fortune!"

Luke nodded solemnly and explained. "They held up the train on the spur line from Rattlesnake Wells. The mine owners were shipping the gold to Cheyenne, and I guess somebody who knew about it sold them out."

"How did it wind up on a riverboat?"

Luke didn't want to take the time to

explain the whole thing in detail, but it looked like he might have to if he wanted to get any help from the marshal. He was about to launch into a brief recitation of the facts when the office door opened behind him.

Kent held up a hand for him to stop. "Mr. Harmon, you'd better come in here and listen to this. It sounds like trouble's about to descend on Pine City."

"If that's the case, I sure want to hear about it." The newcomer was a solidly built man in late middle age with a lined, weathered face tanned to the shade of old wood. Crisp white hair stuck out from under his black Stetson.

Kent went on. "This is . . . What did you say your name was?"

"Luke Jensen."

"Dave Harmon," the white-haired man said as he stuck out a big, work-roughened hand. "My spread's the Leanin' H, not far from here."

Luke remembered Silas Grant at the livery stable mentioning Harmon to him. As he shook hands with the rancher, he said, "This is your town."

Harmon grunted. "Not really. I started it, but it's the good folks of Pine City who have made the place what it is. I can't take any credit for that. Now, what's this about some trouble headed this way?"

With Harmon and Kent both listening intently, Luke explained how the gang had stopped the train and stolen the two strongboxes full of gold ingots. "I just happened to be on the train with a prisoner I was taking to Cheyenne," he concluded. "He escaped and threw in with that bunch."

He didn't add that his old friend Derek Burroughs had gotten killed in the process. There didn't seem to be any need to go into that.

"And you say they're on their way here in a riverboat?" Kent asked.

"That's right. That's how they made their getaway from the place where they held up the train."

Harmon let out a harsh laugh. "No offense, Jensen, but that story sounds loco."

"Maybe it does, but it's the truth. Every word of it," Luke insisted. "I plan to stop them."

"You said you were taking a prisoner to Cheyenne," Kent said. "Are you a lawman?"

Luke shook his head. "Not exactly."

"That's what I thought. You're a bounty hunter." Kent's voice was cool with dislike. "I suppose the railroad and those mine owners will post a reward for the men who stole that gold, too."

"More than likely," Luke admitted.

"I assume that's your main interest in apprehending them."

"You'd be wrong about that." Luke's voice was pretty chilly, too. "I want the man I had in custody because I've got a personal grudge against him by this point. The others I want to stop because they're a bunch of murdering owlhoots and somebody's got to."

Harmon asked, "How much did you say that gold's worth?"

"A hundred and twenty-five thousand."

Harmon looked at Marshal Kent. "Well, Gid, as good citizens I'd say it's our duty to give Jensen a hand with this bunch, wouldn't you?"

"They haven't broken the law here in Pine City, Mr. Harmon," Kent said stiffly. "I don't have any jurisdiction to arrest them."

"Jurisdiction!" Harmon scoffed. "When I helped settle this country, nobody worried about anything like that. We just did what was right and took care of our own trouble."

Luke had known plenty of men with that attitude. It was common among the early settlers of a territory, especially the ones who had become successful, as Harmon apparently was. He had some sympathy with it, too. Sometimes laws had to be bent, if not broken, to accomplish justice.

He could tell that Kent didn't want to argue with the most important man in those parts.

After a moment the marshal sighed and asked, "What did you have in mind, Jensen?"

"I want to sink their boat," Luke said.

"How in blazes do you plan on doing that?" Harmon wanted to know.

"I'm going to be waiting on the bank where the river comes down out of the hills," Luke explained. "From there I can toss dynamite down on the boat and blow holes in the deck. It'll sink, and the outlaws will have to swim for shore. That's where you come in, Marshal. You and a posse will be waiting to round them up as they come out of the river."

"What about the gold?" Kent asked.

"Sinking the boat won't hurt it. Once everything is over, somebody can swim down, attach chains to the strongboxes, and haul them out with a mule team."

A grin creased Harmon's face. "That's a mighty bold plan, Jensen."

"When you're dealing with men like these, you can't worry too much about being cautious," Luke said. "Sometimes you just have to hit 'em hard and hope for the best."

Harmon threw back his head and laughed. "I like the idea," he declared. "It's a little crazy, but I've got a hunch it might work."

"When do you expect this riverboat full of outlaws to arrive?" Kent asked.

"Any time now," Luke answered.

"Then there's no time to waste. How am I supposed to get a posse together on such short notice?"

Harmon shook his head. "Oh, hell, that's not a problem, Gid. I've got half a dozen hands with me. We'll be your posse."

Kent frowned and nodded slowly. "That does make me feel better about the prospects of this scheme working," he admitted. "You say you need dynamite, Jensen?"

"I was told there should be some at the general store."

"Damn right there is." Harmon clapped a hand on Luke's shoulder. "Come on. I'll go over there with you. Cy Herndon, the fella who owns the place, won't give you any trouble if I'm along."

Once the plan was put in motion, things went quickly. Luke was glad of that. The riverboat could come steaming out of the hills at any time, and if it arrived before they were ready, the chances of stopping Mc-

Cluskey and the outlaws would go way down.

Having Dave Harmon on his side really greased the wheels. As the cattle baron had predicted, the owner of the general store was more than willing to provide the half-dozen sticks of dynamite he had on hand.

"Normally I'd have more than that," Herndon told Luke. "I've got an order in for more, but it won't be here for a while yet."

"This should be enough. If it's not, we'll have bigger problems." Luke attached fuses and caps to the dynamite himself, then placed the sticks in a small wooden box.

As he and Harmon left the store, the rancher said, "I'll head over to the saloon and get my boys together. We came into town to blow off a little steam, but this'll be even better. We'll meet Marshal Kent and get ready to corral those varmints from the boat. Better spread the word for folks to stay off the street, just in case there's any gunplay."

"It wouldn't surprise me a bit if there is, so that's a good idea," Luke agreed.

He stopped at the livery stable to get the Winchester from the horse he had ridden into town.

Silas Grant gave him a worried frown.

"What's goin' on, Mr. Jensen? The air's sorta got a feel like there's fixin' to be a thunderstorm, but there ain't a rain cloud in the sky."

"That's perceptive of you, Silas. You'd do well to stay inside for a while. Either that, or go on up to the café and make sure that your wife and Mrs. Walton stay inside, too."

"Oh, shoot," the liveryman breathed. "All hell's about to bust loose, ain't it?"

Luke glanced down at the box of dynamite tucked under his arm. "If everything goes according to plan, that's exactly what's about to happen."

CHAPTER 27

The street was already starting to clear as Luke stepped out of the livery barn. As people scurried inside, they cast frightened looks at the group of men who walked up the street toward the river. Harmon and Kent were in the lead, and behind them came half a dozen tough-looking cowboys, each man wearing a six-gun and carrying a rifle. The sight was enough to warn the townspeople that something was about to happen.

Luke waved at Harmon and Kent and strode quickly to the river. About a hundred yards along the bank, he started up the pine-dotted slope at a fairly steep angle. The trees got thicker the higher he climbed on the hill.

A few minutes later, he reached a good spot — thick with trees and brush — overlooking the river. He estimated it was forty feet below him. The outlaws on the riverboat wouldn't spot him as they approached. He set the box of dynamite on the ground where it would be handy, then hunkered on his heels and leaned his back against a tree trunk.

A couple cigars in his shirt pocket had come through all the commotion of the past few days unharmed. He took one of them out and clamped it between his teeth. From the little tin box he carried, he took a lucifer and snapped it to life with his thumbnail. Holding the flame to the cigar, he puffed until it was burning steadily.

He was ready. All he had to do was wait.

After worrying that he might not have time to get everything in place, the minutes seemed to drag as he smoked and watched the river. What if something had happened to the boat while it was still in the mountains, he wondered? Or maybe McCluskey had decided to change Burroughs' plan. Luke wouldn't put anything past him.

He smoked the first cigar down and used the butt to light the second one, and still there was no sign of the riverboat. He was about to decide he might have to head upriver and start searching for it, when he heard a faint rumble in the distance that steadily grew louder until he could discern it plainly over the noise of the river.

It was the boat's engine, Luke thought. He puffed harder on the cigar until its tip glowed cherry red.

The riverboat chugged into sight, coming around the shoulder of a hill. Spray flew up from the revolving paddlewheel. He drew back a little in the brush to make sure McCluskey and the others didn't spot him.

Luke saw a few men on deck, a couple more in the pilothouse. He couldn't make out who any of them were, nor did he spot Delia.

He felt a few qualms about killing a woman, even one as vicious and bloodthirsty as Delia Bradley, but she was with the outlaws of her own free will. Whatever happened in the next few minutes would just happen, he thought, and the chips would land wherever they fell.

He reached into the box and picked up one of the red-paper-wrapped, slightly greasy sticks of dynamite. He had cut the fuses pretty short. It wouldn't take long for the dynamite to go off after the fuse was lit.

The boat had almost reached his position. Luke held the fuse to the tip of the cigar. Sparks flew in the air as the fuse sputtered to life.

He tossed the dynamite into the air above the river. It spun downward, landed on the deck at the bow, bounced once, and rolled to the edge of the deck. The little lip caught it and kept it from falling into the river.

Yells of alarm came from a couple outlaws near where the dynamite landed. One man foolishly rushed toward the bow, evidently intending to grab the dynamite and fling it off the boat.

The explosive went off just as he reached for it. The blast blew him apart and chewed a big chunk out of the deck.

A second stick of dynamite was already spinning through the air toward the boat. The fuse was timed even better. It blew just as it struck the deck. The concussion picked up one of the suddenly panicked outlaws and flung him into the air. His arms and legs waved wildly for a second before he splashed into the river.

The next stick of dynamite landed on top of the cabins and blew a hole in them. Men were rushing around on the deck, looking for the source of the devastation that rained down from the sky.

Smoke began to boil up from the cabins. That blast had set the boat on fire.

Frank McCluskey appeared on deck, shouting over the tumult and waving an arm at the bank. Luke knew the outlaw had figured out where the dynamite was coming from.

A second later, shots began to ring out as the outlaws opened fire even though they couldn't actually see Luke. Bullets whipped through the brush and trees around him, but none came close enough to make him stop what he was doing.

He lit another fuse from the cigar and flung it at the paddlewheel. The dynamite arched down and exploded. The paddles lurched to a stop, bent and damaged by the blast. The riverboat's momentum kept it moving forward, but it began to slow dramatically.

It was tilting, too, as water gushed through the holes blown in the deck. Quickly, Luke lit the last two fuses and tossed those sticks of dynamite down onto the boat. Some of the outlaws screamed in terror as the deadly cylinders fell among them, but those cries were swallowed up by the unholy roar as the dynamite went off.

Luke snatched up the Winchester and sprayed the pilothouse with lead as fast as he could work the rifle's lever. The two men up there were firing at him, and they had the best angle. One of their shots clipped a branch not far from him.

One man went over backward as Luke's

slugs ripped through him. He toppled through one of the big windows. The other man dived for cover.

The riverboat was nose down in the water. The front half of the deck was awash. Luke knew the boilers might explode when the cold river water hit them, and from the looks of it, some of the outlaws realized that, too. They began leaping off the boat into the stream.

With everything on the riverboat in a state of chaos, the members of Marshal Kent's posse began appearing. They had taken cover so they would be out of sight as the boat approached, but there was no longer any need for that. Harmon's ranch hands had split up between the two banks, and the cattle baron and Kent were on the bridge itself, holding rifles.

The explosions seemed to have knocked all the fight out of most of the outlaws. They were pathetic, bedraggled figures as they crawled out of the river and were swarmed by Harmon's gun-toting cowboys. A couple tried to claw out their guns and put up a fight, but shots hammered into them and knocked them back in the water, where they floated lifelessly.

Luke knelt in the brush holding his Winchester and watched for McCluskey. He had lost track of the man during the confusion, and he still hadn't seen Delia.

A moment later, the outlaw emerged from one of the cabins dragging Delia by the hand. He had a revolver in his other hand, and he emptied it toward the bank where Luke was hiding.

Luke drew a bead on the outlaw and could have drilled him then, but he still wanted to see McCluskey hang, so he held off on the rifle's trigger.

He could tell that Delia didn't want to jump into the river. After emptying the revolver, McCluskey dragged her toward the deck's edge. Frantically, she tried to pull away, but he held on tightly to her. Luke figured she couldn't swim and was deathly afraid of the water.

McCluskey leaped, taking Delia with him. They went under the water and popped back up again. Delia wrapped her arms around McCluskey's neck and clung to him fiercely as he began kicking toward the shore.

They had just reached it and clambered up onto the bank when the biggest explosion of all wracked the riverboat. It split in half as a giant gout of flame and steam erupted from its midsection. The boilers had exploded.

The strongboxes, sturdy enough to withstand the blast, would go down with the boat and wind up on the bottom of the river, where they would be recovered later.

A couple of Harmon's men were waiting for McCluskey and Delia. They herded the two prisoners toward the spot where the posse had gathered the surviving members of the gang — eight of them, counting McCluskey and Delia.

With the stub of the second cigar still clenched between his teeth, Luke took the empty dynamite box and headed down the slope to join the others.

Dave Harmon had a grin on his face as he greeted Luke. "That was quite a show!" the cattle baron exclaimed. "The most excitement we've had around here in a good long while."

Marshal Kent said, "It was more than enough excitement for me, that's for sure. I suppose you want me to lock these men up in my jail, Jensen?"

"I'd be obliged to you if you did," Luke said with a nod. "Can you handle this many prisoners?"

Kent shrugged. "They'll be a little crowded, since I already have the two men in there who delivered the gang's horses, but I doubt if you're very concerned about their comfort."

"Not at all," Luke said.

"As for the lady, I can lock her in the back room so she won't have to share the cell block with these men."

Luke figured that was sparing more thought for Delia's sensibilities than was really necessary, but he didn't argue. As long as they were all locked up securely, it was all that really mattered.

Harmon looked at the shattered husk of the burning riverboat. "One of my men is a mighty good swimmer. I reckon as soon as that boat finishes sinkin', he can go down and locate those strongboxes. I'll get some chain from the store and a team of mules from Silas Grant's stable, and we'll get that gold up out of the river."

"Sounds good to me," Luke said. "I appreciate all your help, Mr. Harmon."

"Oh, hell, that's all right. We'll be well paid for it, after all."

Luke nodded. "Yes, I figured we'd all share the rewards —"

"Rewards, hell!" Harmon said. "That's just chicken feed. I'm talkin' about a hundred and twenty-five thousand dollars' worth of gold!"

Alarm bells went off in Luke's brain as he realized he was being double-crossed. The faint scuff of boot leather on the ground behind him added to the warning. He tried to whirl around and bring up the Winchester.

He was too late. Something crashed against his head, and as he fell, he caught a glimpse of Marshal Kent holding a rifle. He knew the lawman had just slammed the butt of that rifle into his head.

That was the last thing Luke knew for a while. He didn't even feel himself hit the ground.

CHAPTER 28

A familiar odor was the first thing Luke was aware of when he began to regain consciousness. He smelled a distinctive blend of straw, manure, and horseflesh.

He was inside a stable.

The logical conclusion was that he was inside Silas Grant's livery stable in Pine City. However, he couldn't be sure of that. He wasn't sure about much of anything except that he never should have trusted Marshal Gideon Kent or Dave Harmon.

Unfortunately, he hadn't had any reason to think the two men were anything other than what they appeared to be — a small-town star-packer and an honest rancher. He still wasn't sure exactly what had happened out there by the river, but his aching head confirmed the important thing.

They had double-crossed him, knocked him out, and were after that gold for themselves.

Luke opened his eyes and flinched at the brightness that struck painfully against them. It was actually pretty dim and shadowy inside the little room where he lay on a hard-packed dirt floor, but enough light came through cracks around the door to half blind him for a moment.

When his eyes had adjusted, he looked around. He was in a small, windowless room, eight feet by eight feet square. A number of bridles, harnesses, and other pieces of tack hung from nails driven into the walls.

He was convinced that he was in Silas's stable. Biting back a groan in case a guard stood right outside the door, he rolled onto his side and pushed himself into a sitting position.

The pounding inside his skull made him sick and dizzy for a moment. When that subsided, he lifted a hand to his head and gingerly explored his scalp, finding the tender lump behind his ear where he'd been hit. It was sticky with dried blood, and touching it sent fresh waves of pain through his brain.

That died down to a dull ache. Ignoring it, Luke climbed carefully to his feet, bracing a hand against the rough planks of the wall.

Another wave of nausea and vertigo hit him once he was upright, but that soon passed, too. When he felt steady on his feet, he moved over to the door and put an eye to one of the cracks.

His field of view was pretty limited, of course, but he could see enough to confirm that he was in Silas Grant's tack room. In fact, he could see Silas himself, forking some hay into a stall on the other side of the barn's broad middle aisle.

The liveryman was a little the worse for wear, with a scrape on his cheek and a left eye swollen partially closed. Luke wondered who had been knocking him around.

He didn't see or hear anybody else, didn't smell any tobacco smoke to indicate that someone was nearby puffing on a quirly. It seemed he could risk trying to get the liveryman's attention, so he put his mouth next to the crack and hissed, "Silas! Silas, can you hear me?"

Silas paused in what he was doing and leaned on the pitchfork for a moment as he looked around with a frown on his face. Then hurried over to the tack room door. "Mr. Jensen, you're awake in there!"

That seemed pretty obvious to Luke, but he didn't say anything about it. He could tell that Silas was upset and asked, "Is there a guard out there?"

"Not right now." Silas kept his voice low as he replied. "One of Mr. Harmon's men was here until a few minutes ago, but he went over to Herndon's store to buy some tobacco." Silas grunted. "And when I say buy, I mean take it without payin' for it. None of the Leanin' H men ever pay for anything around here. Not with Dave Harmon havin' this whole town right smack-dab under the heel o' his boot."

"It was Harmon's men who beat you up?"

"Yeah," Silas admitted. "Reckon I didn't cooperate quite well enough to suit 'em when they dragged you in here and said they was gonna lock you in my back room. They're used to folks jumpin' whenever they say so, same as Mr. Harmon is."

"You didn't say anything about that earlier."

"Didn't know you was gonna get mixed up with the man. Mr. Harmon, he generally don't hurt nobody unless they get in his way . . . or unless they got somethin' he wants."

Like a small fortune in stolen gold bars, Luke thought with a sigh.

"What about the marshal? He's crooked, too, I take it?"

Silas grimaced. "Not crooked so much as

he won't cross Mr. Harmon. That man owns the bank, so that means he pretty much owns the whole town. Ain't nobody here in Pine City who don't owe him money, me included. Like I said, he lets things go along peaceful-like most of the time."

Luke had run into men like that before — men who considered themselves the monarchs of their own private little domain. Harmon's hearty, friendly, helpful demeanor had been just an act.

And he had fallen for it, leaving him in an even worse position than before.

"All right, let me out of here," he said harshly.

Silas shook his head solemnly. "I can't do that."

"Look, I know you're afraid of Harmon and his men —"

"Damn right I'm afraid of 'em," Silas broke in. "Bad things got a habit of happenin' to men who stand up to Mr. Harmon. That might put my wife Tillie in danger, too, and I ain't gonna do that. But I mean what I say, Mr. Jensen — I *can't* let you outta that tack room. There's a padlock on the door, and I ain't got the key."

"Use that pitchfork," Luke suggested. "You can pry the hasp loose —"

Silas's head jerked toward the barn door.

He grimaced again. "Somebody's comin'!"

Before Luke could say anything else, Silas scurried away. He went back to pitching hay into the stalls, trying to make it look like he hadn't been anywhere near the tack room.

Luke heard footsteps and figured the guard was back.

Moments later, a man's voice drawled, "You hear anything from inside there, Silas?"

"No, sir," Silas answered without hesitation. "Quiet as the grave in there, it is."

Luke heard a match scrape and then smelled tobacco burning, along with the sulfur stink of the lucifer.

"Could be Jensen's dead," the guard said. "Kent really walloped him. Might've stove in his skull."

"If . . . if he's dead, you can't leave him there. This ain't no undertakin' parlor."

"He'll stay in there until the boss says otherwise," the man snapped. "Don't forget who's runnin' things around here."

"No, sir," Silas said, hanging his head. "I sure won't."

A second later, he lifted his head and glared, which made Luke think the guard must have turned away. The hatred on the man's face made Luke realize just how much Silas resented the heavy-handed treatment he got at the hands of Harmon and his men. Many of the other citizens of Pine City probably felt the same way.

That resentment might come in handy, Luke thought — but only if he could get out of there.

McCluskey sat with his back against the wall and his arms around Delia, who was still trembling violently and whimpering now and then. They were in the back room of the marshal's office, which was used for storage and also had a cot in it that looked like it hadn't been slept in for quite some time.

Both of them were still damp from being dunked in the river, but Delia wasn't trembling because of that. She was still on the verge of hysteria.

From everything McCluskey had seen of her so far, Delia Bradley was the most cool-headed woman he had ever known. She had gunned down those guards in the caboose without batting an eyelash, and she had blasted Derek Burroughs.

Yet she had almost lost her mind at the prospect of jumping in the river. He knew that if he hadn't dragged her kicking and screaming off the riverboat, she would have stayed on it until the boilers exploded.

Of course, they had wound up in a pretty precarious position anyway. McCluskey had seen the lawman's badge pinned to the vest of the Pine City marshal and figured they were being arrested. It was worse than that.

They had landed in the hands of another ruthless bunch of outlaws — only those men worked for the cattle baron called Harmon.

The surviving members of Burroughs' gang were locked up in the cells. Marshal Kent would have put McCluskey in with them, but when the time came, Delia refused to let go of him. Still frantic with fear, she clutched him like a lifeline.

Rather than going to the trouble of trying to pry her loose from him, Kent had just told Harmon's men to put both of them in the back room. It didn't have any windows, so it was almost as secure as one of the cells.

They had been there ever since. McCluskey kept waiting for Delia to calm down, but he wasn't sure that was ever going to happen.

As he patted Delia's shoulder and made comforting noises, he thought about Luke Jensen and felt fires of rage burning inside him. The bounty hunter was responsible for their current predicament. McCluskey had expected him to come after them but hadn't figured that Jensen would get ahead of them somehow.

He certainly hadn't expected that Jensen would be waiting at Pine City with a dynamite ambush.

And yet, as soon as he'd heard the first blast go off, he had known in his gut that Jensen was responsible for it. It felt like he was going to plague him for the rest of his life.

Of course, how long that life would be was a good question. McCluskey had no idea what Harmon intended to do with them.

"You're all right now. You made it out of the river," he said to Delia. He heard a key scrape in the lock and sat up straighter.

Delia clutched at him more desperately, but he got hold of her wrists and inexorably unwound her arms from his neck. "Stop it. You don't have to act like this."

Under his breath, he muttered, "Crazy woman."

The door swung open. Marshal Kent stood there, a double-barreled Greener in his hands.

McCluskey thought the man looked like a store clerk or a preacher, but there was no mistaking the evil glitter in Kent's eyes as he warned, "Don't try anything, you two, or I'll splatter both of you all over the walls in here." He motioned with the shotgun. "Get over there in the corner, next to the cot."

McCluskey scooted in that direction, taking Delia with him. Her reaction to being threatened with a shotgun was interesting. If anything, she seemed to calm down a little right away, he thought. It was like she could deal with that threat a lot easier than the thought of jumping in a river.

When the two of them were in the corner, Kent moved out of the doorway and let Harmon come into the room. The marshal stayed there to keep the prisoners covered as Harmon regarded them with what looked like a friendly smile on his face.

McCluskey knew better. He recognized the cold, snake-like eyes of a killer above that smile. He knew that look well. He had seen it enough times in his own shaving mirror.

"Well, now, is the little lady settlin' down yet?" the cattle baron asked.

Delia surprised McCluskey by answering Harmon's question herself. "Don't call me little lady," she spat. "In case you hadn't noticed, I'm not any damn *lady.*"

Yeah, thought McCluskey, she was back to her old self again. And he was glad of it. She was a formidable ally. If they were going to get out of this, he might need her help . . . as he had several times previously.

"What are you going to do with us?" Mc-Cluskey asked.

"How do you know I won't just kill you?" Harmon asked in return. The smile never budged from his face.

"If you wanted us dead, you've had plenty of chances to do it before now. I think you've got something else in mind."

"Well, you might be right about that," Harmon drawled in his folksy ways. "I had a look through the marshal's wanted posters. He told me your name sounded familiar to him, and turns out there's a good reason for that. You're wanted in a lot of places, McCluskey, for a lot of different things — all of 'em bad."

"You're not telling me anything I don't already know," McCluskey snapped. "Get to the point."

"You've got a lot of bark on you for a fella who's in such a bad spot. I sort of like that. Here's what I was thinkin', McCluskey — I might be able to use a man like you."

The outlaw frowned in surprise. "You mean you want me to work for you? I'm no damn cow nurse."

"You know better than that. You're good with a gun, and you don't much care who you use it on. Those are valuable skills to a man like me, who's got a heap of enemies in the world."

"Don't you have enough hired killers working for you already?"

Harmon tut-tutted. "A man can never have enough good workers. But what I really need is a man to take charge of those workers. I'm gettin' up in years. Can't get out and do all the things I once could. And I got to admit" — he looked at Delia, and his smile became more of a leer — "it'd be nice to have a good-lookin' gal around the house again. You could bring your little friend with you."

Delia simpered a little, going from angry to coy in a heartbeat. McCluskey figured that was a purely instinctive reaction with her. Some man — any man — flattered her, and she instantly started trying to work it to her advantage.

He didn't care. Let her play up to the old man as much as she wanted to. He didn't even care if she wound up sharing Harmon's bed. Only one thing mattered to him. "If you want me to boss that crew of gun-wolves for you, I can do that. But there's something I want in return."

"A share of that gold," Harmon said with a knowing nod. "I can go along with that. Probably won't be as big as you would've gotten if you hadn't run into me, but just think of it as a start on a lot more loot."

"Damn right I want a share of the gold, but that's not what I'm talking about." Mc-Cluskey leaned forward and his lips drew back from his teeth as he said, "I want to kill Luke Jensen."

Harmon just smiled and nodded. "Oh, I reckon that can be arranged."

CHAPTER 29

Luke spent some time examining the inside of the tack room, looking for a way out or anything he could use as a weapon if he got the chance. He found a set of reins that might work for wrapping around somebody's neck and choking them, but he would have to get close and take his enemy by surprise for that tactic to do any good.

He rolled up the reins and put them in his pocket anyway, just on the chance that they might prove useful later.

Like the rest of the barn, the tack room was solidly built and in good repair. Silas was conscientious about taking care of his business. Even if he hadn't been, the building was relatively new. There weren't any loose or rotted boards. Luke didn't see any way he could get out unless Silas pried that padlock off or somebody came along to unlock it.

Silas couldn't do anything with one of

Harmon's men standing guard right outside — and if they unlocked the door it would probably be because they didn't have anything good in mind for the prisoner.

The light coming through the cracks around the door had started to fade a little, telling Luke that it was late afternoon when he heard voices outside the tack room. A moment later, a key scraped in the lock.

He stood with his muscles tensed for action. He wanted to be ready if he got a chance to jump one of his captors and maybe get his hands on a gun. Going down fighting would be better than anything they might have planned for him.

When the door swung open, no one was there. They were all standing back well away from the tack room.

"Come on out of there, Jensen," Dave Harmon ordered. "And don't try anything. There are two scatterguns pointed at that door, and if you don't come out slow with your hands in plain sight, there won't hardly be enough left of you to scrape up and bury."

Luke stayed where he was without saying anything.

Harmon sounded irritated as he said, "Damn it, I know you're awake in there by now. Maybe if you heard ol' Silas yellin' in pain out here, you'd be a mite more co-operative. I'd just as soon not do that, since Silas is a good boy, but if that's the way you want it —"

"Leave Silas alone," Luke said. "I'm coming out."

As Harmon had ordered, he stepped out of the tack room in deliberate fashion and made sure his hands were partially raised where they would be visible to Harmon and his gunmen.

The cattle baron laughed. "Got somebody out here who wants to see you, Jensen."

Luke wasn't surprised when he saw Frank McCluskey and Delia standing there. McCluskey had a gun belt strapped around his waist and a holstered Colt on his hip. Delia wore a smirk.

Once again, the outlaw and the blonde had landed on their feet. No matter what sort of predicament they found themselves in, no matter what sort of loco stunt they tried to pull, somehow they survived. Not only survived, but thrived.

More and more, Luke was starting to wonder about that so-called vision McCluskey had had.

Delia said, "He doesn't look shocked to see us, Frank."

"I don't imagine he is. He knows by now

he can't get the best of us. Don't you, Jensen?"

Luke didn't respond to that. He looked instead at Harmon and said, "I thought you were an honest cattleman."

"A man could take offense at what you're implyin'," Harmon drawled. "I *am* an honest cattleman. I never rustled a single head of stock in all my life. Never cheated any man I ever had business dealin's with, either. You can ask anybody in the territory about that."

"But you take over a town and your men run roughshod over its citizens."

"I didn't have to take it over," Harmon said. "It was my town right from the beginnin'. Always has been, always will be. And as such, my men got a right to take what they want. Folks around here understand that."

They might understand it, Luke thought, but it didn't mean they liked it. He knew that from talking to Silas Grant. The citizens of Pine City were ripe for a rebellion.

They just needed somebody to lead it.

"You don't mind stealing a bunch of gold, either."

"What are you talkin' about? I'm not stealin' any gold." Unbelievably, Harmon sounded sincere in that declaration. "Accordin' to what McCluskey told me, your old friend Burroughs and his men stole that gold. What I'm doin' is more along the lines of salvagin' it. You know what that is, don't you, Jensen? There's a law that applies to ships at sea about how anything brought up from a wreck belongs to whomever brought it up. I reckon the same thing applies to a paddleboat sunk in a river, don't you?"

Luke knew there was no point in arguing with the man. Harmon was loco enough — or just plain arrogant enough — to believe what he was saying. Things had gone too far for him to change his mind.

"What are you going to do with me?" Luke asked.

"Well, McCluskey wanted to just march in here and shoot you. I talked him out of bein' quite that hasty about it."

From the look on McCluskey's face, he wasn't too happy about postponing Luke's death. But he didn't want to argue with Harmon. The cattleman could have had McCluskey killed out of hand, too, and surely the outlaw was well aware of it.

"I thought you might like to see what we're doin'," Harmon went on. "You can come with us. Don't try anything, though. You'll die sooner if you do."

Luke had every intention of dying as late

as possible, so he just nodded. "I understand."

Despite that, if he saw an opportunity to escape or to turn the tables on his captors, he would seize it.

The two shotgun-wielding cowboys kept him covered as he followed Harmon, Mc-Cluskey, and Delia out of the stable. Silas was standing right outside the double doors with one of Harmon's men keeping an eye on him.

With his usual smile, Harmon told the liveryman, "You can go on about your business now, Silas. Sorry for the bother and the misunderstanding earlier."

"That's all right, Mr. Harmon. Wasn't no bother." Silas sent a sympathetic glance in Luke's direction, but that was all he could do. Anything more would risk another "misunderstanding" like the one that had left him bruised and battered.

The street was empty, when normally it would have been busy on the pleasant late afternoon. Luke suspected the honest citizens of Pine City knew something bad was going on and were lying low, trying to stay out of the way of trouble. He couldn't blame them.

As they passed the café, he saw a shadow move at the window set into the door. He caught a glimpse of fair hair and knew Georgia Walton was watching.

Being a helpless prisoner in front of a beautiful woman was especially annoying, Luke thought, giving him one more score to settle with Harmon and McCluskey when he got the chance.

They headed toward the river. Harmon didn't stop until he strode onto the bridge. The others followed him and had a good view of the wrecked riverboat. About three feet of the smokestack from the boiler room stuck up from the water at a slant. Other parts of the boat's superstructure were visible just under the water.

Half a dozen of Harmon's men were on the riverbank, including one man who was stripped down to the bottom half of a pair of long underwear. He waved at Harmon, who gave him a benevolent nod in return. The man waded out into the river until it was deep enough to swim, then swam out to the area where the riverboat had sunk.

"McCluskey told us where the strongboxes should be," Harmon explained to Luke. "Rusty there is gonna dive down and locate them."

The man in the river stopped and took several deep breaths, then ducked his head and disappeared under the water. Seconds passed slowly. Harmon rested both hands on the bridge railing and leaned forward to watch with an intent expression on his weathered face.

After about a minute and a half, Rusty's head popped out of the water. He waved to Harmon again to indicate that he was all right, then floated for a few moments while he drew in deep breaths. He went under again, causing ripples in the water that the current rapidly dissipated.

"I hope he's not havin' too much trouble findin' that gold," Harmon mused. He looked over at McCluskey. "You'd better have been tellin' us the truth about where it should be, McCluskey."

"Of course I told you the truth. You let me out of jail, didn't you? I don't have any reason to lie. I want us to work together."

Sensing some friction between the two, Luke wondered if the bond between Harmon and McCluskey was as close as they had acted like it was. One thing was certain, he thought. Given everything that had happened, either man would be a fool to completely trust the other.

With a splash, Rusty reappeared. He cupped a hand next to his mouth and shouted, "Found it!"

Harmon clenched a fist and shouted back,

"Good man!"

Rusty stroked to shore and took the end of a rope that one of the gunmen threw to him. He returned to the center of the river and dived down with it.

The other end of the rope was tied to a heavy chain. With a rattle of links, it began to disappear into the river as Rusty hauled it to him. The rest of the men began attaching the other end of the chain to a draw bar hitched to a couple mules.

The whole process took a while, since Rusty had to come up for air several times while he was working, but finally he gave a thumbs-up and the men leading the mules got them moving. The chain grew taut, and slowly but surely the team hauled the first of the strongboxes out of the stream.

Luke saw pure avarice in the faces of Harmon and McCluskey. It was in Delia's gaze, too, but not as strong. She still seemed more interested in McCluskey than anything else.

No matter how long Luke lived — and that was a matter open to much speculation, of course — he would never understand why Delia had gotten so obsessed with the outlaw so quickly. Some quirk in her brain had caused her to be attached to him, and that bond seemed unbreakable.

By the time the sun was going down, Rusty and the others had repeated the whole business to get the second strongbox out of the river. Harmon's men re-hitched the mules to the wagon and loaded the boxes into the back of the vehicle, grunting and straining with effort.

When that was done, McCluskey said to Harmon, "All right. You've done your gloating. Jensen needs to die now."

Harmon shook his head. "Not just yet."

McCluskey's face darkened with anger. "We had a deal."

"We still do." Harmon's face hardened. "But you need to understand, McCluskey — I call the shots around here. I said Jensen would die, and he will. I didn't say *when.*"

McCluskey looked like he wanted to argue, and Delia didn't seem pleased, either. But neither said anything.

After a moment, McCluskey nodded. "All right. But don't start thinking I'm just some run-of-the-mill hired gun."

"Don't worry. I know that."

One of Harmon's men asked, "Are we staying here in town tonight, boss, instead of heading back out to the ranch?"

"I think so. There's plenty of room at the hotel." Harmon looked at McCluskey and

Delia. "In fact, why don't you and the little lady go on ahead? Tell the desk clerk I said to give you the best room in the house — not countin' my suite, of course."

"I told you, I'm not a lady," Delia said.

"Maybe you should try pretendin'," Harmon suggested. "You might find that you like it."

Before she could respond to that, McCluskey took her arm and said, "Come on."

They walked off the bridge ahead of Luke, Harmon, and the other two men.

Quietly, Luke said, "You don't fool me, Harmon. You decided to keep me alive in case you need to use me against McCluskey."

"A smart man never throws away something that might come in handy later on. I think it'll turn out just fine, McCluskey throwin' in with me, but in case it doesn't" — Harmon shrugged — "it's one more way to remind him who's the boss around here." He regarded Luke thoughtfully for a moment. "You know, if I thought it'd do any good, I might make you the same offer I made him, Jensen. But you'd never throw in with me, and I know that." He jerked his head at the shotgun-toters. "Take him back to the livery stable and lock him up. One of you stay on guard until somebody comes to relieve you."

"Sure, boss." One of the men motioned with the shotgun's twin barrels for Luke to get moving.

The wagon trundled ahead of them, carrying the fortune in gold that had already been responsible for so many men dying.

CHAPTER 30

Luke sat in the tack room, his back leaning against the wall. It was dark in the little room. The only light filtering through the cracks around the door came from a lantern in the stable someone had lit. The feeble yellow glow didn't illuminate much.

Of course, there wasn't much to see.

At least his current situation was much better than it could have been. He was still alive, and Harmon was keeping McCluskey on a tight rein for the time being — or at least attempting to.

The outlaw was too much of a wild card to count on anything, and that went double for his blond girlfriend.

Voices outside the tack room made Luke sit up. Earlier, he'd heard the guard talking to Silas Grant several times, but the voice was different.

It was a woman's voice.

She had come close enough for Luke to

understand the words when she spoke again.

"Mr. Harmon told me I could bring Mr. Jensen some supper. You can check with him if you'd like."

It was Georgia Walton, Luke thought as he got to his feet and moved over to the door. He put his mouth to the crack. "If you've brought me some of Mrs. Grant's excellent cooking, Mrs. Walton, I'll be forever grateful to you."

"Back off in there, Jensen," the guard snapped. "And ma'am, you just stay right where you are. Don't come no closer."

"You can see everything that's on this tray," Georgia said. "It's not like I'm trying to smuggle in a revolver to him or anything like that."

"Well, no, I reckon not," the guard said reluctantly. "Here, let me take a closer look . . . roast beef, taters, greens . . . what's that, some sort of fried pie?"

"Apple," Georgia said.

The guard chuckled. "Can't let you take that in there. It might have a derringer or a knife baked in it. I got to confiscate that."

"You must be joking," Georgia said coldly. "You can see for yourself that tart is much too small to have any sort of weapon in it."

The guard's jovial attitude disappeared as he snapped, "I told you, you ain't takin' it in there, and that's final. Now hand it over or take the whole mess outta here."

"Oh, all right. Here. I know you're just going to eat it, though."

"The boss told me to stay here on guard until somebody comes to relieve me," the guard said with a whiny, defensive tone in his voice. "Ain't no tellin' how long that'll be. A man gets hungry, you know."

"Fine. Now you'll let me in?"

"Hell, no! You're not gettin' anywhere close to that bounty hunter. I'll have to take that tray in to him."

"How are you going to do that and still hold the shotgun on him?" Georgia asked coolly.

"Huh? Oh, yeah, I reckon you're right."

Luke couldn't see the guard, but he could imagine the frown on the man's face as he tried to figure out a solution to the dilemma.

"I got it!" the guard exclaimed, obviously pleased with himself. "Hand the tray to the darky."

"How is it any different if Silas takes it in to Mr. Jensen?"

"Are you kiddin'? The boss would skin me alive if I was to shoot you, Miz Walton, but if Grant or Jensen either one try anything funny, I can paint the inside o' that tack room red with this Greener and nobody'll care that much. Mr. Harmon already told me I can kill Jensen if he tries to get away."

"All right," Georgia said with a sigh. "I hate to trouble you, Silas —"

"Ain't no trouble, Miz Georgia," Silas assured her. "Just let me have that tray."

"What you can do, ma'am, is unlock the door while I cover it. Here's the key." The guard raised his voice. "Jensen, you back as far away from that door as you can get. If you're anywhere close to it when it opens, I'm firin' both barrels o' this scattergun."

Luke backed away and called, "I'm in the far corner. Don't get trigger-happy."

The key scraped in the lock.

"All right. Give it back," the guard snapped. Luke assumed he was talking to Georgia and referring to the key. "Go on in, boy."

Silas pushed the door open with his foot because both hands gripped a wooden tray with a plate of food and a cup of coffee on it. He stepped into the tack room.

"You can get the food, Jensen." The guard had the shotgun pressed firmly to his shoulder as he squinted over the barrels. If he fired at so close a range, the double charge of buckshot would kill both Luke and Silas.

Luke glanced past Silas and saw Georgia Walton standing in the center aisle. The lantern light made a golden halo of her hair. The guard had his back to her, and for a second Luke thought she might try to attack him.

He hoped she wouldn't. Even if she succeeded in knocking him out, he would likely jerk the shotgun's triggers as he lost consciousness. It was too big a gamble with Silas's life.

Georgia stayed where she was with an anxious expression on her lovely face. Silas held out the tray toward Luke, who reached to take it. He paused, but only for a fraction of a second. Silas's eyes were wide with fear, and Luke knew that something was going on. He took the tray so as not to alert the guard.

His fingers touched something *underneath* the tray, at the end where Silas's left hand was holding it. Deftly, Luke slid his right hand under the object so that he held it at the same time he was holding that end of the tray. He could tell by the feel what it was.

With the tray to conceal it, Silas had just passed him a knife.

Luke glanced up and locked eyes with Silas, but again the reaction was fleeting so the guard wouldn't notice it. In that heartbeat, Luke acknowledged what Silas and Georgia were doing. The knife was slender, the sort of thing that would be used in a kitchen, and Luke had no doubt Georgia had brought it with her from the café, holding it under the tray.

The guard's insistence on not letting her into the tack room had thrown a kink into her plan, but she had recovered and managed to pass both tray and knife to Silas without Harmon's man noticing. Silas had been quick to realize what she was doing and got the knife to Luke.

Their attempt to help him was also a way of asking him to help them, he realized. They needed someone to break Dave Harmon's stronghold on Pine City.

Luke wouldn't let them down.

"I really appreciate this, Silas." He hoped Silas and Georgia would understand what he meant.

"All right, Jensen. Back away again," the guard said impatiently. "Come on outta there, darky. You don't want to make me nervous."

"I'm comin'." Silas nodded to Luke, the motion so small it was almost invisible.

But Luke saw it. He knew that if he could

get out of there, he could count on Silas for help.

"Close the door on your way out and put that padlock back on it," the guard told Silas.

Luke thought maybe Silas would try to leave the padlock unfastened but make it look like it was closed. That hope died aborning as Luke heard the guard pull on the lock to make sure it was secure.

So, he was still locked up, but at least he was armed. He stepped over to the door and called through the crack, "Thank you, Mrs. Walton. Your kindness means a great deal to me." He hoped she understood what he meant by that.

"I wish there was more I could do, Mr. Jensen."

"Well, what you've already done will just have to be enough."

If nothing else, the food was very good. The condemned man ate a hearty meal, as the old saying went, Luke thought.

As he ate, he examined the knife. It was slender, with a bone handle and no hilt. The serrated blade was about five inches long. It was an eating utensil, not a weapon, something designed for cutting a steak rather than inflicting mayhem.

But it would slash a throat just fine, and plunged into a man's back it would reach his heart.

A good workman made do with whatever tools were at hand.

The knife's serrated edge put Luke in mind of a saw blade, and that made him glance toward the door. While the lantern still burned outside and he had some light, he got up and moved closer to examine the obstacles facing him.

The door hinges were on the outside, so that did him no good. The floor was dirt. He might be able to dig out eventually, but that would take too long and someone was bound to notice.

That left the lock. He couldn't get to the padlock itself, but the hasp might be vulnerable. It was nailed into the jamb.

He could tell exactly where the lock was. He could see the hasp's tongue blocking the light coming through the crack and that allowed him to estimate closely the location of the nails.

He counted on the sounds of the guard's pacing around to mask any noises he might make, placed the knife against the four-by-four that served as the jamb, and began sawing.

Even if he had the proper tools, it would

be a challenging job. With nothing but a kitchen knife, it was almost impossible. The blade might not even hold up long enough for him to loosen the nails.

But it was his only chance, and he had learned a long time ago that when faced with death, attempting the impossible was better than giving up.

Chapter 31

About an hour later, another of Harmon's men showed up to take over the guard duties. "Has Jensen given any trouble?"

"Nope. He's been quiet ever since he ate his supper. I reckon he might be asleep."

"Well, go on over to the café and get yourself something to eat. The place is doing a good business tonight, what with all of us bein' in town."

The first guard laughed. "Yeah, it's too bad that pretty widow don't make much money off us, ain't it? She brought Jensen's supper over earlier, and I tell you . . ."

Luke tried to shut his mind to it as the man launched into an obscene commentary about Georgia Walton. It wasn't easy. But in a way he was grateful for the offensive rant. As long as the man was spewing filth, he wasn't listening for the steady scraping sound of the knife cutting through the wood around the nails.

Eventually, the first guard either ran out of lustful steam or a different appetite got the best of him. He left, heading for the café. The second guard settled in, probably for the night. Luke heard him moving around some and risked a look through the crack.

The man had pulled up a three-legged stool and was sitting on it about fifteen feet away with his back leaning against one of the pillars that held up the hayloft. He held a shotgun across his lap and kept his eyes on the door to the tack room.

Luke had a hunch the man wouldn't be able to maintain that vigilance, and sure enough, by the time half an hour had passed the guard's head was tipped forward so that his hat brim shielded his face. Snores came from him.

Luke kept sawing, being careful with the knife so that it would last as long as possible before going dull. As it penetrated deeper into the board, he took pains not to let it bind up. He didn't want to risk snapping the blade.

He hadn't seen or heard anything from Silas for a while and wondered if the liveryman had gone home for the night. It seemed likely. Some men who owned stables had living quarters in them, too, especially the single ones. Silas had a wife and, for all Luke knew, children. It was likely he had a house somewhere in Pine City.

Luke hoped Silas wasn't anywhere around when he made his break. If gunplay erupted, at least the liveryman would be out of the line of fire.

Time didn't have much meaning. Despite the hour, Luke wasn't sleepy. He couldn't afford to waste the chance. He continued sawing, seemingly endlessly.

The knife blade struck metal.

Luke had found one of the nails.

He didn't let the satisfaction he felt at that achievement distract him from the job at hand. Carefully, he shifted the knife and started sawing at a different angle.

After a while, he had cut deeply enough. Using a buckle from one of the harnesses hanging on the wall, he pried a rough triangle of wood out of the board. Again, he shifted the knife and began working from a different angle. He could tell the blade was beginning to dull.

The work began to go quicker because he had created some room. He could wiggle the slices of wood back and forth and remove them easier. Even so, hollowing out the area around the nails was a long, tedious task. Luke estimated it was well after midnight before he succeeded in exposing the nails that held the hasp to the wall.

During the time he had been working, he'd had to pause several times when the guard roused from sleep and came over to stand next to the door and listen for any sounds coming from inside the tack room.

During those intervals, Luke had backed away from the door and forced his breathing to be slow, deep, and regular, as if he were sound asleep.

Each time, the guard had gone back to his stool, satisfied that the prisoner wasn't up to any mischief.

Asleep again, the guard's head tilted far forward.

He was liable to wake up with a crick in his neck, Luke thought. But if everything went the way he wanted it to, a crick in the neck would be the least of the guard's worries.

Luke turned the latch carefully so that it didn't make any noise. As he held it tight, he put his other hand flat against the door where the lock was and began to push with a firm, steady pressure.

He knew if he rammed the door with his shoulder, the hasp would probably pull free, but the racket would rouse the guard. If possible, he wanted to get the door open quietly and have a chance to jump the guard and disarm him without any shots being fired.

The nails were held in place only by the outer wall of the tack room. With a slight squeal, they began to come loose as Luke pushed against them. The door moved a little. He hung on to the latch so it wouldn't fly open when the nails came completely out of the wall.

Metal screeched against wood again. Across the center aisle, the guard muttered something and shifted around, but he didn't appear to awaken. Luke paused in his effort and waited for the man to settle back down.

After a minute or two, he resumed pushing again and could see the nails sliding through the holes in the wall. *Steady, steady,* he thought.

The nails pulled loose and the door moved despite Luke's grip on the latch. The nails fell from the holes in the metal plate, but the small thudding sounds weren't loud enough to disturb the guard. He continued sleeping as Luke pushed the door open enough for him to step out of the tack room.

Luke gripped the knife as he cat-footed forward. The edge was pretty dull and the point was blunted somewhat, but it was the only weapon he had. With enough force behind it, it would still penetrate flesh.

The lantern was still burning, but its reservoir was almost empty. The light flickered and dimmed. Maybe even in his sleep, the guard sensed that. He grunted, made a flapping sound with his lips that was half snore, half mumble, and started to lift his head.

Luke had closed half the distance between them. As the guard's eyes flew open, Luke leaped toward him.

As the guard brought up the shotgun, Luke's left hand closed around the barrels and wrenched them toward the ceiling. With his right hand, he drove the knife at the man's chest.

Although half asleep, the guard twisted aside instinctively.

The thrust still landed, but it took him high on the left side, just under his shoulder, rather than in the heart as Luke intended. The man yelled in pain and surged up off the stool, lowering his head and bulling into Luke with enough force to knock him backward off his feet.

As he fell, he shoved the shotgun out to the side. He didn't want it trapped between them in case it went off.

In fact, he didn't want it to go off at all. A shotgun blast would draw way too much unwelcome attention in Pine City. Harmon and the rest of his men were right down the street at the hotel, and Luke was sure they would rattle their hocks to investigate if they heard a shot from the livery stable.

Luke twisted the shotgun back and forth to prevent the guard from finding the trigger.

On top as they struggled, the guard tried to drive his knee into Luke's groin. Luke barely got out of the way of the crippling blow, taking it on his thigh, instead. He had lost his grip on the knife, which was still lodged in the guard's shoulder.

Pain made the guard fight like a madman. He smashed a punch into Luke's face with his left fist, then tried to get that hand around Luke's neck. His movements were fumbling, no doubt hampered by his injury. Luke knocked the man's arm aside and shot a punch up between them that caught the guard under the chin and rocked his head back.

The guard lost his grip on the shotgun. Luke still had hold of the barrels, but the weapon wouldn't do him much good at such close quarters. The guard wasn't going to give him a chance to turn it around.

The best thing to do was get the gun away where neither of them could use it. Luke slung it across the aisle and hoped being jarred around wouldn't cause it to fire.

As the shotgun slid away, the last of the oil burned away in the lantern. Darkness suddenly dropped down over the stable like a shroud.

The deadly struggle continued in the impenetrable gloom. Since Luke's left hand was now free, he used it to throw a couple punches where he thought the guard's head was. Both blows landed, but neither was solid enough to stun him.

The guard brought his knee up again. The vicious blow missed Luke's groin but landed in his belly with enough force to make Luke sick.

Luke ignored it and bucked up from the ground, throwing the guard off. As the man rolled away, Luke leaped after him, guided by hearing and instinct. He landed on the man's back and clubbed a punch to the back of his head.

He remembered the reins he had put in his pocket earlier. He grabbed them, shook them out, and whipped them around the man's neck from behind. Taking hold of the reins with both hands, he planted a knee in the small of the man's back and heaved. The leather lines cut deeply into the man's neck, shutting off his air.

The guard thrashed and bucked, but Luke clung to him for dear life, keeping him pinned to the ground as he put more and more pressure on the man's windpipe. The guard clawed at the reins, but they had sunk too deeply into his flesh for him to get his fingers under. Little whimpering noises were all he could get out through his tortured throat.

It took only a minute or two for the guard to die, although it seemed longer than that. Finally, he slumped as all his muscles went limp in death. Luke smelled the stench as the man's bowels evacuated. He kept the pressure on the guard's neck for a good two minutes longer, just to be sure.

When there was no doubt that the guard was dead, Luke pushed himself wearily to his feet. He left the reins where they were, embedded in the dead man's throat. Bending, he found the holstered revolver on the man's hip and slid it out of its holster.

Feeling around in the darkness, he located the shotgun. As he straightened with the Greener in his hands, he felt better than he had in quite a while.

Now that he was armed again, he could take the fight to his enemies. Sure, he was still greatly outnumbered, but at the moment, he didn't really care. The pulse pounding inside his head might as well have been a drumbeat urging him to war.

Dave Harmon was the key, he sensed. If he could get his hands on the cattle baron, Harmon's men wouldn't be able to move against him. Luke headed to the hotel.

McCluskey and Delia were there, too, he recalled.

Might as well round them all up, he thought with a grim smile.

CHAPTER 32

McCluskey tilted his head back and let whiskey gurgle from the bottle into his mouth. It was a bottle of what was supposedly the finest stuff in Pine City, according to Harmon, but McCluskey thought he'd had better.

Still, the liquor was pretty smooth and kindled a nice warm fire in his belly. He took another drink.

The lamp on the bedside table was turned very low, so the corners of the spacious hotel room were in shadow. The yellow glow spread over the bed, revealing the shape of Delia curled up under the sheet, asleep after their lovemaking.

McCluskey sat in a wing chair across from the bed. He set the bottle aside, picked up the cigar smoldering in an ashtray on the table beside him and savored another few puffs on it. The cigar was a good one, another gift from Dave Harmon.

The rancher was treating them almost like royalty, but McCluskey didn't believe for a second that the man really felt that way. His only interest lay in turning things to his own advantage. McCluskey understood that attitude. He felt the same way.

He didn't trust Harmon. The rancher had spared their lives, but he had the power and that mercy could disappear at any second, with no warning.

McCluskey didn't like that. Whenever he worked with anybody else, he was used to running things.

As he drank Harmon's whiskey and smoked his cigar, he wondered how hard it would be to take over Harmon's outfit. He had managed pretty well with Derek Burroughs' gang — at least until the riverboat had steamed right into Luke Jensen's dynamite trap.

Thinking about Jensen put a frown on McCluskey's face. He put the cigar back in the ashtray and reached for the bottle again.

Harmon shouldn't have double-crossed him about Jensen. There was no good reason to keep the bounty hunter alive. He had a good mind to go down to the livery stable and put a bullet in Jensen's head.

He took another drink.

But there were two good reasons he didn't

do that — the pair of strongboxes still resting in the back of the wagon parked behind the hotel with several of Harmon's men guarding it.

After everything that had happened, the gold ought to belong to him, McCluskey thought. *All of it,* not just a share. With that much money, he and Delia could head for Mexico, disappear south of the border, and never come back.

Of course, he would tire of Delia sooner or later — but the good thing about Mexico was that there were plenty of lithe, eager, brown-skinned beauties to replace her.

She stirred in the bed, which made McCluskey wonder if she knew somehow that he was thinking about her. She sat up and stretched, the sheet falling away to reveal her surprisingly lush nudity.

Maybe once they got to Mexico he'd keep her around longer than he had thought, McCluskey mused.

"What are you doing awake?" she asked him. "Are you all right?"

"I'm fine. Just thinking about something."

"Those strongboxes full of gold?"

McCluskey chuckled. "How did you know?"

"Because I was *dreaming* about them." She pushed the sheet back, stood up, and went over to him. As she draped herself across his lap, she took the bottle out of his hand and drank some of the whiskey. "All that gold ought to belong to us," she said as she gave the bottle back to him.

"You don't want to go in partners with Harmon?"

Delia snorted contemptuously. "Partners, hell. He's the boss, and he'll always be the boss. That's the kind of man he is."

"I'm afraid you're right," McCluskey agreed.

"Besides, I saw the way he was looking at me. Sooner or later, he's going to expect me to come to his bed, Frank."

McCluskey didn't say what he was thinking, which was that he didn't care nearly as much about that as he did about the gold.

Delia evidently mistook his silence, because she went on. "I know, I know. That shouldn't bother me. But that's just it, Frank. Ever since I met you, I haven't been what I was. You changed me. I don't want to be with anybody but you. I'll play up to a man if I have to, for us to get what we want, but other than that I'm your woman and your woman alone from here on out."

She was loco, all right, McCluskey thought, but undeniably useful. He drew her closer to him and kissed her. She responded eagerly, squirming on his lap.

McCluskey drew back. "If we can get our hands on that gold, we can go someplace nobody'll ever find us. We'll be together from now on."

"Yes, yes," Delia panted. "I like the sound of that."

"But our only way out of here with those strongboxes is if we take Harmon with us as a hostage. Otherwise, his men will come after us. They'll be afraid to, though, as long as his life is in our hands."

"What about when we're safe?"

"*Then* we kill him," McCluskey said. "If we don't, that old man would likely hunt us to the ends of the earth to get even."

Delia nodded. "Yes, he would. When are we going to do it?"

"No time like now." McCluskey stood up, not so gently setting Delia on her feet. "It's the middle of the night. He and his men think they're safe in Pine City, so most of them are probably sound asleep." He slapped her bare rump and made her squeal and jump a little. "Get some clothes on. Those strongboxes are just waiting for us!"

Before leaving the livery stable, Luke went through the dead guard's pockets and found six more shotgun shells. It was a distasteful task, but he felt better for having the extra ammunition.

With a man on guard inside the barn, it was doubtful Harmon would have posted another one outside, but Luke couldn't rule out that possibility. He left the place by the smaller rear door, slipping into the alley behind the barn.

Moving like a phantom through the shadows, he made his way around the building, back to a spot where he could look along Pine City's main street. Lights burned in the hotel lobby and the saloon, but the rest of the businesses were dark, long since closed for the night.

He didn't see anyone moving along the boardwalks.

He took a couple steps to cross the street to the hotel when one of the big double doors on the front of the barn scraped open.

Luke whirled in that direction, bringing the shotgun to bear. An icy finger raked down his spine. He wasn't afraid of many things in this world, but he knew good and well the guard he'd left in the barn was dead.

The man couldn't have gotten up and walked and opened that door.

Luke managed not to pull the shotgun's triggers, but it wasn't easy. He was glad he did, though, as the man-shaped shadow stepped out of the barn.

The shadowed man thrust his hands in the air and exclaimed in a harsh whisper, "Don't shoot!"

"Silas?" Luke lowered the gun.

The liveryman was breathing hard from sudden fear as he moved closer. "Lord, I thought you was gonna blow me in half!"

"I almost did," Luke said as he motioned Silas back into the thicker shadows next to the barn and went with him. "What are you doing here? Were you inside when I was fighting with Harmon's man?"

"No, sir. I just got here a couple minutes ago. I came because Tillie and Miz Walton and Mr. McGill were all worried about you. I was, too. Seemed like you might've had time to escape by now, so I decided to come and see." Silas swallowed. "But when I went inside and struck a match, all I found was that dead fella."

"I managed to get out not long ago," Luke explained. "You say you were with your wife and Mrs. Walton and Ben McGill?"

"Yes, sir. Them and some others from here in town are gathered at the café, waitin' to see what's gonna happen."

"You mean waiting to see whether or not I'm going to kill Dave Harmon for them?"

Luke asked.

Silas sounded a little angry as he replied, "That ain't exactly the way it is. All the menfolks have got guns. If we heard shootin', we were gonna come help you. Figured we'd take Harmon's men by surprise that way."

Luke had to admit that strategically, it wasn't a bad plan. His escape would serve as a distraction, giving the townspeople more of a chance against Harmon's hired killers.

"But if I didn't get out, you'd just go on knuckling under to him."

"We're not gunfighters, Mr. Jensen," Silas said. "And most of us got families. Can't expect us to go up against those gun-wolves without much chance of winnin'. We figure if anything'll swing the balance toward us, it's havin' somebody like you on our side."

Luke nodded in the darkness and clapped a hand on Silas's brawny shoulder. "I know. And I'm sorry I sounded a little testy there. What do you say we try to get Harmon's boot off this town's neck?"

"That's all we want," Silas said. "Just a chance to get on with our lives in peace."

"All right. Can you tell me where Harmon and his men are right now?"

"Harmon's in the hotel, as far as I know.

He's got his own suite there, down at the end of the hall on the second floor. Probably some of his men are there, too. But some of 'em are still in the saloon. I had a look as I was comin' down here a few minutes ago. I think they got themselves an all-night poker game goin' on."

"What about Marshal Kent?"

Silas shook his head. "Lawman or not, he ain't gonna help us."

"I'm not expecting him to. I just want to know where he is so I can keep an eye out for him."

"He ain't married. He sleeps in the room back of his office. That's where he is now, I reckon."

"He doesn't have any night deputies?"

"Naw. Never been a need for any. Folks around here know that if they cause too much trouble, they'll answer to Harmon. He's the real law in Pine City. He's judge, jury — and executioner."

"He's killed people?" Luke asked.

"Oh, yeah," Silas said. "Had it done, anyway. How do you think Miz Georgia got to be a widow?"

That took Luke a little by surprise. "Harmon had her husband killed?"

"That's right. Tom Walton got hisself elected mayor and tried to do somethin'

332

about the way Harmon was runnin' things around here. Harmon had some of his men jump poor Tom one night and beat him to death. Thing is, Miz Georgia don't know that. Harmon's men tossed the body in my corral with a bad horse I had at the time. They tried to make it look like Tom had gone in there for some reason and that hoss killed him. That's what Miz Georgia believes. But I've seen men who got kicked and trampled to death by a horse, and I can tell the difference. Tom Walton died at the hands of men, not some horse."

As far as Luke was concerned, that made Dave Harmon just as much a murderer as his men. Since Luke had been in Pine City, the only ones who'd been killed were members of Derek Burroughs' outlaw gang. The law wouldn't see their deaths as a crime. Even Harmon's attempt to hang on to the gold might not get him in much trouble with outside authorities if any ever showed up. He could always claim that he hadn't known the gold was stolen, and no one around here would dare to dispute him.

But Tom Walton's murder — and the deaths of anyone else in Pine City who had opposed Harmon's iron-handed rule — made things different.

Luke would no longer hesitate in going

after Harmon. "You'll testify against Harmon if it ever comes to that?"

"Dang right, and I ain't the only one. There's plenty of wrongdoin' to lay at that man's feet."

"Then let's do it. Go back to the café and tell your friends to get ready." Luke glanced at the sky and saw that it had turned gray with the approach of dawn while he and Silas were talking. "The sun's going to come up on all hell breaking loose in Pine City this morning."

CHAPTER 33

Delia put on the same dress she'd been wearing ever since she got on the train in Rattlesnake Wells. It was the only thing she had to wear.

McCluskey suggested she leave the top two buttons undone. "We might as well distract Harmon a little," he said with a grin. "That might help us get the drop on him."

"I don't mind doing that." Delia adjusted the garment. "Especially if it helps us get that gold so we can find some safe place to spend the rest of our lives."

Not for the first time, McCluskey wondered how she would react when she found out, somewhere down the line, that they *weren't* going to be spending the rest of their lives together. She had a tendency to turn violent when she didn't get what she wanted.

Maybe what he ought to do instead of cutting her loose was to wait until some night when she was sound asleep and put a pillow over her face and hold it there until she stopped breathing. That way she would have spent the rest of her life with him, just like she wanted, he mused.

He put those murderous thoughts out of his head. For now, they were a team, and a good one, at that. He said, "All right. Let's go."

As they went down the hall toward Harmon's suite, McCluskey thought it unlikely the cattle baron had any bodyguards with him. Harmon seemed to feel he was the lord and master, making him absolutely safe in Pine City.

They paused in front of the double doors. McCluskey knocked loud enough to rouse a sleeping man from slumber.

After a moment, a groggy voice asked from inside, "Who the hell is out there? This damn well better be important!"

McCluskey nodded to Delia.

She raised her voice a little and said, "I need to talk to you, Mr. Harmon."

"Oh. Miss Bradley." Harmon sounded surprised but not displeased that Delia had come calling on him in what seemed like the middle of the night. A key rattled in the lock, and one of the doors swung inward.

"Please come on —" The invitation stopped short as Harmon saw that McCluskey was in the corridor, too. "What is this?" the rancher growled.

McCluskey said, "We need to talk to you. It's about the gold."

Harmon looked suspicious, but he opened the door the rest of the way. His white hair was rumpled from sleep. He wore a red union suit and had a revolver in his right hand. "All right. Come on in, both of you."

McCluskey and Delia stepped into the suite's sitting room. With the door to the bedroom open, they could see that Harmon had lit a lamp on one of the tables beside the bed.

Luke and Silas split up, Luke heading for the hotel while the liveryman went back to the café to rally the townspeople ready to throw off Harmon's brutal rule. He moved quickly at an angle across the street so as not to be spotted by any of Harmon's men who happened to be up and about at the early hour.

Reaching the alley beside the hotel, he ducked into its welcoming shadows. The gloom was so thick he had to move slowly to avoid tripping over anything and creating a racket.

He almost ran into an outside stairway that led to the second floor. Holding the shotgun ready, he stayed close to the wall where the boards would be less likely to creak and went up the stairs.

At the small landing at the top, he tried the doorknob. It was locked, but he gripped the knob tighter, put his shoulder against the door, and pushed and heaved.

The lock wasn't sturdy enough to withstand that much force and popped open. He swung the door back, stepped into a dimly lit corridor, and looked around.

The doors nearest him looked like they went to regular hotel rooms. More likely, the double doors at the other end led to Harmon's suite.

"What's this about the gold?" Harmon said sharply.

Even though he was worried about that, McCluskey noted the cattle baron's eyes kept straying to the shadowy, enticing valley between Delia's breasts that the unfastened buttons revealed.

Delia spoke quickly. "Oh Mr. Harmon, we're sorry we woke you. We have some information we think is important."

"Well, get on with it. Tell me what is so important you woke me in the middle of the night." Harmon looked from Delia to McCluskey.

"I think some of your men are planning to double-cross you," McCluskey said. "They're going to take the gold and try to get away."

Harmon snorted. "They wouldn't dare! All my boys are loyal to me. Besides, they're smart enough to know that if they ever did something like that I'd track 'em down and peel all the hide off 'em a strip at a time, just like the Apaches do."

"Maybe, but I swear I overheard some of them plotting to take the gold," McCluskey lied. "I figured it wouldn't hurt anything to go down there and take a look, just to make sure."

Harmon glared at him. "If you're so certain of this, why didn't you come tell me before now?"

Delia moved closer to him. "Frank was going to, Mr. Harmon, but I told him he ought to wait and not stir up trouble. Then I got to thinking about how kind you've been to us, and about how much we owe you, and . . . and I couldn't just stand by and let anything happen that would cause trouble for you." She put a hand on his arm. "It's already going to be hard enough for us to repay you."

Harmon breathed a little harder with Delia standing so close to him. He nodded. "All right. Let me get dressed and we'll go have a look. I still think you're wrong, Mc-Cluskey, but I reckon with that much gold at stake, it don't hurt anything to be careful."

As he turned toward the bedroom door, Delia looked back at McCluskey and smirked in triumph.

Unfortunately, Harmon had paused and swung back around, either to say something else or to get another look at Delia's cleavage, and he saw the look that passed between his two visitors.

Harmon stepped back quickly and raised the gun as his face darkened in anger. "What the hell was that?" he demanded. "I saw that look. You two are plottin' against me, ain't you? This is some sort of double-cross!"

"Oh, no, Mr. Harmon!" Delia cried. "We'd never do that. You're mistaken —"

McCluskey bit back a curse. Delia's overconfidence in her own charms might have ruined everything. His hand moved instinctively toward the gun on his hip as he told her, "Get out of the way!"

Luke eased the door closed behind him so

no one would notice it standing open and started along the carpet runner toward the far end of the corridor.

He kept the shotgun level so he could fire instantly and watched the doors as he approached and passed them. If someone opened a door behind him and tried to get the drop on him, he wouldn't have much warning, so he listened intently.

As far as he could tell, everyone in the hotel seemed to be asleep. He heard snores coming from behind some of the doors. Whether those sleepers were Harmon's men or innocent bystanders, he had no way of knowing, but if they stayed where they were, they would be all right.

Harmon's men wouldn't stay put, though, if they heard shots. They would come to investigate immediately, and Luke didn't think they would likely listen to reason.

If they didn't, they'd have to negotiate with some buckshot.

That walk along the second-floor corridor seemed longer than it was. Finally, Luke reached the doors of Harmon's suite. A tiny sliver of light showed through the crack between them, indicating a lamp was lit inside.

As he leaned closer, he was surprised to hear voices. Harmon wasn't alone. A woman spoke inside the suite, and a man responded.

Delia?

That explanation seemed the most likely. Luke figured she was trying to improve her standing with Harmon the only way she knew how.

But then a second man spoke, and Luke recognized Frank McCluskey's voice even if he couldn't make out the words. The realization that the outlaw was there, too, put a frown on Luke's face.

He ignored the words since he couldn't make them out, telling himself it didn't matter what they were doing. The three varmints he wanted the most were together in one place, so that was a stroke of luck for him. He drew back a little, preparing to kick the door open and get the drop on them.

Suddenly, someone shouted and a gunshot blasted inside the suite.

"Damn it!" Harmon yelled. He pulled the trigger and flame spouted from the muzzle of his gun.

Luke didn't wait any longer. His boot heel crashed against the door, kicking it open. He went in fast with the shotgun leveled.

Instantly, his keen eyes took in the scene.

Harmon was on one side of the sitting room, near the bedroom door, with a gun in his hand. McCluskey was on the other side of the room, also holding a revolver.

Delia was between them with one hand pressed to her breast as crimson blood welled between her fingers.

McCluskey whirled toward Luke, but Harmon was still trying to draw a bead on the outlaw for another shot. Even though she was wounded, possibly mortally, Delia cried out and launched herself at the rancher, ramming into him just as he pulled the trigger again. His shot went wild, smacking into the ceiling.

McCluskey took one look at Luke and thought better of trying to shoot it out with a man holding a shotgun. He kept turning and dived toward the window, just as Luke fired one barrel.

The glass shattered outward as McCluskey crashed into it and toppled over the sill. Most of the buckshot had torn into the wall next to the window, shredding the wallpaper. It hadn't had time to spread much.

Luke didn't know if he had hit the outlaw. He recalled that a little balcony ran along the front of the hotel and wondered if it was outside the window or if McCluskey had fallen to the street.

He got his answer as he started forward. Colt flame bloomed in the darkness as McCluskey, crouched on the balcony outside, fired at him. Luke felt as much as heard the bullet whip past his ear.

He was about to fire the scattergun's second barrel when a shot erupted behind him and plaster leaped from the wall nearby. With McCluskey on one side of him and Harmon on the other, he was caught in a crossfire.

He twisted around and dropped to one knee as he spotted Harmon coming toward him, face contorted with hate. Harmon had pushed Delia aside and was about to cut Luke down at almost point-blank range.

Luke fired first, blasting the second load of buckshot into Harmon's midsection, then rolling across the floor to take cover behind an armchair.

The deadly charge blew the rancher backward, all the way across the room to the far well. He thudded against it and hung there for a second, staring down at his ruined belly in shocked disbelief.

He slid down to a sitting position, leaving a terrible smear of blood on the wall behind him as his head sagged forward in death.

Luke reloaded the Greener.

No more shots came from the window. McCluskey must have fled, Luke thought. With two fresh shells in the shotgun, he snapped it closed.

Delia moaned as she lay in a limp, bloody heap on the floor a few feet from Harmon's body. Luke's first instinct was to go to her and see how badly she was hurt, but two of Harmon's men rushed in, brandishing guns. They caught sight of their boss's gruesome corpse, then spotted Luke and opened fire. Their bullets sizzled over his head as he unloaded both barrels into the gunmen.

They went down like wheat before a scythe. Neither of them would be getting up again. Once more, Luke broke the shotgun open and thumbed fresh shells into it.

Outside, more gunfire erupted in the street. It sounded like a small-scale war had broken out in Pine City. Silas Grant, Ben McGill, and other citizens had launched their uprising against Harmon's men. The hired guns wouldn't know yet that Harmon was dead, so they would fight to protect what they thought were their boss's interests.

Knowing the strongboxes full of gold were still in play, Luke thought it was likely McCluskey had gone after them. The outlaw would use the distraction of battle going on around him to try to get his hands on the wagon.

Luke was damned if he was going to let McCluskey drive away with a fortune in gold. He surged to his feet and was about to leap over the bodies of the men he had cut down when he heard a faint voice calling his name. He turned and saw that somehow Delia had pushed herself up on her elbows even though the front of her dress was soaked with blood.

She had even found the strength to pick up the gun Harmon had dropped, and as Luke turned toward her she pulled the trigger and sent flame lancing from the barrel at him.

CHAPTER 34

McCluskey hung from the balcony and dropped the remaining couple feet to the ground. His right leg buckled under him as he landed, pain shooting through it from the wound in his thigh where one of the buckshot had caught him.

The wound wasn't that bad, he told himself. It hurt like blazes, but that was all. He caught his balance and limped as quickly as he could toward the rear of the hotel where the wagon was parked.

He stopped as more shots rang out along the street. Doubling back, he saw some of Harmon's men trading shots with hombres he didn't know. Must be some of the townsmen fighting back at last, he decided. Jensen probably had something to do with that.

McCluskey turned and headed for the back of the hotel again. He didn't give a damn what happened to Harmon's men or to the people of Pine City. All he cared about was the gold.

Well, he was a little sorry that Delia had gotten in the way of a bullet, he reflected. But she had kept that bullet from hitting *him,* so he was glad about that. She had died helping him, and that was what she would have wanted.

Helping him to be a rich man, he thought with a savage grin as he limped along the alley.

As he came out at the back of the hotel, he saw the wagon immediately, with two of Harmon's men standing beside it holding rifles. As they swung the weapons toward him, he called out quickly, "Don't shoot! It's me — McCluskey!"

"What're you doin' back here?" one of the gunnies demanded.

McCluskey could tell they were nervous and on the hair trigger of shooting him. "The boss sent me," he said, thinking rapidly. "The townspeople have started a war." His eyes fell on the team of mules standing under a shed a few yards away. "Mr. Harmon said to hitch up those jug heads and get the wagon out of here. Take it back to the ranch where it'll be safe."

"How do we know you ain't lyin' to us?" the other guard asked suspiciously.

"Didn't you hear the boss say this

afternoon that he was taking me on as the ramrod of this bunch?" McCluskey snapped as if he were offended by being questioned. "Anyway, you're taking the gold to the ranch. I wouldn't tell you to do that if I wasn't acting on Harmon's orders, would I?"

That seemed to make sense to the men, but still they hesitated.

McCluskey yelled, "Get moving before some of those townies come back here and try to grab the gold for themselves!"

Used to following orders, the guards put their rifles aside and began hitching the mules to the wagon. McCluskey kept an eye on the alley, hoping the battle going on elsewhere in Pine City wouldn't move in their direction and disrupt his plans.

After several tense minutes, one of the men announced, "All right. The wagon's ready to go, McCluskey. Are you comin' with us?"

He strode over to them, stiffening his wounded leg against the pain. "I'm going. You're staying."

"Wha—"

McCluskey shot the guard between the eyes. The other man howled a curse and made a grab for his pistol, but he wasn't anywhere close to fast enough. McCluskey put a bullet through his brain, as well.

Then he hauled himself onto the wagon seat, picked up the reins, and slashed viciously at the team. He knew how balky mules could be, so he didn't give those a chance to do anything except cooperate. The animals surged forward against their harness. As they broke into a run, he wheeled the wagon around and headed away from the hotel.

He was going to be a rich man. Things were going to work out for him again. They always did.

Luke felt the wind-rip of the slug past his ear and brought the shotgun up to return Delia's fire.

That wasn't necessary. She slumped forward and the revolver slipped from her fingers. As the echoes of the shot died away, he heard the blonde's last breath rattle in her throat.

Delia was dead, having fought to the last to help Frank McCluskey.

Luke turned and pounded out of the room. As he turned toward the stairs leading down to the hotel lobby, two more of Harmon's men emerged from one of the rooms. Seeing him armed and on the loose, they opened fire. Luke crouched and swept the corridor clean with another double-barreled blast from the Greener.

He reloaded on the run as he weaved past those crumpled bodies, then took the stairs three at a time on the way down. The lobby was deserted. If there was supposed to be a clerk on duty, the man had wisely hunted a hole.

Luke ran out onto the boardwalk and looked around. He saw muzzle flashes to his right as several men behind parked wagons traded shots with other men in the saloon. He spotted Silas Grant as the livery-man stood up and tried to dash to a better location.

Silas never saw the gunman who emerged from the shadows behind him, but Luke did.

He broke into a run and shouted, "Silas, get down!"

Silas dived to the ground as Harmon's man opened fire. Luke was close enough to let loose one of the barrels. The shotgun went off with a boom and threw the gun-man back against a hitch rack. He flipped over it and landed in the limp sprawl of death.

Harmon's men in the saloon chose that moment to break out, slamming through the batwings with guns blazing. They charged across the street, which turned into a hornet's nest of flying lead. Luke went flat on his belly to avoid the deadly storm and fired the shotgun's second barrel, bringing down two of the hired killers. The other gun-wolves spun off their feet as shots from Silas, McGill, and other townsmen ripped through them.

As the gun-thunder died away, echoing into the nearby mountains, Luke heard hoofbeats. He remembered McCluskey and the wagon loaded with the strongboxes full of gold.

Every instinct in his body told him that McCluskey was getting away.

He broke into a run back toward the hotel, feeling in his pocket for more shotgun shells. When he didn't find any, he threw the empty Greener aside.

He reached the place where the wagon had been parked. It was gone, just as he expected. The sky was light enough for him to spot the vehicle heading south, away from Pine City. He had a revolver tucked into his waistband, but the wagon was already too far away for a handgun to have any chance of hitting its driver.

Two dead men lay on the ground nearby, murdered by McCluskey so he could take the gold. Luke looked around, knowing that cowboys never liked to be far away from their horses, and his heart leaped as he saw two shapes in the shed where the mule team had been kept.

He ran to the shed and swung open the gate in the fence around it. The horses were unsaddled and skittish, but he didn't let that stop him. He managed to calm down one of them enough that it let him grasp its mane and swing onto its back. He dug his heels into the horse's flanks and sent it racing after the wagon.

Loaded down the way it was with the gold, the wagon couldn't go as fast as the horse Luke was riding. He urged the mount on, and slowly the gap began to shrink.

Some instinct warned McCluskey that he was being pursued. He twisted on the seat, and flame spurted from a gun barrel. Luke leaned forward to make himself a smaller target, but he wasn't really worried about McCluskey hitting him. Going fast in a bouncing wagon, that would be pure luck.

Luke was going to trust his luck over McCluskey's. The outlaw's uncanny good fortune had to run out sometime.

Luke drew closer and closer until he could see the strain on McCluskey's face when the man looked back. He emptied the pistol toward Luke, but none of the shots came close.

Luke brought the galloping horse alongside the wagon bed. He could see the strongboxes as he left the horse's back in a dive that carried him into the wagon, landing hard enough to knock the breath out of him and stun him for a second.

McCluskey seized that opportunity to abandon the reins and dive over the back of the seat. He tried to slam his empty gun down on Luke's head, but Luke twisted aside at the last second and grabbed McCluskey's wrist. He banged the outlaw's gun hand against the edge of a strongbox, causing McCluskey to cry out in pain and lose his grip on the revolver.

It was a desperate hand-to-hand battle in the back of the careening wagon as each man gouged, kicked, tried to gain strangleholds, and basically fought for their lives. McCluskey broke away from Luke and surged to his feet. Luke followed and clung precariously to his balance as he and McCluskey stood toe-to-toe, slugging away at each other.

McCluskey buckled first, his wounded leg giving way underneath him. Luke straightened him up again with a left hook and added a roundhouse right that landed on the outlaw's jaw with smashing force. McCluskey went backward, tripped over one of the strongboxes, and flipped completely out of the wagon.

Luke leaped to the seat, grabbed the trailing reins, and brought the runaway mules to a halt as quickly as he could. He turned the wagon and drove back to where McCluskey lay motionless on the ground, afraid the outlaw might have broken his neck in the fall.

He was relieved when McCluskey groaned and lifted his head. Luke picked up the gun that had fallen from his waistband during the fight and checked the cylinder. It still held three rounds. He vaulted to the ground and approached McCluskey. "Get up," Luke said harshly.

"Why don't . . . why don't you just . . . go ahead and shoot me?" McCluskey asked.

"Because I want to see you hang."

By the time they got back to Pine City with McCluskey lying in the back of the wagon next to the strongboxes he had desired so badly, his hands and feet tied with strips Luke had forced him to tear from his own shirt, the fighting in the settlement was over.

It didn't take long to confirm which side had won the war. Silas Grant emerged from the marshal's office, carrying a rifle and grinning. "Mr. Jensen! We were all hopin' you were all right. Did you get him?"

"I got him." Luke looked around. "What about here?"

Silas leaned his head toward the marshal's office. "All the cells are plumb full in there, between the outlaws left over from that riverboat, Harmon's gunnies we rounded up, and ol' Marshal Kent his own self. He ain't the marshal no more."

"I can think of someone else a lot more suited to wear that badge . . . if you think you can fit a lawman's duties in with your work at the livery stable."

"I was thinkin' on it," Silas admitted. "Mr. McGill, he done said somethin' about that already." He looked into the back of the wagon. "What are you gonna do with this one?"

"Think we can cram one more prisoner into those cells?"

"Oh, we'll find a place for him," Silas said, nodding. "We'll find a place. And as soon as we do, you best get over to the café. Miz Walton and my Tillie, they're already gettin' breakfast ready."

Luke looked at the café, thought about Georgia Walton's smile — and her coffee — and decided that was about the most appealing combination he had heard in a long time.

■ ■ ■ ■

None of the townspeople had been killed in the fight with Harmon's men. The element of surprise had helped them, along with the fact that Luke had accounted for several of the enemy himself. Three days later, a rider who'd been sent to the county seat on a fast horse returned with not only the sheriff and a posse of deputies, but also several railroad detectives who were trying to track down that stolen gold.

They promised Luke a sizable reward for recovering it, but he told them, "You'll be splitting that reward between me and the good folks here in Pine City. They deserve it as much as I do. Maybe more."

The sheriff approached him later about Dave Harmon's death. "Harmon was an influential man in these parts," the lawman said. "Some of his friends are liable to say what you did was murder, Jensen."

Luke frowned. "He had just gunned down a woman, and he was trying to shoot me. That's a pretty clear-cut case of self-defense."

"You don't have any witnesses to that. Harmon and the woman are both dead."

"Then there's nobody to testify against

me, is there?" Luke pointed out.

The sheriff looked at him for a long moment. "I've been talking to Ben McGill, Silas Grant, and a bunch of other folks in town. I'm pretty well convinced that Harmon had Tom Walton murdered and had a hand in the deaths of several other men, as well. So I'm not going to push this any further than it's already gone. But I'd suggest that's what you should be, too, Jensen — gone. Get out of this part of the territory and don't come back for a good long while."

"That's all right with me, Sheriff," Luke said honestly, although he was going to miss eating at the café, and Georgia's company, to boot. "I've got a prisoner who has an appointment in Cheyenne."

While McCluskey sat in prison in Cheyenne, Luke returned to Rattlesnake Wells on the train as soon as the railroad bridge was repaired, to pick up his horse and see how Sundown Bob Hatfield and the other friends he had made were doing. He used part of the reward money to pick up a new pair of Remingtons, a new gun belt, and a set of holsters. He was breaking in the weapons, and it felt good to be fully armed again.

There was just one more thing to do before he left that part of the country. With his horse in the animal car, he rode the train back to Cheyenne. McCluskey was scheduled to be hanged, and Luke intended to be there. He took no pleasure in it. It was more like something he had to do to close the last page of a book.

All the way from the jail, up the thirteen steps to the gallows, while a black-suited preacher droned a prayer and the federal marshal in charge of the hanging asked Mc-Cluskey if he had any last words to say, the outlaw looked around, jerking his head from side to side as if waiting for something to happen.

Waiting for someone to come along and save him from his fate.

But Delia wasn't there. She was buried two hundred miles away in Pine City's cemetery, with a plain marker giving only her name and date of death. There was nobody else to help a vicious, two-bit owl-hoot like Frank McCluskey.

McCluskey was still waiting for that miracle, though, as the hangman put the black hood over his head, fitted the noose around his neck, and nodded to the marshal who held the lever. From under the hood,

McCluskey said in a muffled voice, "Wait! This isn't —"

The marshal shoved the lever, the trapdoor dropped out from under McCluskey's feet, and Luke heard the sharp pop of the outlaw's neck breaking as he hit the end of the rope.

So much for visions, Luke thought as he went to his waiting horse. He swung up into the saddle and rode out of Cheyenne without looking back at the figure dangling from the gallows.

J. A. JOHNSTONE ON
WILLIAM W. JOHNSTONE
"PRINT THE LEGEND"

William W. Johnstone was born in southern Missouri, the youngest of four children. He was raised with strong moral and family values by his minister father, and tutored by his schoolteacher mother. Despite this, he quit school at age fifteen.

"I have the highest respect for education," he says, "but such is the folly of youth, and wanting to see the world beyond the four walls and the blackboard."

True to this vow, Bill attempted to enlist in the French Foreign Legion ("I saw Gary Cooper in *Beau Geste* when I was a kid and I thought the French Foreign Legion would be fun") but was rejected, thankfully, for being underage. Instead, he joined a traveling carnival and did all kinds of odd jobs. It was listening to the veteran carny folk, some of whom had been on the circuit since the late 1800s, telling amazing tales about their experiences, that planted the storytelling seed in Bill's imagination.

"They were mostly honest people, despite the bad reputation traveling carny shows had back then," Bill remembers. "Of course, there were exceptions. There was one guy named Picky, who got that name because he was a master pickpocket. He could steal a man's socks right off his feet without him knowing. Believe me, Picky got us chased out of more than a few towns."

After a few months of this grueling existence, Bill returned home and finished high school. Next came stints as a deputy sheriff in the Tallulah, Louisiana, Sheriff's Department, followed by a hitch in the U.S. Army. Then he began a career in radio broadcasting at KTLD in Tallulah, which would last sixteen years. It was there that he fine-tuned his storytelling skills. He turned to writing in 1970, but it wouldn't be until 1979 that his first novel, *The Devil's Kiss,* was published. Thus began the full-time writing career of William W. Johnstone. He wrote horror (*The Uninvited*), thrillers (*The Last of the Dog Team*), even a romance novel or two. Then, in February 1983, *Out of the Ashes* was published. Searching for his missing family in a postapocalyptic America, rebel mercenary and patriot Ben Raines is united with the civilians of the Resistance forces and moves to the forefront of a revolution for the nation's future.

Out of the Ashes was a smash. The series would continue for the next twenty years, winning Bill three generations of fans all over the world. The series was often imitated but never duplicated. "We all tried to copy the Ashes series," said one publishing executive, "but Bill's uncanny ability, both then and now, to predict in which direction the political winds were blowing brought a certain immediacy to the table no one else could capture." The Ashes series would end its run with more than thirty-four books and twenty million copies in print, making it one of the most successful men's action series in American book publishing. (The Ashes series also, Bill notes with a touch of pride, got him on the FBI's Watch List for its less than flattering portrayal of spineless politicians and the growing power of big government over our lives, among other things. In that respect, I often find myself saying, "Bill was years ahead of his time.")

Always steps ahead of the political curve, Bill's recent thrillers, written with myself, include *Vengeance Is Mine, Invasion USA, Border War, Jackknife, Remember the Alamo, Home Invasion, Phoenix Rising, The Blood of Patriots, The Bleeding Edge,* and the upcoming *Suicide Mission.*

It is with the western, though, that Bill found his greatest success. His westerns propelled him onto both the *USA Today* and the *New York Times* bestseller lists.

Bill's western series include *Matt Jensen, the Last Mountain Man, Preacher, the First Mountain Man, The Family Jensen, Luke Jensen, Bounty Hunter, Eagles, MacCallister* (an Eagles spin-off), *Sidewinders, The Brothers O'Brien, Sixkiller, Blood Bond, The Last Gunfighter,* and the new series *Flintlock* and *The Trail West.* May 2013 saw the hardcover western *Butch Cassidy: The Lost Years.*

"The western," Bill says, "is one of the few true art forms that is one hundred percent American. I liken the Western as America's version of England's Arthurian legends, like the Knights of the Round Table, or Robin Hood and his Merry Men. Starting with the 1902 publication of *The Virginian* by Owen Wister, and followed by the greats like Zane Grey, Max Brand, Ernest Haycox, and of course Louis L'Amour, the western has helped to shape the cultural landscape of America.

"I'm no goggle-eyed college academic, so when my fans ask me why the western is as popular now as it was a century ago, I don't offer a 200-page thesis. Instead, I can only offer this: The western is honest. In this great country, which is suffering under the yoke of political correctness, the western harks back to an era when justice was sure and swift. Steal a man's horse, rustle his cattle, rob a bank, a stagecoach, or a train, you were hunted down and fitted with a hangman's noose. One size fit all.

"Sure, we westerners are prone to a little embellishment and exaggeration and, I admit it, occasionally play a little fast and loose with the facts. But we do so for a very good reason — to enhance the enjoyment of readers.

"It was Owen Wister, in *The Virginian,* who first coined the phrase 'When you call me that, smile.' Legend has it that Wister actually heard those words spoken by a deputy sheriff in Medicine Bow, Wyoming, when another poker player called him a son of a bitch.

"Did it really happen, or is it one of those myths that have passed down from one generation to the next? I honestly don't know. But there's a line in one of my favorite westerns of all time, *The Man Who Shot Liberty Valance,* where the newspaper editor tells the young reporter, 'When the truth becomes legend, print the legend.'

"These are the words I live by."

CPSIA information can be obtained
at www.ICGtesting.com
Printed in the USA
FFOW02n0217051115
18361FF